W9-BRI-979

PRAISE FOR *Yannick Murphy*

THE CALL

"A triumph of quiet humor and understated beauty. . . . Murphy's subtle, wry wit and an appealing sense for the surreal leaven moments of anger and bleakness, and elevate moments of kindness, whimsy, and grace." —*Publishers Weekly* (starred review)

SIGNED, MATA HARI

"Murphy is an extraordinarily gifted fabulist. [*Signed, Mata Hari* is] completely original. . . . [A] beguiling evocation."
—Liesl Schillinger, *New York Times Book Review* (Editors' Choice)

"Yannick Murphy, while being one of our most daring and original writers, is first and foremost an exquisitely attuned observer of human behavior. Her characters are so richly imagined and believable that when you're finished with . . . her book, you expect to find her characters' names in the phone book. Murphy's work provides pretty much unexceeded reading pleasure."
—Dave Eggers, author of *What Is the What* and
A Heartbreaking Work of Staggering Genius

"Unself-consciously sensual and achingly beautiful, [*Signed, Mata Hari* consists of] short, exquisite, though never precious, chapters refined almost to a sequence of prose poems. [This] is a profound and profoundly beautiful novel, one that forcefully renews literary fiction's claim to be a laboratory of the human spirit." —*Los Angeles Times*

"[An] alluring novel. . . . Hypnotic [and as] softly poetic as it is insistent, [*Signed, Mata Hari*] entices the reader from the first lines to give Mata Hari what she always craved: not the secrets that are the currency of a spy, but the rapt attention that is oxygen to a performer." —*Publishers Weekly* (starred review)

"In the fictionalized confessional *Signed, Mata Hari*, Yannick Murphy reincarnates the legendary seductress who was accused of being a double agent in World War I, giving her a lyrical voice and an irrepressible vivacity. . . . Most of the twists and gyrations take place on the page, not the stage, [and by] the time her last morning arrives and she walks out to face a French firing squad—*sans* blindfold—we feel as besotted with this passionate, provocative woman as were the rest of her hapless admirers." —*Elle*

"[Mata Hari's] often-overshadowed life provides the emotional core of Yannick Murphy's wondrous novel, *Signed, Mata Hari*. Zelle's death was merely the tragic end of a tragic life, and here Murphy, through exquisite and lush fiction, creates as fully drawn a portrait of her as any biographer could have done." —*Boston Globe*

"In *Signed, Mata Hari*, Yannick Murphy once again treats us to her luscious signature lyric style, its whispers and perfumes, in this time- and space-bending tale of the famous dancer and accused spy." —Janet Fitch, author of *Paint it Black* and *White Oleander*

"In this atmospheric novel of seductively brief chapters, Murphy reimagines the many blanks of Hari's sexed-up history. This compelling mix of erotic poetry, bio, and thriller makes a sympathetic case that Hari was less a spy than a busy courtesan who opted to bed both German and Allied officers."

—*Entertainment Weekly*

"The events leading up to [Mata Hari's execution] still remain shrouded in mystery, but in the intoxicating new novel *Signed, Mata Hari*, Yannick Murphy imaginatively fills in the gaps. The result is a sympathetic portrayal of one of the twentieth century's most vilified women: Murphy's Mata Hari is not a callous femme fatale but an ordinary mother forced to do extraordinary things to survive."

—*Time Out* (New York)

"Brilliant in its structure, beautiful in its language, rich in its characterization, Yannick Murphy's new novel, *Signed, Mata Hari*, also happens to have at its center one of the most fascinating figures of the early twentieth century, a woman who ached deeply and searched intensely for an identity. In Murphy's masterful hands, this quest is tenderly and movingly rendered."

—Robert Olen Butler, author of the Pulitzer Prize–winning *A Good Scent from a Strange Mountain*

"The life of the legendary French dancer and femme fatale is brilliantly captured in this impressionistic novel. [A] compelling portrait . . . [and] mesmerizing read."

—*Seattle Post-Intelligencer*

"Murphy has devised a persona who is willful, dreamy, convinced of the validity of her own perceptions, sexually generous, and incorrigibly naive. The life of the senses coats these pages: textures, smells, flavors. . . . I found myself rushing through the final pages—to an ending that satisfies, opening out into a kaleidoscopic tribute, at once tender and wise."

—*San Francisco Chronicle*

"Murphy's third novel considers the circumstances that galvanized [Mata Hari's] legend, while ruing upon larger issues of womanhood, the burdens of perception, and societal abuse. Murphy has glued together a fine porcelain novel."

—*Chicago Sun-Times*

"Floating along on the exotic current of Murphy's language and imagery. . . . The tragedy of Mata Hari's life—and Yannick Murphy's ambition—pinned me to the couch and kept me there until the story was done."

—*Oregonian*

"Murphy writes like a dream, with vivid sensory descriptions. As for [the question of whether Mata Hari was a spy], the alchemy wrought by both the author and her heroine is so persuasive that you probably won't even care."

—*Dallas Morning News*

"Captivating. . . . Murphy seduces readers with her prose. This elegantly crafted novel keeps you guessing until Mata Hari's last moments."

—*Sunday Express* (London)

"Murphy [writes with a] lyrical tone and imaginative flair. . . . [The novel's] strengths are its beautiful language, love of minute details, and focus on different types of love and loss."

—*Time Out* (London)

"Compelling."

—*Financial Times*

HERE THEY COME

"This is a hell of a book. You might not be able to finish *Here They Come* in one sitting, but it will haunt you till you do. What detail! What characters! I can imagine both Jane Austen and Raymond Carver poring over this masterly novel."

—Frank McCourt, author of *Angela's Ashes*

"Yannick Murphy is a uniquely talented writer who manages to turn everything on its head and make dark, funny, shocking, and beautiful prose out of the detritus of growing up poor, fatherless, and cockeyed. She is fearless."

—Lily Tuck, author of *The News from Paraguay*

"Yannick Murphy's long-awaited *Here They Come* is a unique combination of rare linguistic lyricism with brutal and brilliant prose. It is an unrelenting portrait of family, terrifying for its honesty, its willingness to be ugly and elegant. Haunting."

—A. M. Homes, author of
The Safety of Objects and *Music for Torching*

"Told by a precocious unnamed thirteen-year-old girl who bends spoons with her mind, Murphy's gorgeous third book of fiction recounts the story of a poor family's coming-of-age in 1970s New York. In thick, poetic prose that edges toward stream of consciousness and is peppered with slightly surreal details, Murphy creates a world as magical and harrowing as the struggle to come to grips with maturity."   —*Publishers Weekly* (starred review)

"Yannick Murphy creates a narrator with a unique, sometimes shocking perspective. Murphy's startling language and imagery accumulate great power as they hurtle toward the reader."
                                                            —*People*

"Murphy flawlessly captures a child's-eye view of a battered society and a battered family. The spare elegance of her prose contrasts so jarringly with the sordid physical landscape that it inspires an unsettling sense of disconnect, which is almost certainly the point. Most impressive of all is Murphy's remarkable use of language, the expressive way she puts together ordinary words and images to create surprisingly lovely and moving metaphors."
                                                —*Los Angeles Times*

"A girl on the verge searches for her father in Yannick Murphy's shockingly funny *Here They Come*."   —*Vanity Fair*

The

Call

Also by Yannick Murphy

IN A BEAR'S EYE

SIGNED, MATA HARI

HERE THEY COME

THE SEA OF TREES

STORIES IN ANOTHER LANGUAGE

For Children

THE COLD WATER WITCH

BABY POLAR

AHWOOOOOOOO!

HARPER ⬤ PERENNIAL

NEW YORK • LONDON • TORONTO • SYDNEY • NEW DELHI • AUCKLAND

The

Call

A Novel

YANNICK MURPHY

HARPER ⬤ PERENNIAL

An excerpt from this book originally appeared in *McSweeney's* #29.

THE CALL. Copyright © 2011 by Yannick Murphy. All rights reserved. Printed in the United States of America. No part of this book may be used or reproduced in any manner whatsoever without written permission except in the case of brief quotations embodied in critical articles and reviews. For information address HarperCollins Publishers, 10 East 53rd Street, New York, NY 10022.

HarperCollins books may be purchased for educational, business, or sales promotional use. For information please write: Special Markets Department, HarperCollins Publishers, 10 East 53rd Street, New York, NY 10022.

FIRST EDITION

Designed by Sunil Manchikanti

Library of Congress Cataloging-in-Publication Data

Murphy, Yannick.
    The call : a novel / Yannick Murphy. — 1st ed.
      p. cm.
    ISBN 978-0-06-202314-8 (pbk.)
    I. Title.

PS3563.U7635C35 2011
813'.54—dc22   2010051661

12 13 14 15 OV/RRD 10 9 8 7 6

FOR JEFF, THE BEST MAN, FATHER,
AND VETERINARIAN I KNOW, AND FOR
OUR CHILDREN, WHO TAKE AFTER
HIM IN SO MANY GOOD WAYS.

Part One

Fall

CALL: A cow with her dead calf half-born.

ACTION: Put on boots and pulled dead calf out while standing in a field full of mud.

RESULT: Hind legs tore off from dead calf while I pulled. Head, forelegs, and torso are still inside the mother.

THOUGHTS ON DRIVE HOME WHILE PASSING RED AND GOLD LEAVES ON MAPLE TREES: Is there a nicer place to live?

WHAT CHILDREN SAID TO ME WHEN I GOT HOME: Hi, Pop.

WHAT THE WIFE COOKED FOR DINNER: Something mixed-up.

CALL: Old woman with minis needs bute paste.

ACTION: Drove to old woman's house, delivered bute paste. Petted minis. Learned their names—Molly, Netty, Sunny, and Storm.

RESULT: Minis are really cute.

THOUGHTS ON DRIVE HOME: Must bring children back here some-time to see the cute minis.

WHAT CHILDREN SAID TO ME WHEN I GOT HOME: Hi, Pop.

WHAT THE WIFE COOKED FOR DINNER: Steak and potatoes, no salad. She said, David, our salad days are over, it now being autumn and the garden bare except for wind-tossed fallen leaves.

...

CALL: Sick sheep.

ACTION: Visited sheep. Noticed they'd eaten all the thistle.

RESULT: Talked to owner, who is a composer, about classical music. Admired his tall barn beams. Advised owner to fence off thistle so sheep couldn't eat it. Sheep become sick from thistle.

THOUGHTS ON DRIVE HOME: Is time travel possible? Maybe time is not a thing. Because light takes a while to travel, what we're seeing is always in the past.

WHAT THE WIFE COOKED FOR DINNER: Breakfast.

CALL: Castrate draft horse.

ACTION: Pulled out emasculators, castrated draft horse.

RESULT: Draft horse bled buckets. Pooled around his hooves. Owner said she had never seen so much blood. It's okay, he's got a lot of blood, I said. She nodded. She braided the fringe on her poncho, watching the blood.

THOUGHTS ON DRIVE HOME: What's the point of a poncho if it doesn't cover your arms?

WHAT THE WIFE COOKED FOR DINNER: Nut loaf.

WHAT I ATE FOR DINNER: Not nut loaf.

CALL: Horse is colicking.

ACTION: Drove to farm dodging dry, brown leaves skating across the road because at first I thought they were mice or voles running to the safety of the other side. Gave horse Banamine. Watched him sweating. Watched him rolling on his stall floor. Watched owner cry. Just a few tears down a freckled cheek. Listened to horses in other stalls whinny, worried for the colicky horse.

RESULT: Stayed for hours, until night. Moon was full. Walked horse out to field by the apple tree. Gave him a shot to put him to sleep. Patted his neck. Left owner with her head by his head, not saying anything. Maybe just breathing in his last exhaled breath.

THOUGHTS ON DRIVE HOME: When I go I want to go in a field by an apple tree on a full-moon night.

WHAT I SAW WHEN I PULLED UP TO THE HOUSE: Bright lights in the sky, an object moving quickly back and forth. Not a plane.

WHAT I HEARD FROM CHILDREN WHEN I GOT HOME: Gentle snoring.

WHAT I HEARD FROM MY WIFE WHEN I GOT HOME: Loud snoring.

CALL: Sheep with a cut from a fence.

ACTION: Drove to farm. Inspected sheep. Cut was old. Small white worms were crawling on it. Gave owner some antibiotic.

RESULT: Asked owner if he had seen the bright lights in the sky the night before. Owner shrugged. I go to bed, the owner said.

THOUGHTS ON DRIVE HOME: Since people have become used to seeing telephone wires and telephone poles everywhere, they can get used to seeing wind turbines everywhere. It's just a matter of getting used to something.

CALL: Alpaca down.

ACTION: Drove to farm. Remembered not to look alpaca in the eye.

RESULT: Looked alpaca in the eye by mistake. Got spit in the eye. Alpaca nice and angry now. Alpaca got up. Owner thankful. Handed me a rag that smelled like gasoline. I wiped my eye. Asked owner if he had seen the bright lights, the object moving back and forth in the sky the night before. The owner shook his head, he hadn't seen anything. The alpaca came to me and put his face in my face. I thought he was going to spit in my eye again, but he didn't. The owner laughed, looks like he's trying to tell you something, the owner said. Did the alpaca want to tell me he had seen the object in the sky?

THOUGHTS ON DRIVE HOME: I could have been an engineer or a fighter pilot.

CALL: A prepurchase examination on a Thoroughbred.

ACTION: Brought digital X-ray machine and performed a complete set of X-rays on horse in a barn with ducks, spaniels, and kittens walking about.

RESULT: Owner tried to give me a kitten to take home to the children. No, no, I said. We have two dogs. The dogs will love the cat, the owner said. How about a duck? the owner said. No, they shit liquid, I said. Yes, that's true, she said, but the eggs are golden.

THOUGHTS ON RIDE HOME: Chickens might be nice to have. The children could check for eggs every day. We could eat the eggs. Chickens don't shit liquid. This is the problem today, people don't know where their food comes from. My children will know where their food comes from.

CALL: A sheep needs its shots.

ACTION: Took bottles of vaccines and drew up shots.

RESULT: Old woman named Dorothy called the sheep to her. The sheep's name was Alice. Alice lived in the house with Dorothy. I'd let her live outside, but she's no bother inside, Dorothy said. Alice lay her head in Dorothy's lap. Go on, give the shot, Dorothy said. The sheep was very still while I gave the shot. She is like a dog, Dorothy said. I take her everywhere in my pickup. She waits for me until I get back from my errands. I took her into church one day. I showed the pastor. He made a remark about sheep. He said they were dumb. Go get Alice from the back of your pickup, my friend said, nudging me. I went to the parking lot and got Alice. I held the church doors open for her. She followed me down the aisle. She looked into people's faces as she walked. I'd like you to meet Alice, I said to the pastor. She looked him in the eyes. Now go on, I said. Read the part again in your sermon about how sheep are dumb, I said.

THOUGHTS ON DRIVE HOME: I know some people who will not look me in the eye.

WHAT I SAW WHEN I PULLED UP TO THE HOUSE: The object flying in the sky again. It seemed to circle the house. More likely it was a drone the military used and remotely practiced with in our secluded woods, but still I could not help but think it was otherworldly, the way its lights flashed on and off, the way it flew so low, as if it wanted to see in our windows and check on what my family was doing. I felt that it knew me somehow.

WHAT I FELT EVEN BEFORE I WALKED IN THE DOOR: Warm. Even though it was cold outside, I already began to feel warm as I stepped onto the porch where the glass front door always seemed to be constantly steamed over from the exhaled breaths of my wife, my children, the dogs, and all the other creatures inside.

WHAT CHILDREN SAID TO ME WHEN I GOT HOME: Doesn't Alice pee and poop on the floor in the house?

WHAT I SAID: I suppose she does.

WHAT THE WIFE COOKED FOR DINNER: Omelets with green olives.

WHAT THE WIFE SAID: David, I don't want a sheep.

CALL: A cat.

ACTION: I told owner I don't do cats. The owner asked if I could do this one. The owner had shot the fisher-cats in his barn that had eaten half his chickens. Shoot the cat, I said, you have shot fisher-cats. You have done huge horses, why can't you just do a little house cat whose time has come? the owner said.

RESULT: I did the cat in the belly. I did not need to find a vein. I was paid in sausage and bacon.

THOUGHTS ON DRIVE HOME: This war we are in is a war we started to see how much we can take from another country. It was once not so easy for me to see it this way.

WHAT THE CHILDREN SAID TO ME WHEN I GOT HOME: Mom is not making dinner. Mom is sick on the couch.

WHAT THE WIFE SAID TO ME WHEN I GOT HOME: David, where's the gun? If you just shoot this side of my head, I'm sure it will get rid of my headache. Then Jen laid her head back on the easy chair where the sun was streaming in and the bright light on her face made her look porcelain-white.

WHAT I COOKED FOR DINNER: Bacon. Glorious fresh bacon given to me by the man who shot fisher-cats, not house cats. I showed my children how the bacon did not release injected water into the pan while it cooked because it was fresh bacon, good bacon. Bacon the way bacon should be.

THOUGHTS WHILE TURNING BACON: Why is it legal to inject meats with water? Why is it fair that the consumer has to pay extra money, per pound, for injected water?

WHAT THE CHILDREN SAID: Pop, don't burn the bacon.

WHAT THE WIND SAID AT NIGHT: I can blow down all your trees. I can make the walls of your house fall in.

WHAT THE MORNING SAID: I kept the wind at bay.

THOUGHTS WHILE SHOWERING: Deer season will be here soon. Already it is bear. We have heard the hunters and their bear dogs early on the weekend mornings barking, treeing bears. I will hunt first with a bow for deer this fall season. I will sit high up in a tree in a purchased stand that came with big labels telling me never to use it without wearing a safety harness. I will wear the safety harness. I will check it before I put it on. Are the straps worn? Is the buckle fastened securely? Are the deer gods on my side?

WHAT MY SON SAID AT DINNER: Aren't I hunting with you this fall? He had not hunted with me before, this would be his first time. He was twelve years old now and old enough to carry a gun. He knew the rules well. He had aced his hunter's exam. Gun tip pointed up or down when walking through the woods, never shoot at an animal on a hill, because you never know who might be on the other side of the hill, open your chamber when passing your gun to someone and say, "action open, safety on" while you're passing it.

WHAT I SAID: Yes, I suppose you're ready to hunt with me now.

WHAT MY SON SAID: Yes! I can't wait! and then he chanted, Kill the deer. Eat the meat! Kill the deer. Eat the meat! in time with holding his fork in his fist and banging his fist on the table, making me think maybe we should wait. Maybe he wasn't ready to take a gun into the woods.

WHAT THE WIFE SAID TO ME: Be careful hunting, David. I don't like it. He's still so young. You only have one son, you know.

WHAT I THOUGHT: Maybe Jen is wrong, maybe there are other sons I have. Who knows if the sperm I once donated in college was ever used or simply thrown away after time? The money I received was spent on taking dates to restaurants I wouldn't otherwise have been able to afford.

WHAT I WOULD NEVER TELL THE WIFE: That maybe she was wrong about me not having other sons, because if I told her then I would have to explain why I wanted the money. I would have to explain the other girls, and no matter that I didn't know Jen then, she might become jealous.

WHAT I SAID TO THE WIFE INSTEAD TO CHANGE THE SUBJECT: Did you know that because light takes time to travel, what you're seeing is always in the past?

WHAT THE WIFE SAID: I like that, it's the world's best excuse. The adage "Don't cry over spilt milk" applies to everything then. It's all in the past, there's nothing we can change.

WHAT I THOUGHT: That I could tell Jen not to cry over spilt milk if ever she learned of how I had earned extra money in college and that somewhere in there was a pun she'd pick up on, the spilt milk of me somehow worked in.

CALL: No call. The phone rang and when I answered, whoever it was hung up. Hello, hello, I said and I kept saying hello even after I knew they were gone.

WHAT WE DID AFTER DINNER: Put on sweaters to keep off the chill and went outside and called to the owls.

WHAT THE OWLS DID: Called back and then the spacecraft showed up again, its lights blinking faster than the last time, as if it were trying to sing out its own kind of call.

...

CALL: A choke.

ACTION: Touched the horse's neck. I could feel the ball of food caught in his throat. This could be a tough one, I told Arthur, the hired hand. I gave the horse drugs to relax his throat muscles. I went to fill up buckets. I would need the water to pump through his stomach. I would need to clear the choke. I put the tube through the horse's nose. I asked Arthur, while I was working on the horse, if he had seen the object in the sky, if he had seen the bright lights a few nights before. Arthur, with one hand resting on the horse's neck, looked up at the sky, as if the object I had been talking about could still be seen in all the blue. Arthur shook his head. No, didn't see it, he said. I wasn't out here. Only thing out here were the horses, Arthur said. You see it, Boss? he said into the ear of the horse I was working on, and while he said it he had the flat of his palm on the neck of the horse and I thought how maybe Arthur wasn't doing the talking, that maybe it was the horse doing the talking for him.

A flock of geese came flying down to the pond. Arthur and I watched the geese, their feet out in a pose to brake, their wings not beating, coming down on water flat as glass on a windless day. Who knew geese could walk on water? Arthur said, his hand still on the horse.

RESULT: The drug worked quickly. The water went straight down. The choke had passed. I told Arthur that was good, otherwise we could have been there a long time and he would have heard my whole life story and I his.

THOUGHTS ON DRIVE HOME: What was Arthur's life story? Did he ever have a wife? Kids? What was my life story?

THIS IS WHAT I WANT ON MY TOMBSTONE: He loved his children.

WHAT THE CHILDREN SAID WHEN I GOT HOME: Pop, Mom's in one of her moods.

WHAT THE WIFE WAS DOING: Unloading the dishwasher, but doing it by slamming the pots onto their shelves.

WHAT THE WIFE SAID: Can't anyone else help to do this? Jen motioned with her arm, taking in the kitchen, the messy countertops, the food bits on the floor, pieces of carrots dried and turned white kicked up under the shelves. The books and papers on the table, the loud toy guns, the fishing reels needing line.

WHAT THE CHILDREN DID: Ran outside.

WHAT I DID: Ran outside.

WHAT THE CHILDREN DID: Climbed me.

WHAT I SMELLED: Their hair, a sweet smell and also an outdoors smell, the smell of fall's fallen leaves kicked up.

CALL: No call.

ACTION: Stayed at home.

RESULT: Wished the children were home with me, resented school for taking them away and teaching them nothing. They would learn more at home with me. I would teach them things I want to learn. Violin, German, the possibility of time travel.

THOUGHTS WHILE WALKING THROUGH THE WOODS LOOKING FOR SPOTS TO RAISE DEER STAND: When shooting the rifle, make sure the deer is moving, otherwise he will notice the safety releasing, he will bolt before you squeeze off the shot. Will I even see a buck this year?

WHAT THE CHILDREN SAID TO ME WHEN I GOT HOME: Pop, there was a moose in the back of the house!

WHAT THE WIFE SAID: A cow, not a bull.

WHAT I SAID: Everybody, let's go for a walk and see if we can see her again.

WHAT WE CAME ACROSS: Moose poop. Bear poop. Deer poop. Coyote poop. Fallen over rotting mushrooms that looked like loose poop.

WHAT I POINTED OUT TO MY SON: The barks of trees rubbed off by the antlers of deer. Flattened ferns where deer had lain.

WHAT SAM SAID: I cannot wait to hunt, the deer are all around us!

WHAT WE DID: Put our hands down on the flattened ferns to see if they were still warm and then we walked back home, avoiding breaking spanning cobwebs in our way.

WHAT THE WIFE COOKED FOR DINNER: Spaghetti with meat sauce, black olives, and mushrooms.

WHAT MIA, MY YOUNGEST, MY SIX-YEAR-OLD, SAID TO ME BEFORE BEDTIME: Poppy, I'm going to cold you up. Then she reached her cold hands up under my shirt and touched my back.

WHAT SAM, MY OLDEST, MY TWELVE-YEAR-OLD, SHOWED ME BEFORE BEDTIME: How to exhale when squeezing off a shot to avoid excessive movement and achieve the truest aim.

WHAT SARAH, THE MIDDLE CHILD, MY TEN-YEAR-OLD, SAID TO ME: Lyle got detention for throwing a pencil at Miss Ackerman when she turned her back.

WHAT THE OWLS SAID AT NIGHT: We are in every tree in a five-mile radius.

WHAT THE WIFE SAID IN BED WHILE THE LIGHT OF THE FULL MOON CAME IN THROUGH THE WINDOW: Somebody turn off that light.

CALL: A Dutch Warmblood needs teeth floated.

ACTION: Went to farm where horse is stabled. Brought out floats. Tried floating teeth without giving a drug to the horse. Horse clearly needed drug. Drew up shot, injected horse.

RESULT: Was able to float horse's teeth, but the woman who owned the horse could talk a dog off a meat wagon, and I had to listen to her. Funny how the horses like their teeth floated. Grinding down the back hooks, this horse closed his eyes; if he could purr he would. My arm was sore afterward, was the woman's mouth tired? She talked of gardens and nematodes and the forecasts of the *Farmer's Almanac*.

THOUGHTS ON DRIVE HOME: This is where the horses live, in cozy barns, the pastures here still green, a heron flies across, the cows all standing north to south, the attraction of the poles said to be the reason for their alignment.

WHAT THE CHILDREN SAID TO ME WHEN I GOT HOME: Pop, you smell like horse manure, and what's that on your upper arm?

WHAT I SAID: Why, that's horse saliva.

WHAT THE WIFE COOKED FOR DINNER: Pizza.

WHAT KEPT ME AWAKE AT NIGHT: Pizza.

WHAT I LOOKED FOR OUT THE WINDOW WHILE I WAS AWAKE: The bright lights, the object moving back and forth in the sky, but I didn't see it. I just saw the horizon and what looked to be the sun still setting, only it was the middle of the night and the sun was long gone. I wondered if what I was looking at was just the glow from the moon shining over our back field.

CALL: A one-inch-long curved laceration above the eyebrow on Sarah.

ACTION: Laid out a blanket and a pillow on kitchen table. Told her to lie down on them under the bright light. Blocked her, then began to suture.

RESULT: Sam took pictures with the camera, so close to her face I had to tell him to step back.

WHAT MY WIFE SAID: Maybe we should take her to a real doctor.

WHAT I SAID: I am a real doctor.

WHAT MY WIFE SAID: They have staples, they have glue these days at the emergency rooms. Maybe she won't scar as much with staples or glue, she said.

WHAT I SAID: A scar gives you character.

WHAT SARAH SAID: I want to go to the emergency room!

WHAT SAM SAID: I took eighty-six pictures; want to see?

THOUGHTS WHILE WIFE COOKED DINNER: We must buy a cow. The depression will be upon us soon. No one will be able to afford milk when it happens. Milk will be a thing of the past. And cheese, think of the cheese. We will make our own ice cream, we will no longer have to buy cartons of it from the supermarket, the ice cream whipped with air. Why are we paying for air? When the depression comes we will no longer be able to afford our property taxes. We must sell now, go live in a small house in the woods. We won't have a view. We won't be taxed for our view if we don't have one. We will not have a pond or a stream. We will not be taxed for them if we don't have them. We will continue to heat with wood. We will live off the grid. Our light will come from solar panels. Our woodstove will be our kitchen stove. We will never turn a knob to turn it on. There will always be heat on the range.

WHAT I TOLD MY WIFE BEFORE BED: Let's move to the woods.

WHAT MY WIFE SAID: We already live in the woods.

WHAT I SAID: No, the real woods, way back on the roads where the poles for electricity end.

WHAT MY WIFE SAID: I am not moving from here. I like our house. I like our pond. I like our fields.

WHAT I SAID: You will not have a choice. The calls will stop. People will stop treating their horses, and cows, and sheep. It will cost too much money to treat them. Even if the calls do not stop and I still get called to treat the horse or the cow or the sheep, the bill will not be paid. The people will not pay. Our taxes will continue to rise.

WHAT THE WIFE SAID: How did a bat get in here? Who left the front door open?

WHAT THE BAT DID: Flew low, over Jen's head in bed so that she had to bring the covers up over her head. It reminded me of the spacecraft. Why was everything flying so low? Why did everything want to be so close to us?

WHAT I DID: Opened up the window and let the bat out into the full-moon night. I could see the moon on the grass that was frosting. It reminded me of a Christmas bulb my mother used to put on the tree when I was a child. The bulb was frosted, sprayed on with something white and granular, something like snow.

WHAT I THOUGHT: Something is wrong when something in nature reminds you of something man-made. It should be the other way around. Is this the result of the human race having been around too long?

THOUGHTS WHILE SHOWERING: Maybe we don't need a milk cow, maybe we need cattle raised for beef. A milk cow you have to be at home twice a day to milk. Ah, but the good taste of fresh milk. Maybe we need both dairy and beef.

WHAT THE CHILDREN SAID: Pop, we don't have a barn.

WHAT I DID: I looked around for a place to put a barn. Too close to the house, you would be sorry in the summer for the flies. Too far you would be sorry in the winter, walking all the way across the snow and ice. Besides, put up a barn and they will tax you. They will count the added square footage. They will consider the property improvement. The cost of raising a barn and the added taxes and feeding the cattle the hay that is now so expensive will undermine the profit.

WHAT THE WIFE COOKED FOR DINNER: Steamed squash and rice.

WHAT THE WIFE SAID: I really could be a vegetarian. We would all be better off if we were. Who needs meat?

WHAT I SAID: All those dogs on the meat wagons.

WHAT I THOUGHT: I am one of those dogs.

WHAT THE WIFE SAID AFTER DINNER: Whose sneakers are these on the floor? Who left the butter out? Whose books are these? Whose sweater? Whose crumbs? Can't you clean up after yourselves? Don't leave a wet towel on your bed. Flush the toilet. Can't anyone flush the toilet? These papers will get ruined on the table in the kitchen. Do you want your papers ruined?

WHAT THE CHILDREN DID: Ran outside.

WHAT I DID: Ran outside. We went and looked for trees that would be good for raising my deer stand. There's a hill and ridge below where a stream runs through. There are game trails going down the ridge. There is already a wooden deer stand there someone put up long ago where Sam could hunt from while I hunted from my tree stand at the same time. This would be a good place for my stand. I thought I could use my stand for other things than hunting, too. I could stand in my stand at night and call to the owls. I could stand in my stand at night and look for the bright lights in the sky, the object moving quickly back and forth, but then I remembered there was a warning that came with my stand. The warning said never to strap yourself into the harness in darkness because you may make a mistake, you may not be able to see where your leg should be going through a loop. You could be strapped into nothing. Also, you may not see a rung as you're climbing up to the stand. Your footing will have no purchase. You will fall like a shot bird from a branch, head over heels to the forest floor heavily strewn with needles of pine.

WHAT SAM DID: Imitated me standing in the stand and falling out and landing with my head on a rock.

WHAT MY DAUGHTERS DID: Jumped on top of him as he lay with his head on the rock being me.

WHAT I SAID: Shhh, if you want to see something in the woods you have to be quiet.

WHAT THE KIDS SAID ON THE WALK HOME: Tell us about when you were young. Tell us about the time you hit that kid with a pipe by accident and he had to get five stitches. Tell us about the boy who died after a hard rain in the culvert. Tell it to us again, they said, how he drowned, how the mother stood on the grass, holding her hand to her mouth, her legs giving way, her skirt darkening as she fell to the wet grass, as if she had peed herself, after hearing the news.

WHAT I SAID: Tell me instead what you did in school today.

WHAT THE CHILDREN SAID: Oh, today, some bad kids. Some older kids, they changed the words on the sign outside the school last night. You know the sign that says COME TO THE FALL BREAKFAST, that sign, well they changed the letters and they made the school sign say COME TO THE FALL BOOB FEST.

WHAT I SAID: I would like to go to that Fest.

WHAT THE CHILDREN SAID: Oh, Poppy.

WHAT THE WIFE SAID THE NEXT MORNING WHEN THE KIDS WERE AT SCHOOL: David, have you scheduled your next exam?

WHAT I SAID: Not yet, Jen.

WHAT THE WIFE SAID: You should schedule it soon. What if your levels are high again? Then what will you do?

WHAT I SAID: Cut it out.

WHAT THE WIFE SAID: Cut it out.

WHAT I SAID: I like living. I'll cut it out to get rid of it all.

WHAT THE WIFE SAID: I knew we should have had more sex.

WHAT I SAID: Want to have sex?

WHAT THE WIFE SAID: Now?

WHAT I SAID: It could cure me. It can't hurt.

WHAT THE WIFE SAID: Pleased to oblige.

WHAT THE KITCHEN ISLAND SAID: This is not the usual pounding of dough being kneaded.

WHAT FELT GOOD: Her breasts. The sex.

WHAT HURT AFTERWARD: My dick.

WHAT I SAID TO MY WIFE: That was a bad angle.

WHAT THE WIFE SAID: I should have worn heels.

WHAT I SAID: I made it to the boob fest after all.

WHAT THE WIFE DID: Laughed, hit my shoulder.

WHAT THE HOUSE SMELLED LIKE: Anadama bread the wife was baking.

WHAT WE ATE FOR LUNCH: Anadama bread, butter, and jelly.

WHAT WE ALL SAW FROM THE KITCHEN WINDOW WHEN THE CHILDREN CAME HOME: A spikehorn, too young a buck for me to shoot, behind the house, eating apples fallen to the ground beneath the apple tree. The children were noisy, too noisy, fighting over binoculars. They almost scared the buck away. Sam pretended he was holding his rifle. Bam-bam, he said excitedly, shooting multiple times. I hit him in the chest hard with the back of my hand. Be quiet, I said. I didn't want him to act this way when we would really go out to hunt. It wasn't safe. He ran upstairs, starting to cry, and the moment he ran up, I was sorry, and I wished he'd come back down. I almost ran up after him, but just then the buck scraped the dirt on the hillside with his front hoof, then he turned and stood over where he had scraped and shook his tail, releasing secretions from his glands. He hardly chewed the apples. He mostly swallowed them whole. I could hear Sam upstairs. He was watching the buck from the bathroom window. He had stopped crying now, and I could see the buck lifting his head, listening to sounds coming from our house, from my son above me who shifted his weight on the slate tiled floor of the bathroom, who rested an arm on the top of the clothes washer, who wiped his nose, runny from crying, on his shirtsleeve. Tell no one at school that we have a buck on our land, I told the children. Other hunters will want our buck if they hear, I said. The children nodded their heads.

WHAT THE CHILDREN DON'T KNOW: That their father may or may not need surgery.

WHAT I DID INSTEAD OF MAKING A DOCTOR'S APPOINTMENT:
Cleared land by the stream. If the banks of the stream are cleared,
the children can run to the stream, they can lay their bodies down
beside it, watching the small trout as small as their hands swimming.

CALL: A colicking horse.

ACTION: Drove to farm during snow flurries. Directions from
owner were to keep driving down a dirt road, and when you feel
as if you've missed it and that you're in the middle of nowhere,
then keep driving. Finally found the farm. Gave horse Buscopan,
a new tranquilizer I had just ordered, to ease his pain. Decided
to oil horse to relieve colic. Inserted tube inside his nostril and
pumped the oil in. Stood talking to owner. She told me to guess
what she had seen on her front lawn. I thought she would say the
flying object with the bright lights. I thought I had found someone
else who had seen what I had seen. Instead she said that one day
her husband and her sons took their rifles and went hunting up on
the hill behind the house. She could see them hiking up the hill
through the window. But in the front yard, through the picture
window, she noticed a huge twelve-point buck just standing and
nibbling grass in the yard. She knew that if she opened a window
to yell at her husband and her two sons to come back down the
hill and shoot the buck, then the buck would take off and bound
through the woods. She just sat in her chair in the living room and
watched him through the picture window. He had a broad chest
and a handsome head and when he lifted it every once in a while
it seemed to her as if he could see her watching him from her easy
chair.

It was then that the owner stopped talking and pointed to the floor of the barn by the horse's feet and said, Look at all that oil on the floor.

RESULT: A cold shiver ran up my spine. This is a horse doctor's worst nightmare, that you have inserted the stomach tube through his nose but you put it into his lungs instead of his stomach and now it's coming back out and you have just drowned the horse. You have just bought the horse. I was content listening to the owner talk about the big handsome buck in her front yard. I wanted to keep listening to her telling the story. For a moment, I was her in the nice easy chair positioned in front of the window with a view of the beautiful twelve-pointer lifting his head and looking me in the eyes and her husband and sons far away by now, up over the back of the hill and into the woods. But no, there was now this oil pooled at our feet and the horse with his head down so low it looked as if he would drink up the oil beneath him.

I checked the tube. I blew into it. There was no buildup of pressure. I was able to blow air through it. This was a relief. I knew then that I had not put the tube down the lungs instead of the stomach. It was the new tranquilizer, the Buscopan, that had relaxed the smooth muscles of the esophagus so much that when the horse lowered its head, the oil came out its nose. After a while, the horse seemed better. The symptoms of his colic subsided. I put my stethoscope to him and I could hear the sloshing sounds of his moving gut. He was breathing easier now. The owner wiped up the oil with a towel, and the place on the floor where the oil had been was now clean.

THOUGHTS ON DRIVE HOME: That was scary. That was not good for my levels. Calm your levels, I said to myself. Look how the sun is over the fading green lawns now, raked clean of October's falling leaves, and the sky is blue with passing clouds. The snow flurries are over.

WHAT SAM SAID TO ME WHEN I GOT HOME: Pop, they have given deer eye tests and they have found out what deer can and cannot see. They can see the camo that hunters wear. They roll their eyes at camo. They've invented a new kind of camo, it's not shaped like leaves or branches, it's like computer dots! The tiny pattern matches the colors of the woods, it looks the way the woods would feel to a deer. They learned how to do it from leopards and tigers. Leopards and tigers don't look like leaves or trees, they have spots and stripes, but when the leopard runs or the tiger runs, their spots and stripes blend into the background.

WHAT I SAID: Deer have entered the computer age? I myself have not mastered email.

WHAT THE WIFE COOKED FOR DINNER: Falafel.

WHAT THE CHILDREN SAID: Fal-awful.

WHAT THE MORNING SAID: The deer have already walked through here and you have missed them and next time you should wake up earlier. You should be out here before morning, before my fog has lifted, before the birds have sung.

NUMBER OF DEER I SAW WHILE DEER HUNTING: 0.

NUMBER OF SQUIRRELS I SAW WHILE DEER HUNTING: 6.

NUMBER OF TIMES I WIPED MY HAND ON MY SLEEVE BECAUSE I WAS COLD AND MY NOSE WAS RUNNING: 10.

NUMBER OF THINGS I CAN TAKE TO HELP MY LEVELS GO DOWN: 0. No vitamin A, B, C, D, or E can bring them back down.

WHAT THE CHILDREN SAID TO ME WHEN I GOT HOME: Hi, in German.

WHAT I SAID: Oh, my *lieblings*, you have been paying attention to your Poppy! German is a great language.

WHAT THE WIFE SAID: They should speak Spanish instead. So much of the world does.

WHAT I SAID: Do you really want to know what the Mexicans are saying? I'd rather know what the Germans are saying.

WHAT THE WIFE SAID: To the showers, *mach schnell.* That's what they said.

WHAT I SAID: No, no, they said that only during a fascist regime, but they also strived to do the best. Do the very best, they said. Make the very best, they said. That's what I want my children to learn, I said.

WHAT THE WIFE SAID: Maybe they should learn a little Buddhism. A little maybe it doesn't matter to be the best.

WHAT I SAID: Listen to the children. Hear them say let's race to the car. Let's race up the stairs. Let's race to the end of the field. Who can be the first to finish this book, that meal, brushing their teeth. This is what the children want, I said to my wife. They want to be the best.

WHAT THE WIFE SAID: Dinner? You and the children make your own. I'm sure it'll be the best.

WHAT I COOKED: Tomato soup and grilled cheese.

CALL: No call again, just the caller who hangs up. *Bist du krank?* I said to the caller, practicing my German. "Der Ozean ist blau. Die Maus ist grau." Who are you talking to? the wife and children said. I put my hand on the mouthpiece, shhh, it is Merkel, she wants to know how I feel about health care. Then I took my hand off the mouthpiece and continued talking into the phone. "Ja, die Banane ist gelb."

WHAT THE HOUSE SAID: The house creaks and groans. The house of hemlock, pegged together, framed like a barn so our children can say they grew up in a barn. So they can say they grew up in a house that always sounded like it was coming apart.

WHAT WE HEARD AT NIGHT: Rifle shots.

WHAT SAM DID: He ran into our room and turned our light on. Pop, he said, I can see from my window, they are jacking deer up the road. They are turning their cars into the field and catching deer in the headlights. They should be stopped, Sam said. It's unethical, he said.

WHAT I SAID: When did you learn that word? sitting up on my elbows and rubbing my eyes, "unethical"?

WHAT SAM SAID WHILE STANDING IN THE DOORWAY IN HIS PLAID BOXERS: Pop, I didn't take hours of hunter safety not to know what *unethical* means.

WHAT I SAID: Yes, I forgot. I am living with a walking talking hunter safety manual.

WHAT I FELT: Sad for the deer. They had no chance frozen in the headlights. All right to kill them by day, I mused. But it wasn't yet rifle season. Just coming on bow. What right have they got? I ranted. I shook my wife's shoulder.

WHAT THE WIFE SAID: Call the police.

WHAT I DID: I called the police. Not an emergency, I said right away. The warden came. He went on his hunt for the men who were probably crouching by their dead deer in the woods, slitting it open. The warden would find them. He would arrest them. Go back to bed, I told Sam. I hope they didn't shoot the buck I am going to shoot when it's rifle season, that wouldn't be fair, he said, and then he stomped back to his room and slammed the door shut, only because every door he shut was slammed and every floor he walked across was stomped across because he did not know the meaning of quiet and I wondered if he would really be able to be quiet enough this year in the woods to shoot a deer or if I should wait to take him out next year when maybe he would be more Indian, more light of foot and aware of how to stop his body from crashing against boughs of pine and treading noisily over fallen leaves.

WHAT THE WIFE SAID: Can we go to sleep now? Close the window. It's cold.

WHAT I SAID: Leave the window, Jen. I want to hear for their cars. I want to hear if there are more rifle shots and tires rolling on the dirt road and car engines. I am attuned to those sounds now. They make the hair on the back of my neck stand up.

WHAT I HEARD WITH THE WINDOW OPEN: A whir. Could it be the spacecraft? I opened up the screen and craned my neck to look out the window. It was the spacecraft. It wasn't circling the house this time. Instead it was hovering above it. It stayed that way for a while, and then it quickly sailed away, as if answering to the call of someone else far out in the universe.

WHAT THE WIFE COOKED FOR DINNER: She didn't. We went out. Her idea, not mine. Chinese in what used to be a train car. Sam ordered underwater conference. He picked up a shrimp and a scallop off the platter. How do you do? he said, holding the shrimp so it faced the scallop and moving the shrimp up and down, as if it were talking. Sarah, my Sarah, fell in love with crab Rangoon. Mia learned from her place setting that she was a horse.

CALL: A Belgian cannot breathe.

ACTION: Incised the horse's trachea, looked around for a tube of some sort to put into the trachea to maintain an airway. Asked owner if she had a plastic gallon milk container. Cut off handle of milk container, inserted it into horse's incision.

RESULT: Belgian started to breathe.

WHAT THE OWNER ASKED: How long do I keep the handle in the horse?

WHAT I SAID: Forever.

WHAT THE OWNER DID: She was short. She was probably eye level with the incision and the handle of the milk container sticking out. She could see the wet skin around the horse's neck where I had dunked a towel in water and wiped the blood away. She could see how even though we had rinsed out the milk jug, we did not have time to wash it, and there was still a bit of white watery fluid inside the handle. She nodded. The horse lowered his head toward her and then she put her forehead right against the white star he had there.

THOUGHTS ON DRIVE HOME: Leaves are just mini solar panels. The leaves positioned all around the tree's trunk catching optimum rays all throughout the day. Photosynthesizing all day long. What if you designed a solar panel that looked like a tree? Why can't you plug in a tree? Don't they sell science kits to kids where you can plug wires into a potato and run a watch? Why not plug into a tree?

WHAT THE KIDS SAID TO ME WHEN I GOT HOME: And oranges, you can plug in an orange and run a watch, too.

WHAT THE WIFE COOKED: Carrot soup.

WHAT WE SAID: What else is there to eat?

WHAT THE WIFE SAID: What do you mean what else? She shook her head and looked at us trying to understand.

WHAT I COOKED: Fried eggs and bacon and peanut butter and mayonnaise and lettuce and tomato sandwiches made with toasted bread.

WHAT I SAID TO SAM WHILE I COOKED: Sam, are you ready for youth deer weekend tomorrow?

WHAT SAM SAID: My Mauser and I are ready.

WHAT I THOUGHT: What a lucky boy to already have an attachment to his hunting rifle, as well he should, it being a German Mauser that belonged to his grandfather.

WHAT THE WIFE SAID: Don't wake me up in the morning.

WHAT SARAH AND MIA DID: Ran outside.

WHAT SARAH SAID: I'm going to barf.

WHAT MIA SAID: I'm going to barf.

WHAT THEY DID: Barfed. One in the driveway, one in the flower bed.

WHAT I DID IN THE MORNING: Woke the wife up, looking for pants that would keep out the rain while I hunted with Sam.

WHAT THE WIFE SAID: Fuck, do you have to fucking wake me up in the morning? Can't you find your own fucking pants? How old are you, anyway?

CALL: My son. I can't get to him fast enough. He has fallen from the wooden tree stand on our property. The stand is an old stand whose supports are wooden boards nailed into branches of maples growing close together. This is not the stand I have purchased with the warning labels all over it. This is a stand that has been on our property for years. This is a stand that you climb up to by stepping on slats of gray worn wood nailed with nails now rusty, into the tree. This is a stand where there's a milk crate sitting on its rotting

platform, and you sit on the milk crate and you wait for your buck
to come out and show his face while you notice how sore you are
from sitting on hard plastic for so long.

ACTION: From my store-bought tree stand set up fifty yards away,
I see him fall. I see him and I do what every hunter safety manual
would tell me not to do—I throw my rifle to the ground beneath
me so that I can go down the footholds more easily and quickly,
but nothing is quick with all the gear on. I am a tangle of canvas
straps and plastic buckles that are fastened around my legs and by
my crotch. My son is on the leaves, the rain has stopped but now
there is a brisk wind, the leaves have already blown over him and
there is a bright yellow one on his cheek, as he lies still, his eyes
closed. Oh, Christ. There is no bute or Banamine or injection I
can give him. There is nothing I can do. There was another hunter
in the woods. He was not out for deer. He hunted with a shotgun,
firing off into the sky at the grouse he had flushed while walking
through our woods. These two seasons overlap, grouse and deer.
My son fell twelve feet, on his head. He fell from the force of the
shot hitting his shoulder. I did not see the hunter. The hunter is
gone now, the grouse in more northern woods where I have seen
some cedar waxwings also head, and my son is unconscious with
gunshot peppering the flesh of his shoulder. I can see the holes
in the cloth of his coat, and the goose feathers sticking out from
them, wavering in the wind.

I look around. Where is the hunter? Where the hell is he? But
I do not hear anyone coming toward me through the fallen leaves.
It's quiet now, except for the sound of a squirrel chattering at me
from a few trees away. I put my son over my shoulders in a fireman's carry. I am surprised how fast I can run down the hillside

and back to our house. I am surprised the door is already open to our house. Did the house know what happened and was it ready and waiting for me? There is no one else home. I put Sam on the kitchen table. He is breathing, but he is not awake. I take off his coat and wrap towels around his wound. There is blood, but not a lot of it. There are leaves on the table, too, from when I scooped him up to carry him home and the leaves are mixed with the mail, the bill from the gas company and the catalog from a store that sells seeds and tulip bulbs for spring.

An ambulance isn't smart, not where we live anyway. What is smart is if I put him in the backseat of the truck and drive him to the hospital myself. I will get there that much faster.

On the windy back roads, I reach out behind me, only one hand on the wheel. I make sure he's not going to slide off the seat and onto the floor, I am driving so fast. I drive fast past the Bunny Hutch preschool, even though there are signs everywhere telling me to slow down, telling me there are children at play.

RESULT: My son is being cut out of his camouflage clothes by nurses and I'm standing beside him, my canvas straps from my tree stand safety harness dangling on the hospital floor. I have not had time to take it off, and if I did, I do not know where I would put it. There are no hooks on the wall for coats, nor for the safety harness of a deer-hunting tree stand. He is scanned and there is no sign of brain damage. And a coma, the doctor says, can be, and he knew it sounded strange, not such a serious thing. The body has the opportunity to rest, the doctor says, and on the Glasgow scale, he's scoring high, the doctor says. His chances are good. Ah, the Glasgow scale, I say and look at my son. His face appears pale and yellow, and I wonder if the yellow fallen leaf that had lain on his cheek had somehow left some of its yellow color on his skin, and what comes to mind is the way my girls have played with dandelion flowers, rubbing them on their cheeks because they said the yellow dust was like their mother's blush.

The gunshot is taken out while I sit in the waiting room, head in my hands, thinking of calling my Jen, then thinking to wait until I know more, until maybe he wakes up from his coma and I can tell her how he's better now, how he was unconscious, but that's over. I look up. People walk by, a few men in camo. Is one of them the hunter? I think. I feel the blood rush to my face. Is one of them the one who mistook my son for a bird? Has he come to inquire about my son? Has he come to tell me he's sorry? But these men have not just come from hunting. They are only wearing fashionable camo-patterned pants that are more the weight of jeans than the heavy cloth of real hunting pants that are double-lined and meant to walk through sharp briar and meddlesome branches of pine. The men are wearing sneakers and short sleeves and in the brief moment they walk by me I can smell cigarette smoke on them. They have come from someplace inside and not from the woods. The man who shot my son is not here. The man who shot my son is probably home by now, removing his boots, the dirt from my land falling from the soles to his mudroom floor, his wife inquiring about his luck with game bird. The man who shot my son probably just up the road from where I live and too afraid to come to my door and tell me what he's done.

CALL: An owner needs a health certificate for his horse to travel to North Carolina. I do not respond to the call.

CALL: An owner's horse has a spot of fungus on the pastern. I do not respond to the call.

CALL: An owner's horse has a navicular cyst. I do not respond to the call.

CALL: Jen wants to know where we are. Why is there blood on the table? she says in the same breath and in the background I can hear her pacing in our kitchen, walking across the loose floorboard that squeaks by the kitchen sink. It is a floorboard that is turning black from water sliding off the counter when dishes are washed, and pooling on the floor.

ACTION: There wasn't much blood, I tell her. The hunter was a bad shot, he only hit Sam's shoulder. Thank God, Jen says. I can hear her sigh over the phone and I almost feel the warm breath of it coming through, or is that just my own breath coming back to me that I breathed into the phone? She is on her way, of course, even after I have told her I would stay with him. Even after I told her he would be fine. I go down to the lower level. It is more like a mall. There are shops where I can hear the coffee machines at work, spraying lattes into cups. There are shops that sell baby clothes and there are shops sporting holiday decorations early, white ceramic polar bears hanging by ribbons on the branches of fake trees. The polar bears look smooth and polished, as if they had been tumbled by waves for years at an ocean's pebbly shore. I have an urge to buy something for Sam. I could buy him a Rapidograph. There is one in a stationery store's window. I'd like to see the fine lines he could draw with it. I can see him drawing a submarine, the periscope bending like a goose's neck, observing all there is to see across the sketchbook page.

WHO I SEE IN THE LOWER LEVEL: My own doctor wearing a breast cancer pin buying a Jamba Juice.

WHO DOESN'T SEE ME: My own doctor buying a Jamba Juice.

RESULT: Jen has come and she is with me by his bed now and she is yelling at me. She is telling me she will never forgive me for having done this to our son, our only son. How could you? She's holding my son's hand while she is yelling and I think maybe she is like Arthur the farmhand and all she has to do is put her hand on my son and he will talk through her and my son is yelling at me now. How could you? she yells. I am sorry I said that, she then says and she goes to me so that I can hold her. I am so sorry, I say. I can smell the scent of our Newfoundlands in her hair, and I think how before she saw the blood on the table she must have greeted the dogs and bent down low and hugged Bruce or Nelly, and her hair must have fallen across the dogs' fur. I tell her what the doctor said, that sometimes, not always, the coma can be not such a bad thing. I tell her about the Glasgow scale, how high he's scoring on it and how good that is. Oh, really? she says. She shakes her head. She looks down at our son. She puts her hand on his forehead, as if he were sick with the flu and she was feeling for a fever. She bends closer to him, breathing in different places on his face. It wasn't enough to get shot? she says, and it's to our son she is talking.

WHAT I DON'T TELL HER: That I will find a way to get the hunter who shot our son.

WHAT THE DOCTOR SAYS AFTER WE HAVE STAYED THERE TWO NIGHTS: Go home and sleep. Think of your son as sleeping, too. Go home to your other children. Explain to them what has happened. It's the best you can do.

WHAT SARAH SAYS: Sam likes to sleep. I bet he's happy.

WHAT THE SHERIFF WHO IS ON THE CASE SAYS AFTER HE HAS COME BACK FROM SEARCHING OUR WOODS: Traces of the man are not to be found.

WHAT MY WIFE DOES: Sits up in bed all night with the light on, not even reading.

WHAT I DO: Read the paper.

WHAT THE WIFE ASKS: How can you read the paper?

WHAT I SAY: I can't do anything else. You could so, she says. You're right, I could go out, I say. I get my clothes on and grab a flashlight. I tell her I want to find my rifle that I dropped beneath my store-bought tree stand. What I really want to do is find traces of the man who shot my son that the sheriff, when he came back from his investigation in our woods, said were not to be found. I want to run through the night hitting every branch as I go, kicking up every leaf, punching my fist into the stone-hard bark of all the fifty-foot pines that bore witness, that all saw the man who shot my son, but that cannot speak to tell me his name.

WHAT THE NIGHT SAYS: Go home. There are no clues here, no flattened leaves holding the shape of a boot of a hunter. No evidence, even, of the plate-sized footprints of the half-ton moose that has traveled here before. Your rifle will still be on the ground in the morning.

WHAT THE COYOTES SAY: You have crossed over to where we live and now our howls could be the howls of your own heart you are hearing, or just us, our coats slightly ruffed from the November chill.

WHAT I DO WITH THE FLASHLIGHT: Point it on my son's tree stand, point it on the plastic milk crate, point it at the ground where I found him, point it on the ground where the hunter probably stood who shot him but there is nothing to see, no telltale impression of a hunter's boot in the fallen leaves. I turn and walk to my own tree stand and find my rifle that I only notice because the tip of the barrel is not completely covered in leaves, and it is as if in the time since my son had been shot the leaves were trying to cover up some kind of disgrace, as if it were my rifle that was responsible for the harm done to my son, and the leaves like so many hands of creatures or fairies that live on our land would make the earth swallow it down. I pick up my rifle and head home, the howls of the coyotes flanking either side of me as if they were providing some kind of corridor leading me straight to my home and back to my bed.

CALL: In the morning, a bread machine that needs the belt reattached.

ACTION: Told the wife I could do it. Set bread machine on kitchen table. Unscrewed all the screws in the bread machine. (Number of screws: 62.)

RESULT: Reattached the belt. Screwed back in 60 screws. Two disappeared.

THOUGHTS WHILE WALKING WITH BREAD MACHINE FROM TABLE TO COUNTER TO PLUG IN BREAD MACHINE: It's winter. Snow is falling outside the window. We are living in a snow globe. If there had been snow on the ground at the time my son was shot, the footprints of the hunter who shot him would still be in the snow, but there was no snow and the ground did not hold a man's boot print.

WHAT THE GIRLS SAID WHEN THEY CAME HOME: What's that burning smell?

WHAT THE WIFE SAID: Look at the floor! Take off your boots!

WHAT SMELLED LIKE SOMETHING BURNING WHEN IT SHOULD HAVE SMELLED LIKE BREAD BAKING: The bread machine, whose paddles were not turning because the rubber belt had once again slipped.

WHAT THE RADIO SAID: Beep-de-dah-beep-de-dah-beep-beep-beep.

WHAT THE WIFE SAID TO THE GIRLS: I am getting a transmission.

WHAT I THOUGHT: My wife can save us all. She can save me. She can save our son. She can take us up in her spacecraft. Our son will awaken in the spacecraft and my wife will rub a window clear for him to see down below to our fields covered in frost. She will point out how places in the field hit with morning sun have already melted, and the dead grass showing through is as tawny as the hides of lions on African land.

Part Two

Winter

WHAT WE DO: Visit Sam whenever we can. I sit beside his bed. I bring magazines and newspapers as if I were going on a trip and knew I would need something to read. When I'm done reading them I leave them on the bed and when Jen sits down next to him she becomes angry, pulling out the newspapers and magazines from underneath her and around her, throwing them onto the floor, their pages spreading, catching air, coming down for a slow landing like the geese on Arthur's pond. Can't you put them away? she says. I gather them up and keep them in a stack beside his bed and tell the day nurse not to throw them away. Who knows, I say, if there is an article in one of them I missed. Sam is pale and Jen puts her hand on his cheek and rubs it and I wonder if she's trying to give his face some color. When Sarah and Mia come they play beneath his bed, creating a fort with his blanket and his sheet, exposing him where he lies dressed in a hospital gown. Don't, he'll get cold, Jen says and tries dismantling the walls of their fort, but they protest. "It's hot in here! I'm burning up!" they cry, and it's true, the hospital is overheated. "Let them, it's okay," I say to Jen and she nods her head, letting Sarah and Mia play beneath his bed, every once in a while hitting a hanging blanket, making the blanket move, making it look like just maybe it's Sam doing the moving himself.

THOUGHTS ON DRIVE HOME: My hands are cracking again in this dry weather and I must rub them with Silvadene tonight and wear some gloves to keep them from cracking and bleeding further. I must order more vaccine because I am running low on vaccine. I must teach the children some German. We have not picked up our books in days. I must turn on the German language CD to listen to while driving in my car. The woman on the CD is named Gisela. I have listened to Gisela for months now in her dialogues. Gisela is my good *Freundin*. I wonder if I would be able to understand another woman so well as Gisela. Gisela, on the CD, has let Jürgen know her telephone number. I now know Gisela's phone number, too.

WHAT GISELA SAYS WHILE I AM DRIVING HOME FROM A CALL: Where is an apothecary? I'd like to purchase some aspirin.

WHAT I PASS ON THE ROAD: A diner, a bowling alley, a car dealer, a tax-preparation office. Gisela doesn't need these things. What Gisela needs is an apothecary. I must find one for Gisela. Gisela feels *krank*. Gisela would like to remove her *Kopf* from her shoulders and take a break from it. It is causing her so much pain.

WHAT I NEED TO DO: Order more vaccine. You would think West Nile virus runs rampant through these parts the way I need to vaccinate for it, and maybe it does. Little Egypt, the town, is only a few hours south of here.

WHAT GISELA SAYS: I also need to find the butcher's. Do you know where one is?

CALL: An old horse that needs to be put down.

ACTION: Had owner walk horse over alongside the wide deep grave dug with a tractor. While the horse walked alongside his grave, one of his feet slipped. He almost fell in. I gave the shot. He did not go down. I had to give more. Finally he went down. He fell on his knees, his head in between them. His eyes not so glassy, his eyes looking like he still could see.

WHAT THE OWNER SAID: How do you get him in the hole?

RESULT: Watch, I told the owner. I tipped the horse. He flipped. He fell into the hole sitting up. His head facing forward, his head propped up by the wall of dirt.

WHAT THE OWNER SAID: Is it all right to bury him that way? Shouldn't he be down flat? Isn't his head, even after it's covered with dirt, too close to the surface?

WHAT I DID: I shook my head. There was nothing going to dig up that horse's grave. That horse, with his wise look, would frighten any other animal away.

THOUGHTS ON RIDE HOME: It might happen again. A fascist leader might rise to power here. It might even be a woman. How ironic. Everyone happy to see a woman finally in power, only it comes at a time when the country is broke and the woman is a fascist, her ideals appealing to an economically battered public. Who can say it won't happen? Who will save our country? Who will fight for the good? Who will fight Hitlerina?

WHAT THE WIFE COOKED FOR DINNER: Pulled pork on a bun.

WHAT I HEARD IN THE MIDDLE OF THE NIGHT: A whinny. A horse lost down our road. At first it sounded like an owl or a coyote, or even, Jen said, the sound of Sam crying.

WHAT I TOLD HER: All the way from the hospital we would not be able to hear our son cry.

WHAT THE WIFE SAID: Maybe the horse is injured. Maybe it's his levels. At least he knows when to see the doctor. Have you made your appointment yet?

WHAT I SAID: That's not the whinny of an injured horse. He's just calling to see if anyone's around. He will find his way home at daybreak. A smart horse doesn't travel at night when he might trip and break his leg when he can't see.

WHAT I DID: I turned on the light in our bedroom for the horse.

WHAT THE WIFE SAID: You're leaving a light on for a horse?

WHAT I SAID: He's just like us. He gets scared in the dark.

WHAT THE WIFE DID: She nodded. All right, leave the light on for him, she said. I hope they leave a light on for Sam in the middle of the night. I don't want him waking up in the dark, she said.

WHAT I SAID: Don't worry about the light in the hospital. That place is lit up like an airport. The lights stay on all night.

WHAT THE WIFE SAID: Yes, only too bad he's not going anywhere, too bad he's not getting on a plane. Too bad we are not going to some faraway place with a beach and a bar.

WHAT THE WIFE DID: Fell back to sleep. The flies buzzed. We have flies that winter over in our house. They swarm into the corners of the windows. They fly around the bulb in the lamp that is on. They are noisy. Some die every day, falling from the corners of the rafters and the windows and onto our bed. We shake out the top cover at night before we go to sleep so that they land on the floor instead. Sometimes, while we are sleeping, we are awakened by a dead one falling on our face. I fell back to sleep, too, by the sound, the buzzing lullaby.

HOW SAM WAS LYING DOWN: On his side. The day nurse moved him.

WHAT THE WIFE WANTED TO KNOW: Why she turned him so that he faced the door, and why didn't she turn him so that he faced the window. "At least the trees beyond the parking lot are something to look at," she said.

WHAT THE STATE TROOPER SAID: We've asked around, but if you didn't see the man who shot your son, then we have no lead. Unless your son had enemies, it was obviously an accident. He's okay, isn't he? The gunshot was just to the shoulder, right?

WHAT THE WIFE SAID: In a coma is not okay.

CALL: Another horse to put down.

ACTION: Put the horse down. The owner could talk German. The owner listened to me say a few German words. The owner corrected my accent while the horse fell to his knees.

RESULT: I worked on pronouncing *Strasse*, *fleissig*, and *Goebbels*. *Goebbels* is really difficult to say. We easily tipped the horse into the hole. He went in facedown, his knees bent as if he were in the middle of trying to dig with his hooves an even deeper hole in the ground.

THOUGHTS ON DRIVE HOME: How do you say "Fuck the fucker who shot my son" in German? The only curse word I know in German is *Scheisse*. I need to learn more German curse words. I need to learn "fuck." Then I can say "Fuck the fucker," instead of just knowing how to say *Scheisse*.

WHAT I DID WHEN I GOT HOME: Went to my tree stand. I checked the straps to make sure they were secure. I attached my bow to a long string and I set the bow on the ground and then I climbed up the deer stand with the end of the rope attached to my harness. When I was in my stand I pulled up my bow. I loaded my arrow. Then I stood. My ears turned on. The first thing I heard was my stomach gurgling. The second thing I heard was the wind blowing through what few leaves were left in the tops of the trees. I heard small birds, nuthatches, flitting under the fallen leaves, covered in light snow. I heard cars, far off, driving on the road. But I couldn't tell if they were coming or going. I heard a dog barking that did not sound like any dog I knew. Then it was quiet. Now was the time for a deer to walk past me. No deer did.

THOUGHTS WHILE DEER HUNTING: You may have to be really smart to kill a deer. Where are my antlers to clatter and call the deer in? Where is my doe urine? My grunt call made of plastic in the shape of a tube? My scent-lock coat? My milk jug to piss in so my own urine smell won't be carried in the wind? My camo made of millions of tiny computer dots?

WHAT SARAH AND MIA SAID WHEN I GOT HOME: Did you shoot any deer?

WHAT I SAID: Deer is not for dinner.

WHAT THE WIFE SAID: Good, I could really go for some stir-fry anyway.

WHAT I TOLD THE WIFE THAT NIGHT IN BED BECAUSE SHE WAS CRYING: I love you.

WHAT THE WIFE SAID, STOPPING HER CRYING: What's the matter? What hurts? We laughed. Hers is not a tinkly one, nor is it heavy or gravelly or deep. It is more like a grunt, first an inhalation, then an exhalation along with the sound of her voice, not high or low. What would the deer think of it? Could her laugh call them in? Could we both fit standing on the tree stand? Maybe if we were entwined. Her laugh my call that bags a prize buck?

WHAT THE WIFE DOES: Moves Sam herself so that he is facing the window, but she needs help. It is not easy. There are tubes to contend with. There is the slit in the back of his hospital gown now open, now exposing him to whoever walks in the door. We do it together, moving him, and he feels so much lighter than the last time I carried him, which was after he was shot and I held him in a fireman's carry down the hill. Sarah and Mia, seeing him exposed, dismantle their fort themselves and give back his blankets. Sarah tucks the blanket around his feet and underneath his body so that now he looks like a pale blue cocoon.

CALL: A horse with a lameness.

ACTION: Drove to farm. The poorest farm I have seen so far. Looked at horse. Spoke to owner. There was nowhere to sit outside. There were no lawn chairs, no typical rock walls. The owner's boy sat on the rusted seat of a tractor that did not look like it could move but grew up from the ground where it was, pushing itself through the dirt, and had come to rest. Tall grass grew up high alongside its tires, past the height of the wheel wells. The woman owner sat, too, she sat in the driver's seat of a compact car. She sat sideways in the seat with her legs and knees facing me and the door open. One of the tires of the car was a spare, not meant to be driven on for long, but of course it had been, and it looked bald. These were the only places to sit. Maybe there were places to sit inside the house, but I could not see through the windows. The panes of the windows were missing and in their places were sheets of milky colored plastic stapled to the frames.

RESULT: After I felt the horse's leg, I told the owner about the heat. I told her she would do well to stand the horse's leg in a bucket of ice water. The woman shook her head. "No ice," she said. "Isn't that right?" she said to her son. Her son shook his head, one hand on the steering wheel of the tractor, his sweater sleeves pulled up to his elbows, his arms streaked with dirt, as if he were the one who had driven the tractor up from the center of the earth, as if he did it every day and in a minute he would tunnel back down in his tractor and he would come back holding up a bag of ice, the outside of the bag covered in dirt, but nonetheless ice, because he seemed like the Artful Dodger out of *Oliver Twist*. He could obtain anything his heart desired, and it didn't matter what methods he used to get it. He was easily bought and easily sold. His wide nose was slightly bent to one side, as if the weight of the dirt he had pushed up through had made it bend that way and it could never be bent back. I looked at him and wondered why it was not this son who was in a coma. This son was not lucky enough to have a nose that was straight and thin like my son's and that I thought made my son look smart, even when my son was being stupid, leaving front doors open in the freezing cold, staring at numbers on homework pages for so long it was as if he expected them to rearrange themselves and form the answer when he could not. It was possible that they knew, this son and this mother, the man who shot my son, because it's such a small town, but if I asked them if they knew they would not answer me. Maybe if I paid the son, he would tell me, I thought, but then I just said to the mother, Any hose would do to spray on his leg, to keep the heat down, a constant stream of cold water.

THOUGHTS ON DRIVE HOME: With all the leaves off the trees I'm noticing more houses. When did all these houses appear?

WHAT SARAH AND MIA SAID TO ME WHEN I GOT HOME: Poppy, you look tired.

WHAT THE WIFE COOKED FOR DINNER: Chicken artichoke casserole.

WHAT I SAID TO THE WIFE IN BED: Am I getting grayer? The children told me I have more gray here. (I touched the side of my head to show her where the children had pointed.)

WHAT THE WIFE SAID: No, you don't have more gray than usual. It's just that the children are taller. They can see the gray they have never been able to see before.

WHAT THE NIGHT SAID: Coyotes rule.

WHAT I THOUGHT THE COYOTES WERE HOWLING AT: The spacecraft. I saw it again, this time hovering over our pond, its reflection shining on the dark water rippling in the wind. Was the pilot able to land it on water the way the geese at Arthur's could land themselves? Would the spacecraft submerge and rest on the bottom, the salamanders scooting over to make room for its alien hull?

WHAT I SAID TO THE WIFE: When you drove my truck to visit Sam, you drove too fast. You stop short and all my drugs get tossed around in the back.

WHAT SHE SAID: I don't drive too fast. I've never had a speeding ticket in my life. You, on the other hand, have had speeding tickets. Wasn't it just the other day you were doing 39 in a 25?

WHAT I SAID: Yes, but I did not get a ticket for it. The cop pulled me over and saw I was an animal doctor. He asked if I was going on an emergency call. I told him yes, and he let me go.

WHAT SHE SAID: You lied to him.

WHAT I SAID: I forgot to tell you. This morning, after I drove the kids to school, I saw the same cop in my rearview. His lights were flashing. *Scheisse*, I thought. I pulled over. The cop got out of his cruiser and said, Do you know what I'm pulling you over for? My expired inspection sticker? I said. No, he said, get that taken care of anytime. I just want to know if that horse you were going to see the other night is all right, he said.

WHAT THE WIFE SAID: Our town cop's a comedian.

WHAT I ALMOST RAN OVER THE OTHER NIGHT ON THE ROAD: A deer, a doe. She changed her mind halfway across and turned back into the field she had come from.

WHAT THE WIFE WANTS: I don't know. Haven't I given her all she should ask for?

WHAT THE WIFE SAYS: You're a prick.

WHAT I FEEL LIKE: Not a prick.

WHAT I TURN THE RADIO UP FOR: Celebration time, come on.

WHAT SHE TURNS IT DOWN FOR: Celebration time, come on.

WHAT SARAH AND MIA FIGHT OVER WHEN WE DRIVE TO VISIT SAM: Sitting shotgun, sharing gum, who punched whom too hard after a punch buggy sighting.

WHAT I TELL THE WIFE WHILE WE'RE IN THE HOSPITAL LOOK-ING AT SAM IN THE HARSH WHITE LIGHT: We could sell our place. We could live in Ecuador. We could surf every day. We could eat fresh fish.

WHAT THE WIFE SAYS: This is your levels talking. But I like the idea, change is good.

WHAT I SAY: I don't really want to live in Ecuador. I just want to live in a smaller house way up in the woods.

WHAT I THINK: My levels don't talk. They just go up and down. Why is my wife personifying my levels?

WHAT THE WIFE SAYS: I like the part about surfing. When was the last time we dug our toes in sand? Are there sharks? Is there crime? Will our children be stolen? she said and then she went to Sam and brought the blanket up to his chin even though the hospital was roasting.

WHAT I DID WHEN I GOT HOME: I walked up the hill. I cleared the land. I threw small trees in a pile and started them to burn. Night fell. I heard a coyote close by, howling a small howl outside the circle of my fire. There was no wind, but somehow, opposite where the coyote was, the leaves kicked up. They turned in a circle, forming a cyclone that spun itself into the shape of a man, then as quickly as the leaves started up, they fell to the ground. A moment later I heard the coyote howling again, only this time he had moved, he was howling right behind where the leaves had spun themselves into the shape of a man.

THOUGHTS WHILE WATCHING THE LEAVES IN THE SHAPE OF A MAN: The man looks a little like me. The man looks like a younger version of myself. The man looks the way my son might look when he is older. Where had he come from? The sky? The spacecraft?

CALL: No call. It was another hang-up call. I said, "Jawohl! Jawohl! Ich heisse David Appleton, und du?" but there was no one there. Who are you talking to? Is it about Sam? the wife said. "Der Kapitän, das Boot ist kaputt!" I said and then I said, "Alarm! Alarm! Dive, dive, dive!" and I dove under the telephone table and then Sarah and Mia started screaming it too and the wife put her hands over her ears and the dogs started barking and the wife yelled for me to shut up. It's not funny, she yelled. None of this is, she said, and then she started to cry. Sarah and Mia went to her. They hugged her and I stayed where I was under the phone table, noticing how thick clouds of black fuzzy Newfoundland hair had shored up against the table's spiraled legs.

WHAT I CAN DO: I can swallow my tongue. I can swim fast and for a long distance. I can tie a cherry stem into a knot with just my tongue. I can take a nap and tell myself I only want to sleep for twenty minutes and then I wake up after twenty minutes, without the aid of an alarm clock. I cannot ride a horse. I tried riding a horse. I fell off the horse. I fell from an eighteen-hand Belgian draft horse after he decided he'd rather gallop than walk up our dirt road. I could not see clearly after I fell. For days I could not see whatever was to the side of me, as if I were a horse wearing blinders. It was ironic, falling off a horse and then walking around like a horse with blinders on. Jen said I was not missing much, but still, I would have liked to have known what was about to come up from behind.

WHAT THE WIFE SAYS: Can we drive to see Sam again?

WHAT I SAY: No, we have been there once already today. Nothing has changed in him. The only thing that might have changed is his sheets, maybe, and the angles of the shadows on the fucking tiles of the floor.

WHAT MY WIFE CAN DO: Make me angrier than I have ever been.

WHAT OUR NEWFOUNDLAND DOGS DO: Never make me angry. Sneeze when they're on their backs. Drink out of the toilet. The other day Bruce drank out of the toilet and then stood by the woodstove and shook his massive head and sprayed water so far that it hit the woodstove with a fire in it and the spray of water popped and fizzed on the woodstove like a greasy spoon's griddle.

CALL: A woman needs her horses' teeth floated.

ACTION: Ate a big breakfast. Floating teeth is hard work. Drove to farm.

RESULT: Filed down the hooks in the back of the horses' mouths. Told the woman they were very polite horses, which they were, and let me float them without giving them any tranq.

THOUGHTS WHILE DRIVING TO HOSPITAL: How do the animals survive in the winter? I mustn't cut the milkweed I left to grow in the field for the monarch butterflies, because now I am sure the stand of milkweed I left is home to mice and voles. I could keep driving. Where would I go? I have already been west. I have walked the streets the nights filled with the smell of palm trees, dusty with car exhaust particles caught in the tapering fronds in the dry desert wind. The streets slick on nights of a fast rain that ended quick, the mornings a blooming rose color in the sunrise.

WHAT THE WIFE SAID AT HOME AFTER WE WALKED IN THE DOOR, AFTER WE HAD BEEN TO THE HOSPITAL AND HAD SEEN HOW SAM WAS IN EXACTLY THE SAME POSITION HE WAS IN THE DAY BEFORE, HOW NO NIGHT NURSE OR DAY NURSE HAD BOTHERED TO MOVE HIM: What about Ecuador? Tell me again about the surfing?

WHAT I SAID: No, Ecuador is out of the question.

WHAT THE WIFE SAID: Bali, then?

WHAT I SAID: No, not Bali, not Fiji, not Maui or Palau. Here, right here, where we live is where we'll stay.

WHAT THE WIFE SAID: This is not an island, we're surrounded by trees, not water, and then she stood at the window looking out over the parking lot.

WHAT I SAID: Then that makes it some kind of island, and the trees some kind of danger, a thing to drown in, the crowns of pines so thick no daylight passes through to the forest floor below, no air visible to breathe. Panic is just steps away. Feel better now? I asked.

WHAT THE HOUSE SAID: I have let the mice come in for the winter to live in the walls, for if I don't they will be cold and hungry and I am not that kind of house to shut them out.

CALL: A man with an old Appaloosa he wants to put down. (See, I told the wife, how now there are so many of these calls.)

ACTION: Drove to farm. Tranqued the horse so the owner could walk him calmly alongside the hole that had been dug with a backhoe.

WHAT THE OWNER SAID: I want him in the hole facing east.

WHAT I SAID: East?

WHAT THE OWNER SAID: Yes, east.

RESULT: The owner turned the horse facing east and held on to the horse's halter. Did the horse love the mountains facing east, did he go for trail rides there his entire life? I wondered. Or was it something Asian, something feng shui I had never heard of before that the owner believed in. I thought how if I hadn't myself seen an object with bright lights floating in the sky, I would have thought feng shui was bunk, but now feng shui quite possibly contained a kernel of truth. I felt ready to accept feng shui, and maybe even the yeti. I looked behind my shoulder, into the woods, but there wasn't anything nine feet tall crashing through them. What was crashing down, more dangerously, was the horse. After I gave the series of shots, the horse started to fall, he was going down, but the owner was standing too close to the horse. The owner was going to fall in the hole with his horse because he forgot to let go of the horse's halter. The owner was old. He had white hair and gray stubble. I did what I had to do. I pushed the owner back with a swing of my arm. The horse then turned his backside, he swung his hips so that instead of facing east, he was now facing west. He was going in the hole the opposite way. After he fell in, I turned to the owner. He was on the ground. He was just looking up. His name was Jack. Did Jack know the man who shot my son? I looked around. What clues were there to tell me that he did know? It did not seem the old man hunted, himself. It did not seem the old man could even see so well. It did not seem the old man had the strength to even raise a shotgun in the air. Jack, I said, I am going to give you a hand up. I held out my hand to Jack, but he still looked up. I looked up, too, thinking there was something other than the sky to see. I grabbed on to Jack's arm and pulled. When Jack was standing he took his cap off his head and put it on again. Then he looked down into the hole. He nodded when he saw his horse, as if to say even in your moment of death you have done what was contrary to what I wanted you to do. And I thought on these mountains facing east, on these trails his horse so often rode, was Jack the one who had to yank his horse's reins hard, get him going where he wanted him to go? Was Jack's horse that kind of stubborn mule?

THOUGHTS ON RIDE HOME: If my levels get too high, if they talk too much, then put me out of my misery and burn me on a pyre, that's how I want to go. Don't bother with a backhoe to try and dig the hole. Take down the trees to build the pyre off our land. Let the Newfoundlands have my bones. Let them walk the property drooling with my femur between their massive jaws. I am renewable energy.

WHAT THE WIFE COOKED FOR DINNER: Meat loaf with sweet pickle.

WHAT SARAH AND MIA SAID: We love sweet pickle.

WHAT THE WIFE SAID: Sweet pickle is so sweet I might as well put candy in your meat loaf instead.

WHAT THE HOUSE SAID AT NIGHT WHILE WE LAY IN BED: I am just made of wood. I can break.

WHAT SARAH SAID THAT WE COULD HEAR HER SAY FROM HER BED WHILE WE LAY IN OURS: Mom, Pop, the house is coming apart.

WHAT THE WIFE SAID: Is it true, can the house break apart?

WHAT I FELT: That it was my heart that was breaking in two. I turned over, switching sides.

WHAT I SAID: The house will be the last thing to go, I said, now facing the wall.

WHO IS NICER THAN THE DAY NURSE: The night nurse. The night nurse brings Sarah and Mia extra blankets and lets them create a very dark fort without having to use Sam's blankets. The night nurse sees the stack of papers and magazines on the floor and admits that that's what her house looks like and she is always afraid to throw them away for fear she has missed reading an article in them, an article that will save her life maybe. A recall on her brake pedal, a recall on ground meat, a recall on a faulty crib railing, even though she doesn't have a baby. The night nurse has glasses with pink rims the color of the eyes of an albino pet mouse I had as a child. I would let the mouse run up and down my arms, liking the way he tickled my skin.

CALL: A prepurchase exam on a horse.

ACTION: Drove to farm. Owner's daughter held the horse while I took X-rays of the horse.

RESULT: Horse, thankfully, stood very still. The X-rays came out clear. The daughter was a young woman. She talked about snowboarding. She talked about competing as a snowboarder. I told her about surfing, how she should really try it. I told her how I had lived by the ocean out west and surfed the waves and when there weren't waves to surf, I still went out on my board, lying flat and eyeing orange garibaldi in the clear water. I told her how waves are not like mountains, and how every wave is different and every ride is different and the ocean always changes. I told her that surfing is learning to spot where the wave out on the horizon will be coming from. She laughed, she threw her head back, mountains are like that, too, she said. The conditions are never exactly the same. Her mother brought me out a scone to eat while I X-rayed the horse, a small Morgan with his winter coat beginning to grow in woolly so that he looked more like some Mongolian pony. The scone was delicious. Bits of orange were grated into the batter. Fresh cranberries and bits of apple were mixed in. I asked the owner for the recipe and after I X-rayed the horse, she invited me into her house. Her husband was a carpenter and had carved the doors between the rooms, and he had carved the moldings and the cupboard doors. He had carved the shapes of trees into the wood, not trees you'd expect to find here, but trees, maybe, from the likes of Indonesia. Their canopies were spread wide and their branches thin and delicate and numerous below the canopies, leading down to trunks that were not smooth but ropy in appearance, as if the trunks were twisted strands. Your house is beautiful, I said, and I feasted on the details, wishing everyone's house I entered could be so distinct and interesting to walk around in. The owner folded up the paper she had written the recipe on and she handed me a check and I put them in my coat pocket. I wanted to ask her if she had heard about Sam, but I knew she had, everyone had heard by now. When she handed me the recipe, she folded it up right after she wrote it, so I could not see the letters. I hoped walking back to

my truck that what she had written was the name of the man who
had shot my son.

WHAT I DID DRIVING HOME: Unfurled the recipe. There was no
name in it, even though I studied the words "grated orange peel"
thinking it was some kind of anagram for a man's name, but what
could it be? I came up with "Pete Darlan George" and reminded
myself when I got home to look up the name in the phone book.

THOUGHTS WHILE DRIVING HOME: This is a good feeling, a check
and a good scone recipe in my coat pocket. What more could a
man ask for? Then I answered the question myself, alone in my
truck. "For my son to be awake," I said and as I said the words I
passed by a man jogging down the road and he must have seen my
mouth moving and he must have thought I was talking to him,
because he waved and he smiled as I drove on by.

WHAT THE SPACECRAFT WAS DOING WHEN I GOT BACK HOME:
Moving quickly up and down, then back and forth, the way a child
would wave a sparkler on the Fourth of July, trying to spell his
name out in the air with the burning tip. Was the message the
name of the man who had shot my son?

WHAT SARAH AND MIA SAID WHEN I GOT HOME: "Father" in
German sounds like "Farter."

WHAT THE WIFE SAID: They got that right.

WHAT WAS NOT IN THE PHONE BOOK: Anyone named "Pete
Darlan George."

WHAT THE FIRE SAID IN THE WOODSTOVE: You have loaded me
with wet wood. You did not cover my log piles over the summer,
and now I will smoke instead of burn.

WHAT THE WIFE SAID I DID IN MY SLEEP: Cried.

WHAT THE WIFE DID IN HER SLEEP: Snored.

WHAT THE TRUCK IS TELLING ME: Check engine.

WHAT I TOOK THE TRUCK INTO THE SHOP TO BE REPAIRED FOR: The CHECK ENGINE light.

WHAT THE TRUCK COST ME AT THE SHOP TO BE REPAIRED: $300.

WHAT THE TRUCK IS STILL TELLING ME AFTER $300: Check engine.

WHAT I HAVE DECIDED: That having a light on all the time telling me to check something is a good thing and it will make me check my levels more often. It will make me more aware and alert and maybe I need this constant state of alertness to feel alive. Maybe, just maybe, my high levels are keeping me young in ways I never knew. I have my levels to thank. To show my appreciation, I make the appointment with the doctor when I'm at the hospital visiting Sam. I stand by Sam's bedside and talk to him and tell him I will be right back, I am going down to floor 5 to make an appointment with my own doctor. I feel stupid talking to Sam. I am too much like my wife for a moment, and I do not want to be like her. Talking to him, having him smell food she has brought for him that he cannot eat, brushing his hair for him when it did not have the chance to get messy—he was not running through the pastel yellow walls of the halls, the window was not open letting through winter's blustering wind, he was not wrestling with his sisters the way he did before.

WHAT GISELA SAYS: Meine Telefonnummer ist zwei, sieben, neun, null, neun.

WHAT JÜRGEN SAYS: Do you play chess? (You see Jürgen is always trying to get Gisela to go out with him and do something. He suggested playing table tennis earlier, but Gisela, can you blame her, hasn't got a thing for table tennis.)

WHAT MY WIFE CALLS GISELA: A slut, and then my wife wants to know how you say slut in German, and my wife guesses it's something like a *Schatz*, but she's not sure, considering how anything she ever learned about German was from the movie *Das Boot*, which we have seen several times over and over, because we love *Das Boot* and we and our children are known, every once in a while, to walk around the house and belt out the piercing cry of "Alarm! Alarm!" in German accents, as if we were not living in a house with creaking timbers, but living in a U-boat about to be attacked by the Allied forces and we have to quickly descend to crush depth in order to save our tails in our beloved tin can.

CALL: No call. Just the caller who hangs up. Jen wants to know who it was. I don't know, I say. Was it the hospital? she says. I don't know, I say. Well, who was it? How do you know it wasn't the hospital? she says. Why would the hospital hang up? I say. The hospital hung up? Jen says, then call them back. And then she calls the hospital and talks to the day nurse asking if we had been called, if there had been any change in our son.

WHAT THE WIFE SAYS AFTER SHE GETS OFF THE PHONE WITH THE DAY NURSE: Well, he's fine. There's been no change. Thank God, Jen says. But I've been hoping for a change, any kind of change.

WHAT THE CHILDREN DO IN THE MORNING: Climb into bed with us. Sarah curling around me, pulling hairs from moles off my back. I tell her not to. She reads, her eyes close to the page, words from *The Secret Garden* somehow hard for her to see. Propped up on her elbows, the small muscles in her back pop up, and off her skin comes the faint smell of chlorine from when she had her practice swim the night before. A heavy header on the team, her face looking down at the tiles and the drain, rather than where the coach would have her look—up and out and toward the wall. Who can blame her, not wanting always to swim into a wall, when looking down is where one might want to go. At least down there in the holes between the hairs tangled in the drain there is a possible way out.

OTHER THINGS GISELA DOES NOT WANT TO DO BESIDES PLAY TABLE TENNIS: She doesn't want to play chess, she doesn't want to go to a movie, she doesn't want to lift weights. Gisela is too tired for all of this. Perhaps, another day, she tells Jürgen, she will go in-line skating when she is feeling better.

THINGS I DO NOT WANT TO DO: Cut the limb off the big maple that leans on the asphalt shingle roof covering my wife's office and threatens to rot a hole all the way through to the timbers. Oil the windows so the sun and rain and snow don't ruin the wood. Fix the drawers in my wife's desk. She tries to pull them out and they don't work, the bottoms fall through, and the drawers' runners are broken or out of line, so that in order to open them she has to pull hard, making her stapler, and three-hole punch, and black Sharpies all jump from the drawer and onto the floor. I don't want to bring in more wood for the fire. I really don't mind the hearth turning cold under my butt, at least not for a while. It is still only fall and the clutch of winter not yet here and besides the last time I went to the log pile to get more wood, I stepped in dog shit and I don't feel like having to shovel up the dog shit now so that I can get more armfuls of wood. Maybe I will feel like going in-line skating in a few days, but not right now. Not right now, Jürgen. I am so tired right now, and I can say that in German. I have learned that much.

WHAT I DO: I lie down and close my eyes. What I see is an outline on my eyelids of the spacecraft and I wonder if that's where it's been all this time anyway, and it's never even been in the sky.

WHAT WE HEAR ON THE RADIO: That the animal shelter has an overabundance of cats. Cats are being brought in by the sackfuls, quite possibly, and now there is no more room. The shelter is full. Owners can't afford their cats anymore. What will happen to the cats? I wonder. They will be turned out into the woods. The coyotes will make meals of them. They will try to survive. They will band together, they will roam in cat packs. Cars will have to stop and let them cross in packs across the road, yellow-eyed in the headlights and silent except for the flicking speech of the ends of their tails.

WHAT ELSE I HEAR ON THE RADIO: Transmissions from Mars. It's a break in the reception, the show that's on is interrupted by a series of broken beeps. Beep-di-dah-beep-di-dah-beep-beep-beep. When it happens, my wife puts her fingers up on her head like antennae of an alien and says in a monotone to the children: I am getting a transmission . . . the next flight to Mars is scheduled to lift off soon. This is a very important mission. We need to fill a number of vital posts on board. We are searching for a loyal and dedicated Head Potty Cleaner. We are pleased to announce that you, Sarah, have been especially selected for this high honor. Welcome aboard, Sarah, Head Potty Cleaner.

WHAT WE DON'T HAVE: Cats.

WHAT WE HAVE: The two dogs, of course, fish, crayfish, and a rabbit. The rabbit is now wearing diapers. Pampers, sized newborn. Because the rabbit wears diapers, it gets to come out of its cage and run around the house with us while we cook, while the children do their homework, and we are not worried about it peeing on the furniture. Rabbit pee smells worse than cat pee. The rabbit likes to stand on its hind legs in the easy chair and look out the picture window. The rabbit is really cute wearing diapers and my wife looks fondly at the rabbit, remembering when our children wore them, too.

WHAT THE RABBIT SEES: The pond, maybe, down our field. The chairs we sit on in the summer that I have not yet brought in. The rope swing I made for the children that hangs from the apple tree, now apple-less, now leafless.

WHAT THIS WEEKEND IS: Still bow season. I sit in my tree stand. I sit and listen and watch. It is raining. The drops of rain are good, masking any noise the turn of my head may make, the creak of a neck joint, a sigh I may exhale.

WHAT I DO: Go to my doctor's appointment.

WHAT THE DOCTOR, MY DOCTOR, WORE WHEN I WENT FOR MY EXAM: A pink ribbon brooch. Anti-AIDS, anti–breast cancer sentiments pinned to his white coat lapel. And I wanted to ask where the pin was he might have had for anti-coma, and what would that look like, because I wanted to tell him about my son on floor 9, whom I had just come from visiting, still with his eyes closed.

WHAT THE DOCTOR OFFERED ME AFTER MY BLOOD WAS DRAWN: Orange juice.

WHAT I TALKED TO THE DOCTOR ABOUT AFTER MY BLOOD WAS DRAWN: A parallel universe, one that was created at the same time ours was. I had read this.

WHAT HE SAID: Yes, yes, that's all very interesting. Now, about your levels.

WHAT I AM: An anomaly. A man my age with such high levels unheard-of. It's only in older men, the doctor has told me, that we have seen these kinds of numbers. The doctor is a little giddy with the news he reads on the chart, and maybe he wouldn't let his giddiness show if he were talking to someone who was not also a doctor, but being a doctor myself, he can let me join in on the wonderment of it all, the beauty in the numbers.

CALL: The alpaca that spit in my eye is dead.

ACTION: Drove to farm. The owner wanted to know what had done it. There's no blood, the owner said, and there wasn't, only the barn floor strewn with the neat balls of alpaca dung. He looks like he's sleeping, that's all, the owner said and he bent down next to the alpaca, putting his knees into the balls of dung, and stroked his belly. I looked around the barn and then I stepped outside and into the paddock where the alpaca used to stand and look out across the field. The field was wet from a storm in the middle of the night before. The storm came back to me and how the rain started to pour right after a deafening clap of thunder as if the rain had been kept inside a huge metal bin that spanned the sky and was suddenly released with the pull of a handle. He died from fear, I said to the owner. Your alpaca died when the thunder clapped.

WHAT THE OWNER SAID: Yes, it was loud here. I could see the lightning strikes start in the middle of the sky and then reach all the way down to the ground. We lost some trees and the phone even, he said. My heart raced, too, he said, and he stood and put his hands on his hips and shook his head while he looked at the alpaca. Then the man looked at me. Wait right here, he said. He went outside the barn. He looked left and then right. He is about to tell me something secret, I thought. Something no one else should know. He is about to tell me the name of the man who shot my son. I tried not to look too anxious. I looked at the dead alpaca, its cleft hooves filled with dirt and a bit of straw. I wrote down the name and number of a man I knew who could dig a hole for the alpaca on the property with his backhoe. The owner came back into the barn.

RESULT: The man looked around his barn. He spoke in a whisper. Maybe someday I'll get another one. I'm whispering so the wife doesn't hear. You see, they're no trouble to keep. Have you seen their manure? It has no smell. It's easy to clean. They do it all in the barn, not inconsiderate like a horse or a cow, going wherever and whenever it pleases in a field. No wonder he died of fear. He was gentle. He will go to alpaca heaven, the owner said, and I tried to picture what alpaca heaven would look like but all I pictured was the same barn I was standing in and the owner petting the dead alpaca's side.

THOUGHTS ON DRIVE HOME: If I could time-travel in only one direction, would I go forward or backward?

WHAT THE WIFE COOKS FOR DINNER: Turkey soup with rice. I wanted noodles, but we had none. I helped her with the dinner. I pulled out the bag of basmati rice from the pantry. I washed the rice well. There were no Indian stones or bugs I wanted to find in a mouthful of soup.

WHAT THE WIFE SAID: Your levels will love this soup.

WHAT SARAH SAID WHILE WE ATE THE SOUP: Sam would hate this soup.

WHAT THE WIFE SAID: He would not! Then she stood and dumped her soup into the kitchen sink and let the water run over it and watched it for a very long time.

CALL: A woman who needs a prepurchase exam on a Dales Pony.

ACTION: Drove to farm. X-rayed pony, checked his legs, did a spavin test, and, bending his leg at the knee, held knee bent for a while, looking to see how much it could flex.

RESULT: Dales Pony was in fine shape. Owner was thankful, asked, before I left, if I wanted to see her Mammoth Mules. Mammoth Mules? I asked. She led me to her back field. There they were, all sixty-five of them. The tallest maybe fifteen hands high. The last of their breed, she told me, and if it were not for her farm they would be extinct. I touched their huge, mammoth ears. Your mules are the horse for me, I said to her. They were so cute. I wanted to take one home.

WHAT I TALKED TO SAM ABOUT IN THE HOSPITAL: How, when he was better, we could build a chicken coop big enough to keep a Mammoth Mule. He would protect the chickens from the coyotes, from the fisher-cats. We could come to visit the Mammoth Mule throughout the day, feeling up along the backs of his mammoth ears, the soft hairs.

WHAT THE HOSPITAL SAID: Visiting hours are over.

WHAT THE NIGHT NURSE SAID: No, not you, you can stay. You're family.

WHAT I WISHED: That I wasn't. That I was one of the ones who could leave. That I was just a friend, an acquaintance, anyone else but the father, and that in the bed it was anyone else but my son with the tubes in his nose and the legs that were beginning to look thinner every day so that who would know they weren't arms except for the fact that they were at the foot of the bed?

WHAT THE WIFE COOKED FOR DINNER: Ham steak with mashed yams and green beans.

WHAT SARAH SAID: We are eating pig for dinner.

WHAT MIA SAID: Pig is good.

WHAT WE ALL DID: Agreed how cute pigs were and how good the ham steak was, and then I told the girls how I had read that pigs were one of the few animals that used mirrors the same way we did, and that pigs could look into a mirror and see their food behind them and turn and find the food. And then I thought how I would tell Sam this when I saw him next, and that I hoped I remembered to tell him since he had always talked about having a pig for a pet.

WHAT WE DID AFTER DINNER: Sat by the fire and took turns reading *Jane Eyre* out loud.

WHAT THE RABBIT DID: Wore her diaper and hopped around and on top of the girls as they lay flat on their backs on the carpet.

WHAT JANE EYRE HAD: A really sad life.

WHAT MIA SAID: She should have had a bunny, then she would not have been so sad.

WHAT WE ALL AGREED: That Jane Eyre, that anybody, would be better off if they had a bunny, especially one who wore diapers.

WHAT SARAH ASKED: Can't we bring the bunny to see Sam?

WHAT THE WIFE DID: Shook her head, but it was so slight, it looked as if it was just her eyes that moved from side to side.

CALL: No call.

ACTION: Went deer hunting instead while the wife and children went to visit Sam. Thought maybe I would see the hunter who shot my son. Maybe that hunter always hunted the same spot of land. I was that hunter's hunter. I had images of shooting him in the shoulder when I found out who he was, just so he would know how it felt. I gritted my teeth in anger while I stood in the stand, and at first I didn't even know I was doing it. I thought it was a squirrel chattering and making grinding noises next to me, warning me to stay away from his tree and his nuts.

RESULT: Saw no one, not even a deer. Saw the trees in front of me, so many of them dead, so many of their limbs down. Bits of leaves sticking up between a lightly fallen snow and after my anger I became sad and it hurt in my heart and I wondered if people's hearts would not hurt when they were sad if people hadn't always said things like "their heart was heavy" or that there was a pain in their heart.

WHAT I SAW ON MY WALK BACK HOME AT DUSK: Not the rock wall I had followed to get to my spot against my beech.

WHAT I FELT: Fear. I was lost, but I knew where the sun had set. I knew which direction to follow, but still, where had the rock wall gone? I had no light. My clothes would not be enough to keep me warm throughout a night until daybreak. Would I freeze to death? I was lost and would never be found. Hunting deer will kill me, I thought, and I thought didn't the deer know already how high my levels were? Didn't the deer already know what had happened to my son and it was already killing me and that there was no need to kill me like this, and then, in that moment, I loved the deer more than I had before, because of course they did not care about my levels, or feel sorry for me about my son. The deer would kill me the same as any other man, with the fever, buck fever.

WHAT I DID: I walked downhill, through woods I swore I had never walked through before. My feet on thick, carpeting needles of pine I could not remember having felt before beneath my boots. I listened for the sounds on the road, for the cars that might be driving up or down to steer my way. There were no sounds, just the sound of the wind in the trees, creaking tops. I walked on, going down, not sure which side of the ridge I was on, thinking I could have turned myself around completely when I had stood up from my spot against the beech. Finally I saw the bright lights. I thought it was the object from the sky that had landed. I followed it. It turned out to be my house. I felt stupid to see it. It was so large, the light in the kitchen window so bright. Inside I went to the bathroom. I looked at myself in the mirror. I should have known I was never lost at all but just letting myself enjoy the thrill of fear, a thing that seemed to be alive. It was so strong I thought that if I were smart enough, if I were pig enough, then when I looked in the mirror I could have seen the fear standing there and I could have turned to it and dealt with it the way the pigs could understand a mirror and turn and find their food when they looked in it. I was not pig enough, I decided, nor was I man enough, I thought, because I wasn't any closer to finding the man who had shot my son.

CALL: A Weimaraner that was listless and had stopped eating.

ACTION: Had owner, my neighbor, bring the dog to my garage. Turned on X-ray machine, laid dog down on blanket. X-rayed belly to see if there was an obstruction.

RESULT: Noticed significant signs of bloat. Dog had eaten a "greenie," a processed dog bone, two days earlier. There was a substantial amount of air in the dog's stomach. Told Sandy, my neighbor, whose hair was coming undone from her ponytail, that the dog was not in good shape. I pulled back the lips of the dog and showed her his gums. They were not pink, they were gray, almost the same color as the dog's coat. I told Sandy she had best take the dog for emergency surgery at the small-animal clinic. I helped lift the dog into the back of the car. Sandy asked how much she owed me and I told her nothing. I told her she better get going, the dog was very ill. I also told her that the surgery works sometimes, and sometimes it doesn't. She nodded her head. Let me know how it turns out, I said, and then she drove off.

THOUGHTS ON WALK BACK INTO HOUSE: I wonder if Sandy has German in her blood. She looks like she knows about kugel and schnitzel. She looked strong, like I think German women would be. She hardly needed my help carrying that dog to her car. She probably could have lifted Sam as easily from the ground when he had been shot and carried him back to our house. I could have sworn that when she drove off she said "tschüss," good-bye, to me and maybe I said "tschüss" back and maybe she thinks I'm German too and maybe next time she has to come over because her dog has bloat, or whatever, we will practice our German together. Maybe she has a good German accent. Maybe she can help me say the things I cannot say.

WHAT THE WIFE SAID WHEN SHE SAW SANDY DRIVE OFF: Will the dog be all right?

WHAT I SAID: The dog is in good hands, I said. Feeling for sure now that Sandy was German, that Sandy would drive as fast as she could, as fast as one would on the autobahn, to get to the animal hospital, that she would not waste time at the front desk, that she would probably, on her own, carry the bloated Weimaraner in her strong arms into the surgery and onto the table. Maybe Sandy even could help me find the man who had shot my son. She could come with me to every house near our house. She could hold my son in her arms while I knocked, she could lay him on my neighbors' kitchen tables, his eyes still shut, and she could say, look, who has done this to this man's son? "Gott im Himmel," she could say, pounding the table, making plates and cups jump, "answer me!"

WHAT I DID: I called the animal hospital and told them to expect her and the dog. I told them that I was sure she would be there very soon.

WHAT THE WIFE SAID: What do you want for dinner?

WHAT I SAID: Bratwurst.

WHAT THE WIFE SAID: Well, we don't have bratwurst. How about chicken?

WHAT I SAID: Then why did you ask?

WHAT THE WIFE SAID: I was being polite, wanting to know what you felt like eating tonight. That's polite, she said.

WHAT I SAID: If you already know the answer, then how is that polite?

WHAT SHE SAID: It is, it just is.

WHAT SARAH SAID: Poppy, there have been eighty-two deer bagged in our town so far. We read it on a piece of paper hanging on the wall at Phil's, beside the shelf for videos, above the special soup for the day.

WHAT I SAID: I am going out now. And to myself I said what Sam would say, "Kill the deer, eat the meat, kill the deer, eat the meat."

WHAT I SAW GOING UP TO MY SPOT: Three coyotes. They were beautiful and big. Their silver-tipped winter coats, already in, made them appear fluffy. They turned and looked at me, as if waiting for me to come along, and then they trotted east, over the ridge, where I couldn't see them any longer.

WHAT I HEARD WHILE AT MY SPOT: Three rifle shots.

WHAT I SAW WALKING BACK HOME: Two hunters who told me that earlier they had shot three coyotes for fun.

WHAT I WONDERED: Why everyone is shooting everything that shouldn't be shot.

CALL: The caller who hangs up. The caller who my wife thinks is always the hospital when it's not. The caller who lets me listen to the dial tone of our phone. The caller who makes me turn the phone off and on again and say "hello, hello, hello," even though the dial tone drones on.

CALL: A retired veterinarian who needed some bute for his horse.

ACTION: Drove to his farm. Saw that he was combing his horse. Handed him the bute. He would administer it to his horse himself. He talked very quietly, so quietly I had to stand very close to him. I could see the short hairs of his horse on his sweater, sticking to the woolen sleeve. I used to work at Suffolk Downs, he said. Really? I said. I had worked at the racetracks in Southern California for years, before moving here, I told him. He nodded his head. I think he began to speak even more quietly, and so I leaned in even closer to him, my chin now almost touching his shoulder. Is that so? he said. Well, then we have something in common. Tell me, he said, do they still use as many drugs on the track as they used to? Even more, I said. He shook his head again. You know, when I started practicing near here, I saved my clients money on the goners, I carried a Colt .45 pistol in my truck. It was much cheaper than that fancy euthanasia solution.

I wondered if my clients would think that was okay, to step out of my truck with a pistol instead of a syringe. People these days, I told the retired veterinarian, might not like me putting a hole in their horse's skull.

You tell them they can save some money, they'll do it, he said, nodding his head at the same time.

You're probably right, I said.

Yes, I'm right, he said. I'll tell you something else, he said. I'll tell you how to kill a horse with just a scalpel. Think, he said, how would you do that and not leave a mess of blood?

I liked this. It was a mystery I had to solve. I thought about it. I stood back from the retired veterinarian's horse and looked at it, thinking how I could kill it with just a scalpel. The horse was calm right now, but I knew that if I pulled out a scalpel and tried to stab into its throat, it would rear and strike and run, and besides, even if I were able to cut into the horse with a scalpel, he would bleed profusely. I thought of all the orifices a horse has. If I were able to stab it in one eye, it would still bleed copiously before it died. Then it struck me, of course, where I could cut the horse. If I reached up inside the anus with my scalpel, I could cut into the large artery there. In less than an hour he would be dead, and there would be no blood on the outside that anyone could see, just a horse lying on fall's carpet of gold and red leaves.

RESULT: I told the retired veterinarian I had figured it out. He smiled and nodded while I told him. You've got it, he said quietly. And then he said how he bet it would work on humans, too, and I told him I wasn't planning on killing any humans and then the moment I said it I realized I had lied. I had imagined my son wasting away hooked up to machines. I had imagined the mass of him disappearing beneath the white hospital sheet. I had imagined having to put an end to my son when the time came. I told the retired veterinarian I had a riddle for him now. A riddle I haven't been able to answer myself. I told him you go hunting in the woods with your son and your son gets shot in the shoulder, and who did it? I ask. Who knows who did it is what you should be asking, the retired veterinarian said, his voice even quieter now, and the tail end of the word *asking* sounding like a whisper that sailed away in the cold afternoon wind.

THOUGHTS ON DRIVE TO VISIT MY SON IN THE HOSPITAL WHILE MY WIFE AND SARAH AND MIA DRIVE WITH ME: I no longer need my doctor visits. My doctor will have to find someone else to share his amazement with over my high levels. I will not be going back. I can't think about myself. I can only think about my son.

WHAT THE WIFE SAID TO MY SON AFTER SHE FIXED A PLATE FOR HIM THAT SHE KNEW HE COULD NOT EAT: The Thanksgiving turkey is cold. The marshmallows on the yams caved in. Then Jen told our son how she had seen a man's stand in the back field. He left a little wooden plaque with his name on it and his address, she said. The stand was deluxe. There was a wide padded seat. I would not be surprised if there was a drink holder in the stand. I felt like climbing up the stand and sitting in it and taking a picture of myself in it and sending the picture to the man, so he could see me sitting in his deer stand on our property, then I would like to take a picture of me with a buck I had shot from his deer stand, and I would like to tell him thank you for setting up his deer stand on my property because I have now shot the biggest buck in our county. But, of course, Jen said, there is no buck I can spread out before you. I did not climb the stand. It was up too high, and there was dinner to cook, the green beans to watch over, this oyster dressing, now cold, to prepare. Then Jen lifted a forkful of turkey and gravy and held it beneath our son's nose. At least smell it, she said.

WHAT I SAID TO MY WIFE IN BED THAT NIGHT: Oysters are an aphrodisiac.

WHAT THE WIFE SAID IN BED: I am so stuffed. And then she rolled over.

WHAT THE COYOTES SAID: What have you done with our brethren?

CALL: The caller who hangs up. Who needs to reach me but can't talk when I say hello? Who is this? I'm listening, I say, but no one answers, only this time I don't hear the caller hang up. I think I can hear him breathing. It sounds restful. It is the sound a seashell makes when you hold it up close to your ear.

WHAT SARAH AND MIA SAID: Pop, figure this one out. You're out in the wilderness in the freezing cold, you come across a cabin and go inside, there's a match, a candle, a kerosene lantern, and a woodstove. Which one do you light first?

WHAT I THINK: Is Gisela in the cabin? Is she across the bearskin rug?

WHAT THE CHILDREN SAY: Well?

WHAT I SAY: Uhm.

WHAT THE CHILDREN SAY: You light the match first!

WHAT THE SMOKE ALARM SAID: Beep-beep-beep. Wake the hell up, you have left the windows open and now the smoke from your chimney has blown back into the house on this night of no wind where the smoke is not carried far away.

WHAT MIA WOKE UP SAYING WHEN THE SMOKE ALARM WENT BEEP-BEEP-BEEP: Is Mommy getting a transmission?

CALL: Arlo has a fresh cow that needs calcium.

ACTION: Drove to Arlo's. Noticed how there was scarcely any snow on his roads. There was a milky mist but it lay loosely over fields that were still green, where plants in summer gardens, although dry, still stood, as if fooling themselves thinking a short-lived sun on an autumn day could warm the green back through their withered leaves and shrunken stalks as thin as fingers of the sick and old.

RESULT: Handed Arlo the bottle of calcium. Admired the fresh Chianina cow, a white tall giant of a breed from Italy, standing here, strangely, the backdrop of the white-peaked mountains framed between its bony haunches. Arlo's cattle were always healthy-looking, their weight perfect and their fields nicely draining so that they were not muddy seas. Arlo also kept the Chianinas clean, and bathed them so that their whiteness was impressive and made the cows appear majestic, like huge ghosts walking slowly through the valley and along the mountain face where the borders of their fields spanned. Arlo then showed me an eight-point buck he had shot. It hung from his tree, nicely cleaned, twirling in a moist wind that started to come in from the east. I could almost smell the salt of the ocean in it and Arlo said how he had sat in his tree stand for ten hours before the buck walked down beneath him and he had a shot to the neck that knocked the buck flat down. Oh, he's a fine buck, I told Arlo. Arlo shook his head and his hair that was as black and as shiny as licorice shook also, and I think how he even smells a little like licorice or some kind of pipe packed with licorice-smelling tobacco. Nah, he said. He's just a normal buck and I will eat him all winter, that's all, he said. Not like some other guys, he said. Some who kill an animal and throw away the meat.

WHAT I SAID: What other guys, Arlo? I thought he was trying to tell me the name of the man who shot my son. I listened carefully, as if I were hunting, feeling my ears even slightly move, slightly lift up, opening further the diameter of my dark canal to hear his words.

WHAT ARLO SAID: Justin Ays.

WHAT I SAID: Justin Ays?, thinking it was the name of a man.

WHAT ARLO SAID: No, just guys, I said. Any guys. Clean your ears out, Doc, he said.

THOUGHTS WHILE DRIVING OUT OF ARLO'S PAST HIS FIELDS: There are no happier cows I know of.

WHAT I HOPED TO SEE WHEN I DROVE UP THE DRIVEWAY: Another car, the one that belonged to the hunter who had shot my son, the man coming out to tell me he was sorry. Where was that man?

WHAT I SAW INSTEAD: The lights on in the house. Jen at the stove.

WHAT WAS NOT IN THE PHONE BOOK: Anyone by the name of Justin Ays.

WHAT SARAH AND MIA SAID: We saw Arlo's name up at Phil's. We didn't want to tell you he was one of the eighty-two who had shot a buck in our town. Don't worry, Poppy, you will get a buck someday. Go on, Poppy, practice your bow in the house. It is almost bow season again. We will go upstairs and out of your way.

WHAT I DID: I shot the bow in the house at a target I set up fifty feet away because bow season was coming again and I wanted to be ready. One arrow hit the twelve-inch hemlock post. I could unscrew the arrow shaft but I could not remove the tip. It remains embedded in the post.

WHAT THE WIFE SAID: Well, the deer aren't going to be nervous with you in the woods, but the trees might be quaking.

WHAT THE HOUSE SAID: Don't worry about the tip. I will close up around it and swallow it in oh, about one hundred years.

WHAT I REENACTED FOR SAM AT THE HOSPITAL: The arrow's

flight into the post. Thwack, I said, jabbing my finger into the pastel yellow hospital room wall, beside the metal door, showing him how it was at our house, an arrow tip embedded in the hemlock and my wife now leery of my peephole, my arm pull, my overall aim. Sam, I could have sworn, moved his foot. I wanted to open the metal door, call down the hall for the night nurse. I have seen his foot move, I wanted to yell, but I didn't, because maybe it was a trick of the eye. Instead I knelt down beside the bed and pulled back his covers and stared at his foot.

His foot was huge for a twelve-year-old boy. There was dirt in his toenails that was dirt from our house from where he had always walked barefoot even on days of winter's most frigid cold, and I looked at the dirt and thought how because of it he belonged now at home, and not here, surrounded by the yellow pastel walls. The dirt under his huge big toenail was dirt from our house, where he rightfully belonged. His foot, for a moment, looked like it was moving, but it was not, I realized. It was just me leaning on his bed and the beating of my own heart and the workings of my own lungs that was making the mattress move up and down, ever so slightly, making him move in turn. I breathed harder then, I willed my heart a faster beat, there was the possibility I could jump-start his foot into motion. My wife walked in the room and I jumped instead. I covered my son's foot up again, I did not want her to see the dirt beneath his big toenail, if she had seen it she would have gone after it with a clipper, with a file's curved point, somehow ashamed of dirt on her own son, and I wanted to keep that dirt there. As long as it remained, it somehow meant there was a possibility of my son coming home.

She did not talk. She sat on the end of the bed drinking tea, the bag's small postage stamp–sized tag and its thread-like string twirling in some slight breeze by the Styrofoam cup's side. She held the cup with one hand and rested her other hand on his ankle, her hand some kind of cuff, some kind of shackle to keep him prone, laid out flat, on his hospital bed so he would never rise. Look at this, I said, to get her away from him. I wanted her to see the first heavy snow in our region, the flakes fat, falling heavily, on the ledge of the window that could not be opened.

She stood from the bed, letting go her grasp on him, and joined me at the window. I looked in the reflection. Maybe my son, thinking we weren't looking, would turn his head, would smile, would raise his hands in the air and look at them. He had done this as an infant, turning his hands in the air while he lay in his crib, mesmerized by the motions he made, the thumbs that could rotate, the wrists that could turn, they were his first toys. My wife's breath steamed the window glass. My son did not wake. "Snow now makes it seem like he's been here so long. He came here in late fall, and now it's winter weather already," she said, and then turned back to our son.

The door handle turned and a tall man came in. I'm sorry, wrong room, he said shaking his head and leaving, letting the door shut.

MY FIRST THOUGHT: Could he be the hunter who shot my son, who has come to my son's bedside to tell us he's sorry it has taken him so long to come?

WHAT THE WIFE DOES: Puts her tea on the tray table, gets under the covers, and lies next to our son.

WHAT I SAY: What are you doing?

WHAT THE WIFE SAYS: He's my son. I nod my head. I wanted to do it earlier, too. I wanted to crawl in beside my son and hold him. The wife closes her eyes.

CALL: A standardbred that has a cut on his neck. Owner says it definitely needs stitches.

ACTION: Drove to the man's house. His name was Brody. His property bordered mine.

RESULT: Brody was wrong. Standardbred did not need stitches. The cut was only a scratch. Brody invited me into the house while he found his checkbook to write me a check for coming to his house to do nothing to his standardbred but shine a flashlight on its neck while standing in the freezing-cold barn. Brody had books on his shelves that looked like they had never been opened. Brody's house was so clean. Brody had pictures of his grown children on the shelves. His wife, he said, had died. Brody said, Stay for dinner. No thank you, I said. I'm sure my wife is waiting at home, keeping a meal warm for me. But then I thought maybe this is the man who shot Sam. He has called me here for no reason because it's a ruse and he wants to confess. I touch a wooden duck decoy he has on his mantel.

WHAT I SAY: You hunt? Brody laughs. He says his wife bought him the decoy in a gift shop when they visited Cape Cod. The decoy was signed by the artist, and Brody flipped the body of the duck, showing me the letters painted on the wood. I am afraid of guns. I have heard too many stories, he says.

WHAT I THINK: Brody is pulling my chain. Brody really did shoot Sam and now he thinks he can toy with me.

WHAT I SAY: Oh, come on, surely living here where we live you have an understanding of guns. You must hear them go off all the time the way your woods back up onto mine. There is game all around us, I say. Brody shakes his head. No, I just don't hunt, he says.

WHAT I DO: I start to leave, but really I want to stand in Brody's mudroom. I look at the hooks on the wall and see if there are any camo-patterned coats or hunting pants. I see old dark-colored cardigans with holes in the weave and looping bits of yarn. You're hell on sweaters, I say. Is that from walking in the woods, all the branches? I say. Brody laughs and points down to a skinny cat sidling between his legs. No, it's from her darn claws, he says. I think about the word *darn*. I think how either he said it and knew he said it in place of *damn* because he wanted me to think he wasn't the one who shot my son, or he said it because he really is the type of man who could never shoot a gun.

WHAT GISELA SAID IN GERMAN THAT SHE NEEDS FOR HER DORMITORY ROOM ON THE DRIVE HOME: Gisela needs a new desk. Gisela needs a new lamp. Gisela needs a new bed. Gisela needs new curtains. Gisela, maybe, is shy, and cannot have all the boys on campus peering up at her through her dormitory window while her *Kopf* is hurting her so, because, as of yet, she still feels *krank* and has not found the apothecary to buy her aspirin.

WHAT THE WIFE KEPT WARM FOR ME ON THE STOVE: Chicken stew made with dried apricots, cinnamon, and honey.

WHAT I SAID TO THE WIFE: I'm okay without the apricots.

WHAT THE WIFE SAID: The apricots are good. The apricots are part of the dish. Eat the apricots. Your levels are begging for fruit.

THINGS MY WIFE THINKS MY LEVELS CAN DO SO FAR: Talk, appreciate food, beg.

WHAT I DON'T CARE ABOUT: My levels. I just want Sam to wake up.

WHAT I DID: Forked up the apricots and laid them on the rim of my plate.

WHAT SARAH AND MIA SAID: Did you sew up the horse?

WHAT I SAID: No, the horse did not need sewing. The horse did not need a vet. There was nothing I could do. Now go back to bed.

WHAT SARAH AND MIA SAID: Come kiss us good night.

WHAT I DID: I kissed them good night. I pulled the covers up to their necks.

WHAT MIA SAID: Poppy, you have so many drugs in your truck. Couldn't you just give Sam some to make him better?

WHAT I SAID: No, there's nothing I have for him in the back of my truck.

WHAT I DID: I covered the rabbit's cage with a cloth, so she could sleep without the light of the full moon glaring onto her through the metal bars. Then I stood and looked out the window, searching the sky.

WHAT SARAH SAID IN THE MORNING: A deer has walked on our porch. It was true. There were hoofprints in the snow covering the boards that the wind had blown up under the roof. Why had the deer come to our front door? the children wanted to know. I did not know. Maybe the deer had seen the hunter who shot my son. Maybe he wanted to come and tell me who the man was. The deer was a messenger. He is a messenger, I said to my wife and children. Jen laughed, Yes, come to tell us to brush the snow off our porch before someone gets hurt, and then she fetched the broom and began to sweep.

CALL: No call. I went out to my deer stand with my bow and arrow. How can you still hunt? Jen said before I left. I shook my head. I might find the hunter who did this to our son, I said. Then what? she said. She lifted her hands, her palms facing up to the ceiling where some cluster flies clung to the beams. It was like she was beckoning them, asking them to jump into a fireman's net from a burning building. You don't get it, do you? I said. You don't just go into the woods and hunt and hit someone instead of an animal and think you can get away with that. You don't let a man do that, I said, and I left. I stood the entire time in my tree stand because I knew that a buck would be hard to shoot from a sitting position. Standing, I was ready.

WHAT I SAW: A buck, far away, so far that if I shot him with my arrow, the arrow would never reach him. It would hit the ground first, tunneling through the snow and then down under the flattened leaves of dirt.

WHAT JANE EYRE HAS RECENTLY DONE: She has saved Rochester from a fire in his bedroom. She has doused him with water. What, has there been a flood? he asked.

WHAT THE WEATHER BECAME: Freezing rain that made me not want to go out and deer hunt.

WHO CAME TO VISIT: My brother and his family. He believes that there is a good Lord, that he made us all.

WHAT I BELIEVE IN: Evolution, that a thing even as complex as the eye, for example, can have developed, must have certainly developed.

WHAT HIS WIFE BELIEVES IN: The good Lord.

WHAT SHE TELLS US TO BELIEVE IN WHILE VISITING SAM WITH US IN THE HOSPITAL ROOM: The good Lord.

WHAT JEN SAYS REALLY LOUDLY: Good Lord! Jesus Christ! and I laugh, because she's making them sound like curse words, but my brother and his wife, they look down at the tops of their shoes.

CALL: A woman with Icelandic ponies needs a prepurchase.

ACTION: Drove to farm through roads along the stream where the water was mostly frozen, making the water flowing beneath the ice appear light green.

RESULT: Examined horse. Decided I was glad I didn't bring my daughters with me, as the Icelandic pony was so cute, they surely would have wanted one. The owner said she would never own a different kind of pony because the Icelandic ponies had such good temperaments that they were more like golden retrievers than ponies. The dog she owned, however, who trotted at her side, was an Australian shepherd.

WHAT I ASKED THE WOMAN: Do you know a man named Brody?

WHAT THE WOMAN SAID: Brody?

WHAT I SAID: He lives near me. His woods border mine.

WHAT THE WOMAN SAID: He has a horse?

WHAT I SAID: Yes! He has a horse! That's the man.

WHAT SHE SAID: No, I don't think I know him.

THOUGHTS ON DRIVE HOME: With all this snow, how will the deer find food? Can the spacecraft fly in all this snow? Can the cold air wake up my son? If only I could open up the windows in his hospital room.

WHAT SARAH AND MIA SAID WHEN I GOT HOME: Pop, Mom said the transmission was coming in loud and clear. It would be meat loaf for dinner.

WHAT THE HOUSE SAID AT NIGHT: The banging you hear is not dead bodies falling to the ground from a great height, but rather the snow sliding off the panels between the standing seams of the copper roof and onto the ground.

WHO I CALLED IN THE MORNING: Brody. I wanted to know if his horse was all right. I wanted to know if I could hear in his voice that he was the man who shot my son. Brody, it's me, I said, hoping to catch him off guard. Pardon? he said. The vet who came the other night, I said. Oh, yes, he said. The horse is much better, he said. Thanks for calling, he said, and he sounded like he had to run out the door.

CALL: No call. I drove up the road. I knocked on the neighbor's door. Nate, I said, you weren't out hunting a few weeks ago, were you? Yes, I was, I sure was, Nate said. For grouse? I said. Oh, no, for buck. I don't go out for grouse, he said. Then I told him what happened to my son even though in this small town he already knew. He shook his head while standing outside his door. I'm sorry to hear that, he said, as if he hadn't heard at all. Any idea who it was? I asked Nate. Nate said he didn't know anyone who went out for grouse anymore. He said maybe twenty years ago he could give me some names of men who hunted grouse around here, but not anymore. They were no longer around. Nate's wife came to the door. Annabelle said what about the caretaker at the farm on Cemetery Road, didn't he still go for grouse? she said to Nate. Nate shook his head. No, he don't go out for it anymore, Nate said. We heard about your son, we're sorry to hear it, Annabelle said. I nodded. I'd better get going, I said.

CALL: A horse that has a cut on his neck.

ACTION: Drove to farm.

RESULT: The horse had suffered the cut hours ago. I blocked the horse. Then I sewed up the horse cold. I was cold. The horse was cold. The cut was cold, and strange to my fingers to feel bloody flesh that was not warm, that did not have mist coming off the incision when it came into contact with the cold winter air.

WHERE I DROVE AFTER I SEWED UP THE HORSE: To the farm where the caretaker lived up on Cemetery Road. The view from the farm on the hill was beautiful and when I got out of my truck I stood looking at the mountains in front of me and wondering if that was a view I'd like to see every day or if living up on a hill like that would make me feel too unprotected, and like the wind could blow me down. The caretaker wore glasses that looked like they hadn't been cleaned in a long time, and wasn't that a waste, I thought, a man living up here who did not even bother to clean his glasses so he could see the view. He was large and I thought how walking through the woods he must scare the grouse out far ahead of him because his heavy steps would surely alert the grouse a long way off. I introduced myself and he shook my hand and I asked him if he had been hunting recently and he said that in fact he had been and showed me on a picnic table behind the house some grouse he had shot earlier in the day and that he was now just cleaning out. I admired the birds and held one in my hand, letting the head drop back, and touching the soft feathers at its neck. Around here? I asked. The caretaker shook his head. No, down south, I hunt at my brother's place. He has rock walls all over his property, the grouse like to roost behind them. I'm always lucky there, he said. I told him about my son. I asked him if he knew who that might have been that day, hunting on my property. The caretaker shook his head. You're asking me something I don't know the answer to, he said, and he took the bird from me and said he had better get started on them if he wanted to wrap them in bacon and roast them for dinner.

WHAT SARAH AND MIA SAID TO ME WHEN I GOT HOME: Poppy, look what your hat has done to your hair.

WHAT I DID: I looked in the mirror. It was true. The hat had done something to my hair. It was sticking straight up.

WHAT SARAH SAID: It looks like an ax blade stuck in your skull.

WHAT MIA DID: Played with my hair so that instead it looked like a palm tree swaying in an ocean breeze.

WHAT THE WIFE SAID: Lasagna for dinner. But I don't like the cow we ordered this year. The ground meat is full of gristle and rubbery veins.

WHAT I SAID: Tastes fine to me. And it did.

WHAT THE NIGHT SAID: A cold front is coming through and the sky is so clear you can hear sounds from very far away. Hear the branches breaking on the hillside? Hear the grouse in the thicket? Hear the chipmunk running across the wood pile? Hear the blood in your own veins? Hear the height of your levels? You can hear them, can't you?

WHAT THE PHONE DID: It rang. It was the hospital nurse. I saw your son move his foot today, she said. This is a good sign, she said.

WHAT WE ALL DID: We piled into the car. We drove to the hospital. We sat in metal framed chairs by his bed and threw back his covers and stared at his foot.

WHAT THE WIFE SAID: Oh, God, look how dirty his toenails are, how come I didn't notice before. She went digging in her purse for a nail clipper, but I stopped her. It's okay, it's dirt from home, I said. Yes, it's not like he's been walking around here, she said, and looked around the room at the tiled floor with gray flecks in the pattern. Put the clippers away, I said, and she did. We stayed until Sarah and Mia's bedtime and then we drove home. We never saw Sam's foot move.

WHAT THE WIFE SAID ON THE RIDE HOME: Tell me again what the day nurse said. Did she say she saw it move herself? How much did it move, did she say? Was it a twitch or a kick, or just a side-to-side motion? I told her I didn't know. I didn't ask all that of the day nurse. You didn't ask? How could you not ask? Jen said.

WHAT I DID: I turned the radio on. I listened to the news.

WHAT THE WIFE SAID: There's something wrong when you have all these actors and actresses promoting world peace when they're starring in movies that are awful and violent and will surely affect our youth in a negative fashion.

WHAT SARAH AND MIA SAID THEY SAW: A great horned owl.

WHAT THE SEASON IS NOW: No season. Not bear, not turkey, not deer, not moose, not grouse.

WHAT THE TRANSMISSIONS ARE DOING: Coming in more frequently. We can hardly listen to the news without being interrupted several times. My wife says the request is urgent now, more urgent than ever for the Head Potty Cleaner on her spacecraft. She looks at Sarah imploringly, with her forefingers from each hand held up by her ears, to look like antennae poking from her head. Oh no, Sarah giggles, her eyes slanting upward, nearly closing with her smile. I am not going to be Head Potty Cleaner!

WHAT THE TOY PIGGY BANK IN THE SHAPE OF A BANK VAULT SAID IN THE MIDDLE OF THE NIGHT: Beep-beep-beep. Who has broken open my doors? Who has plundered the cash? Made away with the goods? Is it the mice who crawl across our loft boards at night? Is it the cluster flies, their beating transparent wings strong enough to turn a combination?

WHAT THE WIFE ASKED IN THE MIDDLE OF THE NIGHT: What is that noise?

WHAT I TOLD MY WIFE: It's just a bird. Go back to sleep.

WHAT THE WIFE SAID: That is not a bird. No way that is a bird. That's the bank, she said. The fucking bank.

WHAT I SAID: Think of it as a bird. A tropical bird. A bakonga bird.

WHAT THE WIFE SAID: What is a bakonga bird?

WHAT I SAID: Ah, the rare bakonga bird, you have never heard of this bird?

WHAT I THINK FOR A MOMENT: That the light flashing from the smoke alarm reflected in the window is a light from the spacecraft, but it's not. I think what the sheriff said, that if I did not see the man who shot my son there is no way to find him, but maybe someone did see. Maybe the pilot of the spacecraft saw. If only he could tell me. I look again into the darkness, waiting to see if the spacecraft will show up. I think how the next time I see it I'll run outside to the snow-covered field. I'll flail my arms, I'll land it in. If it doesn't come close I'll write in the snow in large letters like those written by men stranded on deserted islands, only I won't write "Save me," I'll write, "Tell me who did it!" and hope that the pilot can read my words formed in three feet of hard crusted snow.

CALL: The caller who doesn't talk. I know because Sarah answers and she says hello, hello, and then she holds the phone up in the air and then out to the side, still saying, hello, hello, but louder every time, until she is yelling. I run to grab the phone away from her. There's no one there, she tells me, and then she hangs up. Quickly I pick up the phone. Hello, it's me, I say, out of breath from my running across the room, and I'm thinking maybe if he hears my voice he'll start talking and I'll find out who it is. But it's too late. No one's there now, just the dial tone of our phone, but I keep talking anyway. Brody? Brody, is that you, you fucker? Brody? I say.

CALL: Dorothy's sheep, Alice, seems to be sick.

ACTION: Drove to Dorothy's on a bright, sunny day. Snow still sat on the lower branches of the pines, but the winds over the past few days have blown the snow from the topmost parts.

RESULT: Alice wasn't sick. Dorothy was keeping Alice in the kitchen. There was straw on the floor, over the tile. She is not sick, I told Dorothy, but Dorothy shook her head. I know something is wrong with her, she said. I patted Alice's head. I looked into her eyes. Dorothy sighed. I could feel the breath from her sigh reach my face. How are you feeling, Dorothy? I asked. Dorothy shook her head. I have things going on with me; at my age, who wouldn't? she said. I nodded. I told her I thought how Alice was the luckiest sheep I knew. Yes, lucky. But who will take care of her when I'm dead and gone? Dorothy said. You can't go anywhere, not while she's alive, I said. You wouldn't want someone else taking care of her. Who else would have a sheep in their kitchen? Who else would take their sheep to church? No, I said to Dorothy. You are not allowed to check out anytime soon. And I thought of Sam and how maybe if I brought him here to Dorothy's kitchen, he would awaken. I could lay him down next to Alice under the kitchen table, and the warm breaths of Alice could bring him back.

WHAT DOROTHY SAID: How are you, Doc? Are you all right yourself? she asked. I'm okay, I said. I've been busy. It seems that people are calling me who don't even really need me. I got a call from a man named Brody, lives near me. You know him? I said. Dorothy shook her head. You're up a ways from me. I don't go north of here much. He must be new to here, she said. Anyway, I said, he had a horse with nothing wrong with him. Don't you think that's strange? I said. To spend the money on a call to a vet when nothing's wrong? Dorothy laughed. Well, Doc, she said, that's just what I did here to you. Seems that Brody isn't the only one to blame, she said.

WHAT I TOOK THAT TO MEAN: That Dorothy didn't think Brody was the one who shot my son and I could now narrow it down to only 599 people instead of 600.

THOUGHTS ON DRIVE HOME: In order to cut costs on health insurance, everyone should be enrolled in an exercise program. Everyone enrolled should receive a discount on the cost of their health insurance. Everyone would be healthier. Everyone would live longer.

CALL: A horse who is depressed.

ACTION: Drove to the farm in the arctic cold. My truck's thermometer said it was minus 17 degrees. The girl who owned the horse was a checkout girl at the grocery store. The girl said she had seen me in there before with my wife and children. You buy a lot of eggs, the girl said. You should buy yourself some laying hens. I couldn't agree more, I said. I thought the girl was good. She could help in my search. She probably knew the man who had shot my son. She had probably sold him beer, slid the six-pack across her conveyor belt, swiped his card through the machine. She knew his name, had seen it printed on the back of the card, had seen it printed on the receipt she handed back to him along with the points he had earned in the "fill-her-up for free" gas program. I bet you know a lot about the people around here, I said.

WHAT THE GIRL SAID: You can tell some things about what people buy.

WHAT I SAID: Like what?

WHAT SHE SAID: Like things you don't want to know. Like when they're on the rag and when they've got hemorrhoids. The druggies, they used to buy the baby formula in the huge cans, but we've stopped that now, only so much allowed per customer. I hate watching it, she said, their veiny, dirty fingers holding the can, covering the picture of the cute baby. You know how a woman's mad at her husband? she said. No, tell me, I said. She buys tons of stuff. She buys stuff that's mostly not even food. You don't buy frying pans, something to remind you of how you have to cook for him, when you're flaming furious at your husband. You buy makeup and hair product. You buy the body oil and bath beads, she said.

WHAT I SAID: What about the guys? I mean, how do you know when they're feeling angry or guilty? Or a criminal, I said, what do they buy? But the girl looked at her horse. I had spent too much time on the subject. I had not timed it right. I would have to wait for another time. The girl was done talking about the checkout line. Is he going to be all right? she said.

The horse was an old Thoroughbred. The horse had his head hanging down, but the strange thing was the horse had his tongue hanging out of his mouth. I reached in and felt his tongue. I could move it from side to side. The horse did not or could not pull his tongue back in. I went to the back of the horse and lifted his tail. He let me lift it up high. He let me swing it from side to side. Swinging it that way created a breeze. The checkout girl wrapped her arms around herself. The checkout girl tucked her head down, into the collar of her parka. Look at this, I told the checkout girl, this isn't right, I said as I kept swinging the tail back and forth and lifting it high and letting it drop. Wow, the girl said. I took the horse's temperature. It was normal. These are classic signs of botulism, I said. The girl nodded. Do you know what botulism is? I said. The girl shook her head. It affects the horse's central nervous system. That's why he's sick, but he doesn't have a temperature. That's why his muscles are affected and his tongue sticks out and his tail is so easy to move.

RESULT: I took a blood on the horse. It could be botulism, I said. I'll let you know soon, I said. If he goes down in the next twenty-four hours before the blood results come back, he will not get up again. You cannot get a horse sick with botulism up from the ground if he has decided to go down. They will almost always die.

THOUGHTS ON DRIVE HOME: What if I send this blood off and it freezes in the mail before it reaches the lab? Is it too cold for the spacecraft to fly in this weather? Is this why I haven't seen the spacecraft for days?

WHERE I STOP ON THE WAY HOME: Phil's. I walk the three aisles of the store, my feet making the wooden floorboards creak as I look at items like gravy in jars with dusty lids and I think if I stand around long enough, maybe the man who shot my son will walk in and will tell Phil something as Phil stands behind the meat counter, slicing roast beef. He will tell Phil how he was out hunting for grouse weeks ago and has to admit he hit something he thought might not have been a grouse, and has Phil heard of anyone hurt in the woods? When I realize the likelihood of that ever happening is zero, I buy some milk and drive home.

WHAT THE HOUSE SAYS: I have been tricked by the wind.

WHAT THE THERMOMETER INSIDE THE HOUSE SAYS: 53 degrees.

WHAT SARAH AND MIA SAY: Add more wood, Poppy. Add more wood.

WHAT THE WIFE COOKS FOR DINNER: Roast chicken with giblets alongside the chicken, all of it roasted. All the giblets dry and brown.

WHAT I TELL THE CHILDREN: Don't eat the skin. It's fatty. Don't eat the liver. Do you know what the liver is? Do you know what the liver does? The liver stores all of the toxins inside the body. Why would you want to eat it?

WHAT THE CHILDREN DO: Eat the liver and the skin. The skin especially. They can't get enough of it. They fight over it. The good meat, the white meat, they don't like. They leave it on their plates, but on the bones they chew off the cartilage and suck on the marrow.

WHAT MIA PULLS OUT OF HER POCKET FOR SAM WHEN WE ARE VISITING HIM AT THE HOSPITAL: A wizened cooked chicken heart she saved from her meal. The heart is his favorite, she says, and she puts it next to his ear on his pillow. Ugh! Sarah says and turns away.

WHAT THE NURSE SAYS WHEN SHE COMES INTO THE ROOM: It happened again today. It's here in the notes. His foot moved again.

WHAT MY WIFE DOES: Grabs the notes from the nurse and reads them. It's not just his foot, she says. It's also his eyes! We all look to Sam's eyes. The lids are closed, but Sarah says she swears she saw his eyeballs moving back and forth.

WHAT MIA SAYS: It's the chicken heart, I know it. It's giving him dreams.

CALL: Helga Bartlett says her old dog needs putting down.

ACTION: Drove to Helga Bartlett's house. The dog ran up to me and wagged his tail. The dog sniffed my pants and wagged his tail. The dog looked up at me with smiling eyes and wagged his tail.

RESULT: I could not put Helga Bartlett's dog down. Helga, I said, maybe it's just not his time.

WHAT HELGA SAID: Yesterday, it was his time. Yesterday, he could not walk. He lay on the floor by the fire hardly breathing. Yesterday, he did not eat.

WHAT I SAID: He got over yesterday.

WHAT HELGA SAID: I guess you're right. Yesterday is behind him.

WHAT THE DOG DID: Fetched a stuffed-up toy, a green fuzzy spaceship from one of the children's rooms in Helga's home. The dog held it in his mouth and cocked his head while looking at me. He thinks that's his spaceship, Helga said. It's really my son's, she said. He's a fine dog, Helga, I said, and for a moment I thought the dog was trying to tell me he'd seen the same spacecraft I'd seen, the object with bright lights flying back and forth in the sky. I know, she said. Yesterday was his time, but today is not. I'll call you again, when yesterday comes—when it will be his time again, she says. Good, I said. Call me when yesterday comes again.

WHAT I TELL SAM WHEN I SEE HIM AGAIN AT THE HOSPITAL: I tell him about Helga and her dog. I tell him things that are not about anything. I recite for him the foodstuffs I see down the three aisles at Phil's. The marshmallows, the soup cans, the replacement arrow tips, the Day-Glo fletchings, and the Whisker Biscuit rests. I whistle for him *Appalachian Spring* and still there is no response, the only change in the room being the light that goes from weak sunlight to dusk to darkness.

CALL: A woman says she found her horse on the barn floor rolling his eyes and paddling his legs. It's a seizure, she said.
ACTION: Drove to farm. I knelt down next to the horse. I felt his pulse. He stood up abruptly.
RESULT: The horse was awake now. He was just sleeping, I told the woman. Sleeping! she said. Yes, I said. He must have some kind of sleep disorder. It happens to horses as well as to humans. He may not be able to sleep well at night because of a predator in the area, or too much light, a full moon maybe, and so he is so exhausted and the next day he falls asleep suddenly, and falls to the barn floor instead of kneeling to lie down. Once he's down, he falls into a deep REM state. He rolls his eyes in a dream, and the leg paddling, that too is from galloping in his dreams. It's not really a seizure, just a deep sleep, I said.

The woman shook her head. Hard to believe, she said. She invited me into her house while she wrote me a check. It was a nice house, unusually large. There were so many knickknacks and ceramic figurines on the shelves that I was sure if Bruce or Nelly were inside the house, with one swipe of their bushy black tails the woman's entire collection would have been smashed. I told the woman it was a nice house. She raised her forefinger. Upstairs there's a bowling alley, she said. Really? I said. She nodded, saying she had bought the house a year ago and she never used to bowl, but now, after dinner, she takes her drink and her cigarette upstairs, and she bowls. The part she likes best is the sound the pins make when they fall, and she swears that on bone-chill cold nights, when the sound carries farthest, the entire town can hear her strikes. I think how the man who shot my son can hear the strikes. While cleaning his shotgun, he could smell the gunpowder that smoked after he took the shot that injured my son, and down the road he heard this woman's pins falling down. That's not so strange, I say to the woman. I think there are stranger people around here than that, don't you? I say to the woman. The woman nods her head. Oh, no doubt there are stranger people around here. What about that man with those cows, she says. The cows who live in the man's basement? How's he ever going to get those cows out in the spring-time when they've grown so big they won't fit up the stairs?

WHAT I SAY: The man with the cows?

WHAT SHE SAYS: Yes, you know, old Greg Springer, wears overalls all the time with the straps down and his gut pouring out.

WHAT I SAY: Ah, yes, old Greg Springer.

WHAT SHE SAYS: Now there's some guy I wouldn't trust as far as I could throw him. And what he's done to those cows, letting them stand up to their necks in their own shit every day. I think that's criminal. He's a criminal, she says.

WHAT I DO ON DRIVE HOME: Realize that in order to spell "Springer" out of grated orange peel I need an *s*, but that maybe the recipe I was given for scones was really asking for "grated orange peels."

WHAT I NOTICE WHEN I DRIVE HOME: That I have not seen the spacecraft in days and that I will never know now who shot my son if I cannot ask the pilot in the spacecraft if he saw anything.

WHAT I DIG THROUGH THE JUNK DRAWER FOR IN THE KITCHEN:

The scone recipe, to check and see if it really asks for "grated orange peels." I find the rabies tags for Nelly and Bruce, I find a magnifying glass (which I think might come in handy and slip it into my pocket even though it's a kid's cheapo magnifying glass, the quality no better than a cereal box trinket). I find wildflower seeds whose envelope is torn and the seeds litter the bottom of the drawer, I find a dried-up glue stick and a turkey call and an owl call, I find receipts for dental work done years ago, but I do not find the scone recipe.

WHAT I AM BEGINNING TO THINK: That my son will never awaken, even though his score on his Glasgow coma scale was a 14, even though his SPECT scan showed normal cerebral blood flow, even though his foot, according to the day nurse, has moved now and then, approximately a millimeter to the right, and another millimeter to the left. I look up while driving home on our driveway at night. I'm looking up the whole time, seeing if I can see it, and then because I'm not paying attention, I drive off the driveway and partly down the side of the road.

WHAT THE WIFE SAYS IN THE MORNING: Some drunk kids from town must have driven down our driveway last night and gone off the road.

WHAT SARAH SAYS: Oh, those must be the same kids who changed the sign to COME TO THE FALL BOOB FEST.

CALL: A cow with milk fever, down and doesn't want to get up.

ACTION: Drove to farm past huge old maples that lined the road. Met farmer and his son out behind the barn, where the cow was lying on a mixture of frozen mud and ice. In the barn, on some hay, was her newborn mooing for her, and the farmer's wife was trying to feed the calf colostrum from a bottle. Clipped to the side of the stall was a heat lamp, shining down on the calf. Outside,

though, the mother would not get up. I had brought my bottle
of calcium with me and stuck a needle in the vein in her neck
to inject her with some. This might take a few minutes, I said to
the farmer and his son. But the farmer could not hear me, and he
yelled, What's that? and held the top of his ear, red from the cold,
and pushed it out toward me so that I would know he could not
hear so well. I leaned up close to him. I could see where the yarn
from his sweater collar was coming undone and hung in a loop of
scalloped waves. It will take a while for the calcium to take effect.
She may not get up for a while, I said, loudly. The farmer nodded.
In the meantime, I asked the farmer's son if there was a flat board
around. I wanted to drag the cow onto it so that when she did try
to stand up, she wouldn't slip on the ice. He brought me a sheet of
composite board, and then the three of us, the farmer and his son
and I, all tried to push the cow onto the board. She was a heavy
cow, and I was pushing from her rear, which was all bloody from
birthing her calf and expelling her placenta, so that if I pushed too
hard, my hands would slip. I had to find the right strength to push
her with, not too hard so that my hands would slip off her hind,
and not too easy so that she wouldn't budge. The farmer, though
old, was strong and his son even stronger, so the three of us were
able to get her onto the board. Once she was on it, she seemed ap-
preciative to be off the cold frozen mud, and she lifted her head
and looked around, taking in the sight of me and the farmer and
his son, but her interest didn't last long, and maybe the dry surface
beneath her was too much of a comfort, because she suddenly lay
down and sprawled across it and closed her eyes. Doesn't look like
she wants to get up now at all, said the farmer, loudly. His wife, who
was still in the stall in the barn with the newborn calf, thought he

was talking to her, and I could hear her yell from the stall, What's that, Michael? But the farmer didn't answer her.

It was true, the cow didn't look like she wanted to get up. She looked like she wanted to take a long nap instead. Come on, old girl, I said, and I pulled on her rope halter, but she just opened her eyes and looked at me. I hope she won't be a downer, the farmer said. She's my best milker, he said.

Let's give her a few more minutes, I said. There was not much to do but look at the cow and then look out across the farmer's snow-covered hills. On the closest hill there was a sugar shack.

How many trees do you tap? I asked.

Oh, about fifteen hundred, the farmer said.

That must keep you busy in the spring, I said.

The farmer nodded. We sell the syrup here. Between that and the cows, we stay alive.

Then the farmer's wife came out of the barn. She held the empty bottle of colostrum. She didn't wear any gloves, and I could see how red her fingers were from the cold.

How's it doing? the farmer said.

Okay, for now. It needs its mother, though, she said.

The farmer nodded. We're working on that, he said.

I hope she ain't a downer, the farmer's wife said. She's our best milker, she said.

The doc already heard all that, the son said, shaking his head and then spitting on the icy mud. I didn't want to hear the family squabble. I interrupted with a little conversation.

You have a nice place here. Nicer than I've seen in a while. I recently heard of a guy named Greg Springer. I heard he keeps his cows in his basement. Can you believe that? I said.

The farmer nodded.

You know Greg Springer? I said. The farmer spat. I looked at the wife and she turned away. I looked at the son and he spat then, too, right on top of where his father had spat. It was enough of a clue for me. I would head to Greg Springer's. I would see if he was the man who shot my son.

I'll get her up, I said. I went to my truck. From the back I pulled out my bullwhip. I had ordered it from Australia. It was made of braided kangaroo hide. I knew how to crack the whip so that it sounded like a gunshot. When the farmer saw me walk back to the cow with the bullwhip, he didn't say anything. He just put his hand on his chin and felt some gray stubble that was growing there. The farmer's wife stuck the empty bottle of colostrum in her back pocket, and then she folded her arms in front of herself and watched.

RESULT: I pulled the whip back and laid it right next to the cow, so that the tassel end struck by her ear. When the whip made the crack, the cow jumped to her feet. The minute she was up, I pulled her off the composite board. I didn't want her getting comfortable again on it. Put the board away, I said to the son, and he did, quickly. I wished that my whip could wake Sam up the same way and I pictured myself cracking it in his yellow pastel hospital room beside his ear on the stiff white pillowcase and him rising from his bed and holding out his arms to me.

When she was up the farmer said to her, Come on and take care of your youngun', and then he walked in front of her and she followed him into the barn. The calf was mooing for her and she mooed back and when she was close enough, the calf came up under her and started nursing. She turned to it and started licking it, turning the hairs on its backside into a wet swirl.

The farmer's wife called to me from the porch of their house. "Come inside so I can write you a check," she said.

We stood in the kitchen. The only stove in there was a wood cookstove. The floors were beautiful old wide planks that had begun to slant with age and time and made me feel as if I could lose my balance any second and fall over. This is a nice house, I said. The farmer's wife nodded. It's been in the family for four generations. My son was born in the room above our heads, and Michael was born there, too, and his father before him and his father before that.

I looked up at the ceiling. It was tin. The pressed shapes in it had a leaf pattern.

When I walked back to my truck to head home, there was a large jug of maple syrup on the driver's seat.

THOUGHTS ON DRIVE HOME: Is it true what they now say about the Big Bang, that they believe the universe really isn't expanding, but that it's all really heading for one place? What is that place?

WHAT SARAH AND MIA SAID WHEN I GOT HOME: The place is a magnet. The place is warm. Mom's spacecraft can take us to the place. When everything gets to the place, it will collide again. The Big Bang will have a sequel.

WHAT I TELL THE CHILDREN: Did you know that gravity is not a constant? Did you know that gravity bends light?

WHAT THE WIFE SAYS: What is this mess? This room is not the laundry room. This room is the living room. Whose coat is this? Whose hat? Whose dirty socks?

WHAT MIA SAYS: Don't worry, Mommy, everything you're seeing is in the past, because light takes time to travel.

WHAT THE FLIES SAY AT NIGHT: Thank you for this warmth. We are happy here in your home. We like sharing it with you. We will try not to buzz in your face. We will keep our distance. When, in death, we do fall from your beams above your heads and onto your beds while you're sleeping, please forgive us. Forgive us for sometimes clinging to the television screen. We like the extra warmth. It soothes us.

WHAT I CHECKED FOR OUT THE WINDOW: The spacecraft, but it wasn't there, just a clear night with so many stars they seemed to make the sky white. I left the house then. I didn't even need to turn my lights on, the sky was so bright. Where are you going? asked Jen. I'll be back, I said. It's just a horse, I said. It wasn't a horse. I drove to the hospital. The night nurse was reading *Ulysses*. It's like I'm in this guy's head, but the problem is I don't always want to be there, she said when I asked her how the book was. I brought Sam the maple syrup. I opened the bottle and took a sip out of it as if it were a whiskey jug, and it was cold from having been in my truck and I thought how I could almost drink the whole thing like it was water. I threw back the cover and checked his foot. It was still and seemed to glow in the light that the hospital used at night. Then I read a book I had brought. It was about B-24 bombers during World War II. My father was a pilot on a bomber then. I read Sam the part about how in training men had to fly in formation and another pilot had to come at them head-on and be able to lift up just in time to miss flying into the formation, but in training there were many accidents and one man missed, crashing his plane as well as four others and all the men on board died. I told Sam I had figured out what had happened. That the pilot going three hundred miles an hour did not take into consideration that the formation was also flying at him at three hundred miles an hour. When he did pull up, it was already too late. There was no way to judge, I said, and then I cried, thinking of those men, thinking of Sam, the tears falling into the binding of the open pages of the book, magnifying letters.

CALL: A Morgan foundering. I had to go, even though I wanted to check out Greg Springer and drive to his place.

ACTION: Drove to farm, was greeted by a woman with a British accent named Lillian and her King Charles dog and her springer spaniel dog. Lillian was bundled in two sweaters and a scarf and a hat and a down coat. She had just been in the ICU with a lung infection. She was not about to land in there again. Good heavens no, she said. Lillian showed me to the barn. In a stall was the Morgan lying down, his front legs tucked under him. The first thing I noticed about him was that he had a very thick neck. The horse was fat. When I lifted up his blanket, I checked his hind end and there were thick pads of fat there, too. Have you been feeding him extra grain? I asked Lillian. Lillian coughed. Well, yes, with this cold weather, I thought he'd need it.

I explained to Lillian how in the winter, when a fat horse isn't being exercised much, it doesn't need much grain. Too much grain and it builds up too much glucose. In turn this can cause an overgrowth of bacteria that can cause laminitis in its hooves and make it painful for a horse to stand. Cut back the grain, almost to nothing, I told her. Oh dear, Lillian said. He's been getting two big scoops of it a day, on top of his flakes of hay. He won't like being cut back. I nodded. I knew how hard it was to cut back on an animal's feed. I always fed the dogs too much myself. Yes, but he'll only get worse if you don't, I said. In the meantime, Lillian said, what about drugs? Can't you give me something for his pain? I want lots of drugs. When I was in the ICU, I told them I'm as old as the hinges of hell and I feel like shit and I want all the drugs you can throw at me, and so they did. I love drugs, Lillian said. I walked out to the back of my truck. I handed Lillian some Banamine pills and bute paste. Lovely, she said, taking them in her leather-gloved hands. We were standing on a nice spot of her property. A number of snow-covered hills could be seen from where we were. The sun was shining, and the snow looked like ice, slick and glistening. The King Charles dog was looking up at us while Lillian and I talked. He had soft brown eyes, and his little tail wagged gracefully, as if the words we said were words directed toward him. I bent down and petted him, and he smelled my pants at the knee, and smiled up at me. Then the springer spaniel took off, jumping over the snow-covered stone wall, and Lillian called to him, telling him to come back. I don't need him running out into the road and getting run over, though at least you'd be here to patch him together again. What's he after anyway? Lately he's been going batty at night. He runs back and forth in the field and barks at the sky for hours. Do you think he sees things we can't? Lillian asked. I told Lillian I didn't know. What about drugs? Do you have something I can give him that will make him stop? she asked. Try exercising him more in the day. He'll be too tired at night, I said. No drugs? Lillian said sadly. No drugs, I said. Besides, he might really be seeing something in the sky. You don't want him doped up. He could save your life, I said. I didn't want to tell her about the spacecraft I'd seen in the sky at our house. I didn't want her to think her veterinarian was as batty as her springer spaniel.

WHAT I SAID: He might be a tracker. He might be able to solve a crime, he might be useful around here, don't you think? I said. Lillian looked right at me. Maybe so, she said, but I don't think it takes any genius to figure out who's committing all the crimes around here. It doesn't? I said. No, look at that John Bennett's driveway and you can tell he's up to no good. He's got six Saabs sitting there. I heard his bear dog ripped the throat of the sheepdog next door. He hunts bear? I said. Bear, coon, coyote, buck, duck, hell, anything that moves, she said. Grouse? I said. Oh yeah, he's a louse all right, she said. What about Greg Springer? I said. Greg Springer? He's a kind soul. Everyone makes fun of him keeping his cows in his basement, but I've gone down there in that very basement. That's the nicest cleanest driest basement in the whole town. He's got those cows right up cozy against the water heater. Those are the happiest cows around, Lillian said. No, that Greg Springer gets hell because of how he looks and how he dresses, but people shouldn't be shoving their noses into other people's business. It's that John Bennett they should be pointing fingers at.

WHAT I DO INSTEAD OF DRIVING STRAIGHT HOME: Stop at John Bennett's. Lillian's right. He's got six Saabs sitting in his driveway, but none of them has tires. There's no smoke coming from the chimney and no one has shoveled the walk since the last snow. I start thinking John Bennett must have skipped town.

WHAT'S NOT IN THE SKY WHEN I DRIVE HOME: The spacecraft.

WHAT SARAH AND MIA SAY TO ME WHEN I GET HOME: Pop, a deer was killed in Brownsville. It was hit by a car while trying to cross the road. The police came and shot it because its leg was broken. Will they eat the deer?

WHAT I SAY: Yes, I hope so.

WHAT THE WIFE COOKS FOR DINNER: Beef soup made with okra and corn, and biscuits. The children poked their fingers into the middle of the biscuits, and then poured honey into the holes they had made.

WHAT THE WIFE SAYS: Easy on the honey, we need it for other things.

WHAT WE SAY: Like what?

WHAT THE WIFE SAYS: I don't know, just other things. And another thing, stop leaving your shoes in the living room, stop leaving the bathrooms for me to clean, stop leaving the dishes for me to do, and stop leaving the dinners for me to cook.

WHAT I SAY TO THE WIFE: Leave the room. We don't want to hear it.

WHAT THE WIFE SAYS: I don't know. I stopped listening to her. I watched the children filling their biscuit pools with the golden honey.

WHAT WE HAVE TO WATCH OUT FOR NOW: Peanut butter jars and mayonnaise jars where the bottoms are concave, saving the manufacturer money so he doesn't have to use as much food to fill up the jar, but can charge the same price as the old jars where the bottoms were flatter.

WHAT MY CHILDREN DO: Run to the pantry and pull out jars we have recently bought. Look how they're cheating us, the children say, holding up the bottoms of the jars to me. How can they cheat us like this? the children say. The children shake their heads. We are all sad, for a moment, about the injustices in our world.

WHAT MY DOCTOR DOES: Catches me at home. I pick up the phone, thinking it's a call from a client. Before I know it's him, I think it's my father on the phone, just from the sound of his voice. I think my father is calling me, and I'm happy to talk to him, and I forget the impossibility of the situation, the fact being my father is dead, has been dead for a number of years. Died of lung cancer in a senior home called Sunrise, but I was always forgetting the name and calling it Sunset. The doctor has a gentle reminder for me. That is what he calls it, a gentle reminder. I'm past due for coming in to have my levels checked. He is looking forward to seeing me. He hopes that my family and I are well. Well? I want to say. I think of Sam, his eyes unopened in the yellow pastel room. I think of my wife, slipping into bed next to Sam, who still sleeps with a wizened chicken heart by his ear. I think what I hate to think about, that Sam may never wake up. I think about Sarah and Mia, interrupting their dinner to run to the pantry to find plastic jars and hold up their bottoms so I can see how we're being robbed on a daily basis. Yes, we're all fine, I say. I tell him I'll be holding off on being retested. I tell him I don't see the point in doing it again so soon. It's sometimes good to know these things, he says. I tell him I know what he's trying to say, but sometimes, I tell him, it's also good not to know these things. He tells me it's my choice. Why is he telling me that when I already know it's my choice? Thank you, I say. You're welcome, he says, and I know by the tone of his voice that I've disappointed him.

CALL: No call. I drive to John Bennett's house. I sit parked, looking at it, waiting for signs of life, maybe his dog bouncing and barking, trying to look out a ground-floor window at who has parked on the side of the road, but there is no dog, and still no smoke coming from the chimney top.

ACTION: I drive to town hall. The clerk is named Jean and she's sitting at her rolltop desk wearing sheep fleece slippers. Do you know John Bennett? I ask.

WHAT JEAN SAYS: I know everyone. I'm the town clerk, remember?

WHAT I SAY: What's he like?

WHAT JEAN SAYS: He pays his taxes. He buys dump stickers. He put an addition on his house in '89. His dog's name is Howie, a sweet collie mix that has seizures. He takes two pills a day for the seizures, but sometimes they still don't work.

WHAT I SAY: How do you know?

WHAT JEAN SAYS: I take care of Howie all winter while John's in Florida.

WHAT I SAY: All winter?

WHAT JEAN SAYS: He's a snowbird. He leaves before Halloween frost.

WHAT I SAY: That's before hunting season.

WHAT JEAN SAYS: Yes, before hunting season. He doesn't buy a hunting license. The only license he buys is a dog license. You're barking up the wrong tree with John Bennett.

WHAT I SAY: Who do you suggest I search out?

WHAT JEAN SAYS: I don't suggest that kind of stuff. I can tell you what your taxes will be next year, though. I can tell you what the taxes were on the place in the 1800s. I can tell you if you add a twenty-by-five porch to your place what the taxes will be. But I can't tell you what I don't know.

WHAT I DO: I walk behind her. I look at the town map hanging above her desk. I look at all the houses that border my property. I see a house in the northeast corner I didn't know was there before. Whose house is that? I ask.

WHAT JEAN SAYS: Anne Thompson's. She's the daughter of Sleeping Mary.

WHAT I SAY: Sleeping Mary?

WHAT JEAN SAYS: Yes, she would go into a trance and tell the future. If someone wanted a session with her, they would go down to the library on Friday afternoons.

WHAT I SAY: Does she hunt?

WHAT JEAN DOES: Pulls out a book of every licensed hunter in our town. She copies the page for me. No, these are the people who hunt in this town, but anyone could have been walking on your property that day who had a hunting license. That's all you need is a license, and some people don't even bother to get one.

WHAT I SAY BEFORE I LEAVE: What about Howie? Did he bite the neck of a sheepdog?

WHAT JEAN SAYS: Howie's a kitten. That sheepdog got his head cut up trying to limbo a barbed-wire fence on John Bennett's property.

WHAT THE HOUSE SAYS AT NIGHT: "David," it wakes me up, calling my name with a huge creak of its timbers. I look over at Jen, who is sleeping. It was not she who called out my name in her sleep. It must have been the house. What? I say in a whisper, but the house doesn't answer.

WHAT GISELA SAID WHILE I WAS DRIVING: David, check your levels. When I listened to the CD again, she was talking about taking a visit to Tübingen. She was talking about buying more coffee because she had run out. She was talking about where to buy sweet bread. Now she was telling me to check my levels. Repeat after me, she said: Check your levels.

WHAT I THOUGHT ABOUT DOING: Checking my levels because both the house and Gisela had told me to.

WHAT I THOUGHT WAS FUNNY: That my wife and a doctor had

told me to go check my levels, but I didn't want to do it, and now that a house and a German language CD are telling me to do it, I am considering it, especially if it means I might see the spacecraft again.

WHAT WE CAN LEARN FROM RABBITS: That wherever you are, you must look for a place where you can run to and hide.

WHAT I TELL THE WIFE: Have you thought anymore about where we can live when we can no longer afford the taxes here?

WHAT THE WIFE SAYS: I'm not leaving this place. I already told you that.

WHAT THE FLIES SAY AT NIGHT: David, David, David.

NUMBER OF RESIDENTS IN OUR TOWN: 600.

NUMBER OF PEOPLE WITH HUNTING LICENSES: 100.

NUMBER OF FLIES IN OUR HOUSE: Probably 6,000.

NUMBER OF FIELDS ON OUR PROPERTY: 5. The front field, the field to the pond, the middle field, the fern field, the back field. The pond is frozen now, but it is spring-fed and still the water bubbles up from it. We have told the children to stay off it, but Nelly, the Newfoundland, sometimes walks across it and we hold our breaths, scared she will break through the ice and drown. We had a beaver in our pond, and he chewed down seven of our trees that surrounded the pond. In the warmer months, the trees that the beaver felled are visible as they lay submerged at the bottom of the pond. I have put on my wet suit from my days of riding ocean waves and waded into the pond and tried to pull out the trees that I could—the small, thinner ones, but the larger trees I have had to leave where they are, with brown algae growing on their bark.

NUMBER OF TIMES I'VE LOOKED AT THE LIST OF ONE HUNDRED NAMES OF LICENSED HUNTERS: 60.

NUMBER OF TIMES MY WIFE HAS TOLD ME TO PUT IT AWAY: 10.

NUMBER OF MARKS WHO HAVE LICENSES: 3.

NUMBER OF JASONS: 3.

NUMBER OF CALEBS: 1.

NAME THAT ISN'T ON THE LICENSE LIST: Greg Springer.

WHAT NELLY TELLS BRUCE, WHO IS TRYING TO MOUNT HER: Not yet, you brute!

WHAT THE WIFE SAYS: If we really want puppies we have to hire someone who helps breed dogs and this someone has to masturbate the dog.

WHAT I SAY: I am not spending money on hiring someone to come masturbate my dog. I know how to masturbate, for Chrissakes. I'll do it for him.

WHAT THE WIFE SAYS: Oh, that is soo disgusting.

WHAT BRUCE LIKES: Me masturbating him wearing rubber surgical gloves and holding a Ziploc freezer bag nearby to catch what I can whenever it comes spurting out, reminding me of my own days when I donated sperm.

WHAT DOESN'T GET HARD: Bruce.

WHAT STARTS TO REALLY HURT: My arm.

WHAT MY WIFE AND I DECIDE IS NOT GOING TO HAPPEN: Nelly getting pregnant.

WHAT NELLY IS: Still in heat, but now she wanders. Bruce is not man-dog enough for her. She wants to find someone who can do the deed. Bruce, though, follows her when she wanders. They head down the driveway, Bruce trying to mount her the entire time she is trotting away over the frozen road.

WHAT THE NEIGHBORS DO: Call us to tell us our huge black Newfoundland dogs are on their back porch and that the male is trying to mate with the female.

WHAT I DO AFTER I PICK UP THE DOGS: Drive to Greg Springer's with the dogs in the back of the truck and Bruce still trying to mate Nelly. I yell for him to get off her, because every time I look in the rearview all I see is a pumping mass of black fur and my truck's rocking side to side.

WHAT HAPPENS WHEN I OPEN THE DOOR OF MY TRUCK TO KNOCK ON GREG SPRINGER'S DOOR: Nelly runs out and Bruce runs after her up the road and I have to get back in the truck and chase them until they listen and get back into the truck. I am far from Greg Springer's now, and almost home, and so I go home, doubtful that Greg Springer with the nonhunter's license is going to talk to me about hunting, is going to talk to me about anything at all.

CALL: No call.

WHAT THE HOUSE SAYS: You could stain my windows now. You could fix your wife's desk.

WHAT I DO: I make meringues. I can bring Sam the meringues. You use four egg whites, a cup of sugar, and cocoa if desired. I desire the cocoa.

WHAT THE MERINGUES ARE LIKE: Chocolate-flavored air. I need them to live. I can already feel my levels going down. The meringues will wake up Sam.

WHAT SARAH CALLS THEM: Remingues.

WHAT I DO WITH THE MERINGUES: Drive with them on my lap on a plate covered with plastic wrap to the hospital and put them by Sam's head, next to the chicken heart. I tell the night nurse to give *Ulysses* a rest and try one of them, that they're light as clouds and so she tries one, the crumbs falling down her white front and onto *Ulysses*.

WHO EATS ALL THE MERINGUES: The night nurse and I. Between bites she tells me I'm right, they are like clouds.

WHAT SARAH IS READING NOW THAT SHE'S FINISHED WITH *JANE EYRE*: *Heidi*.

WHAT THE CROWS SAY IN THE BACK FIELD WHEN I TAKE THE DOGS FOR A WALK: Call, Call, Call.

WHAT THE WIFE COOKED FOR DINNER: Moose steaks a hunter gave me because I let him hunt on my land.

WHAT THE WIFE ATE FOR DINNER: Not moose steaks.

WHAT THE WIFE SAID: Oh, no, I'm not getting that disease, that crazy brain disease. Why do you think that hunter gave you the moose? It was infected, she said.

WHAT SARAH SAID: Here's a joke. Two cows were talking. One said, "What do you think about this mad cow disease?"

WHAT THE OTHER COW SAID: "Why should I care? I'm a helicopter."

CALL: No call, just the one who doesn't answer back when I say hello. If it's a scammer, hang up, Jen says, who's sick of it not being the hospital. I shake my head, to tell her it's not a scammer. I make up answers to questions of a survey never being asked of me. Yes, I own my own house, I say. No. Yes. No. Yes, we have pets, I say. Two dogs, I say. A rabbit, fish, I say. Oh, it's one of those surveys, just hang up on them, Jen says, but I don't. I want the caller to have enough time to change his mind; maybe he'll talk to me after all. Then I'm quiet, listening for the sound of his seashell breathing again.

WHAT SARAH GETS FROM HER TEACHER: Six baby chicks. The day we get them we put them in a box with a heat lamp shining down on them. We put them in a room separated by a gate so the dogs will not get to them.

WHAT WE HEAR AT NIGHT: Gentle peeping.

WHAT WE SEE IN THE MORNING: No chicks, not even a sign of feathers, and the gate we put up to separate the dogs from the chicks is knocked down. Bruce and Nelly lower their eyes. Have they eaten them whole? Even the claws? Jen says.

WHAT I FIND IN THE CORNER OF THE ROOM: One claw, but that is it.

WHAT SARAH DOES: Cry.

WHAT THE WIFE SAYS: What did we expect from the dogs? We put these yummy morsels in a big tray for them and even heated them to the perfect temperature with a heat lamp. It was just a nice Newfoundland hot lunch we prepared for them.

WHAT SARAH DOES: Continue to cry.

WHAT THE WIFE SAYS: It's just as well. There was no place to put those chicks. Your father had not built a chicken coop even. The next time we get chicks, we will be ready for them. We will have their coop built.

WHAT I LEARN AND WHAT I TELL SAM IN THE HOSPITAL: You can make a chicken coop out of bales of hay. You can make one called an "eggloo."

WHAT THE NIGHT NURSE SAYS: I had a pet chicken I used to swing in a swing when I was a girl.

WHAT THE HOUSE SAYS AT NIGHT: David, check your levels. I woke up and turned to my sleeping wife again. It was not she who had said it this time, either. It was still the house talking to me. I whispered back to it. Check my levels? Is that what you said? The house did not answer. I could hear the rabbit far away in the other room scratching at her newspaper. Maybe it was the rabbit who was talking to me.

WHAT JANE EYRE DOESN'T DO: Marry the young, handsome missionary.

WHAT SHE DOES DO: Marry Rochester, the invalid, blind old man.

WHAT THE RABBIT IS: Maybe lonely because we have just one. I have heard budgerigars are good pets for rabbits. The budgerigar sits on the back of the rabbit and keeps it company, and the rabbit is not afraid of the budgerigar because the rabbit knows the budgerigar is too small to hurt the rabbit.

WHAT THE LAST HUNDRED PAGES OF *JANE EYRE* IS: A lot of talk.

WHAT I HAVE BEEN ABLE TO DO: Collect sperm from Bruce and inseminate Nelly.

NUMBER OF DAYS UNTIL PUPPIES MAY BE BORN: 72.

WHAT SARAH THINKS IS DISGUSTING: That I collected sperm from Bruce and inseminated Nelly.

WHAT I TOLD SARAH: Every living thing you see was created by an act of sex.

WHAT SARAH DOES: Covers her ears.

CALL: No call. I will substitute-teach to put food on the table.

WHAT A STUDENT SAYS: You cannot hand test grades back like that. You have to hand them back so that we can't see each other's grades. We are not supposed to know each other's grades. That is not how it is done. You cannot do that.

WHAT I SAY: It's okay. I can do that.

WHAT ANOTHER STUDENT SAYS: I have to see the counselor.

WHAT I SAY: Not right now. We are in the middle of algebra right now. See this quadratic equation?

WHAT THE STUDENT SAYS: No, you don't understand, I really have to see the counselor. I want to see the counselor. I need to see the counselor.

WHAT I SAY: No, you are going to be fine. Take a deep breath. Look at the numbers on the board.

WHAT THE STUDENT SAYS: I can't do this. I have to see the counselor. Can I please see the counselor?

WHAT I SAY: Go, go and see the counselor.

WHAT I DO AFTER CLASS: Stop and see the counselor to see if the student ever made it to see the counselor. The counselor wasn't in. I noticed how the waiting room was huge. It had paintings on the walls and carpeting, and enough cushioned chairs for thirty kids. It was nicer than my doctor's office. I remembered my own counselor's office in school. It was next to the closet where the buckets and mops were kept. It was a tiny room, with no window. There was only one counselor at my school, but this school had four counselors, all with their own offices, and they all had their names on the doors. I felt like I was inside a hospital instead of a school. And maybe, I thought, this is what schools have become, hospitals, and the teachers are really just hospital staff, making sure the students with problems are taking their meds. And maybe, if I just see one of these counselors they can help me with my levels. Maybe that's all I need is a little Ritalin, a little fix for my ADHD, my ADD, my IEP status. And maybe they've got something for Sam in one of their desk drawers, a smooth coated pink or robin's egg blue pill that will make his eyes flash open and his foot start jumping.

Part Three

Still Winter

WHAT I TELL SAM THAT I'M TRYING TO FIGURE OUT: Gravity. I'm not sure it's a constant. I think it changes. I'm reading books about it, but I'm not any closer to knowing. I think it's like light. You don't see light bend. What you're seeing is space bending around light. I'd like to see gravity. I'd like to try, I said, and then I looked out the hospital window at the moon rising yellow over the mountains.

WHAT THE WIND SAYS AT NIGHT: If I wanted to I could rip your roof off. I could break every goddamned tree next to your house. I could send your truck up over and into the next town. Gravity? I laugh in the face of gravity, the wind says.

WHAT I HEAR AT NIGHT: The rabbit. I am convinced she has escaped out of her cage. I turn the light on in the hall and check on her, but she is fine and still in her cage. When she sees me she sits up, thinking I'll open the cage for her and maybe give her some food. She is so cute, I have to reach in and pet her, because after all, she is a rabbit and there is no comparing her soft fur to anything else. I tell her not to worry about the wind, the wind is out there and we're in here and just listen, I tell her, to the flies gently buzzing. Go back to sleep, I say. All is safe here.

WHAT SOME PEOPLE WANT TO KNOW: If I keep my bullwhip in my bedroom.

CALL: No call. I have to go to a conference. The other vets and I sit at a table. We tell each other stories. One vet, he tells the story about the very first call he had.

WHAT I TELL SAM IN THE HOSPITAL: The vet's story. How a horse grazed on a vast field. There were no trees on the field, no trees except one. The owner had recently trimmed the branches on the tree, and one of the branches was only partially cut so that its point was now sharp. The horse had run straight into the tree and straight into the branch, where it plunged through his forehead and then broke off. The horse then had a branch, larger around than the handle of a broom, stuck through his head. The vet was able to pull the branch out, and the wound healed. To this day he refers to it as the case of the unicorn.

WHAT THE NIGHT NURSE SAYS: She has not seen Sam's foot move lately at all. She has seen another boy down the hall come out of his coma, though, and I want to hear everything about it. I sit down in a chair. Tell it to me the way Leopold Bloom of *Ulysses* would, I say, and she does. She leaves out nothing. I know the blond-haired mother wore snow boots and the snow from the bottom of the boots melted on the hospital room floor and that was the first thing the boy saw, and then he looked into everyone's eyes and the mother held his hand and cried, and the boy, even though weak, tried to move her aside, he wanted everyone to move aside, because he wanted to see more clearly a painting that was on the wall of the ocean, with a killer whale breaching and the sun setting behind him. The doctor then took the painting off the wall and held it up close to the boy so he could see it better, and so now the painting sits propped on the seat of a chair, right beside the boy's bed, so he can see it more clearly.

WHAT I SHOWED SAM: The flight of the spaceship, my hand flat, moving through the air of the room that smelled of rubbing alcohol and urine.

WHO WALKED INTO THE HOSPITAL ROOM WHILE I WAS MOVING MY HAND LIKE THE SPACESHIP: The night nurse, holding *Ulysses* to her chest.

WHAT THE NIGHT NURSE ADMITTED TO: Sometimes reading *Ulysses* out loud to Sam because it helped her to understand it better if she read it out loud.

WHAT I ADMITTED TO: Making my hand into a spaceship.

WHAT THE NIGHT NURSE SAID: I hope you don't mind.

WHAT I SAID: Can you read some now? And I sat on the edge of Sam's bed, his huge feet with the dirty nails next to me, and I put my arm over his two feet and I held them close to me while the night nurse read through her red-rimmed glasses.

WHAT NELLY PROBABLY IS NOT: Pregnant. She is no bigger around the abdomen than she was four weeks ago.

WHAT I ULTRASOUND: Nelly. She's very calm and I lay her on her back and she stays there, with her long legs splayed out even while I apply the cold gel all over her abdomen.

WHAT THE ULTRASOUND SAYS: Nothing. There are no pups in here. Here is a full bladder, maybe. Here is a blood vessel, maybe. But there are no pups.

WHAT THE NIGHT SAYS: Here, here is your snow you have been waiting weeks for. I will cover the yellow stains from your dogs

on the old snow in front of your house. I will cover the gray snow
piles on the side of the roads. I will sit in the trees again, frosting
the branches.

WHAT THE CHILDREN DO AT THE TABLE: Compare an actual
cheese cracker to the photo of the cheese cracker on the box to see
if they are being cheated. The actual cheese cracker turns out to be
larger than the photo on the box of the cheese cracker.

CALL: One of Greg Springer's horses is colicking.

ACTION: Drove to Greg Springer's farm thinking how maybe it was
fate that made his horse colic, and now it would be easy for me to
meet him and easy to see if he were really the man who shot my
son. Maybe he had even wanted to meet me and confess, and his
horse having a colic was just an excuse to call me and talk to me
in person. It was late. I used my flashlight when I got out of the
truck to see my way to the barn, but I didn't really need it. The
moon was so bright it glowed yellow, like a flame from an oil lamp.
I could see Greg Springer's house. I could see his basement light
on, where I had heard he kept his cows nice and warm by the water
heater. Greg Springer came out of the barn to meet me. The bottoms of the legs of his overalls were soiled with horse manure. He
saw me looking at them and said, "I've been lying next to my horse
and praying while she's in pain." I nodded my head. As I walked to
the stall, Greg Springer walked ahead of me, waddling side to side
because of his girth. A man that size walking in the woods would
have made a huge crashing sound, I thought. I walked into the
stall, and I looked at the straw beside the horse. The imprint didn't
clearly show where Greg Springer's legs or arms had been, it just
showed a hollowed-out place in the straw, a dip where something

heavy had been. It could have been anything, it could have been the spacecraft that had been sitting here instead, I thought. I knelt down in the place. I could feel the warmth that was left there and then I started to work.

RESULT: I put my stethoscope on the horse's belly. I could hear a few gut sounds, which was good, but still the horse seemed in pain. She kept reaching up with her rear leg to kick at her belly, as if she wanted to kick the pain away. Greg Springer stood very close to me. I think he was trying to hear what I was hearing. So I let him listen to my stethoscope. He nodded his head after he listened for a while, and then the two of us just stared at the horse. We watched how she shifted her weight from hoof to hoof and how she didn't seem to care whether we were standing there, her pain all that mattered. I gave the horse Banamine and Greg Springer and I just waited awhile, keeping an eye on the horse. I looked up at the sky through the open barn door and told Greg Springer it was probably going to be a cold night because of all the stars that were already showing. I told him it was too bad it wasn't still hunting season, as the nonexistent wind would make for good conditions. He shook his head and said, With my horse the way she is I would not be able to go out and hunt anyway. Yes, that would be distracting, I said. Going out to hunt with something on your mind was a dangerous thing. You never know what you could shoot instead, I said. Once, I said, I was hunting and my mind was not on it and then I heard a deer walking toward me, but I couldn't see it yet. Then all of me was listening for it and waiting for it to show its face. My finger was ready to pull the trigger the moment I saw it because I knew I would not have many chances to shoot it, there being so many trees in the way. Suddenly I saw a dark shape through the trees, and I almost shot, but I hesitated, and it was a good thing, because what came out into the clearing wasn't a deer at all, but a man, another hunter, walking carefully through our woods, but it was scary to think how close I was to shooting him. Greg Springer nodded his head. The horse made a low whinny and then Greg Springer shook his head and reached out and touched the side of the horse's neck. It'll be all right, girl, he said. I told Greg Springer to call me in the morning if the horse didn't show signs of improvement. I told Greg Springer it was going to be a cold night, and that he might want to sleep inside. He shook his head. I've a warm sleeping bag. I'll just bring it out here and sleep beside her and pray, he said, and then I thought how maybe Greg Springer could go to the hospital. Floor 9, I could tell him, get off there, the fourth patient door on the left, that's my son. Would he lie next to him and pray?

THOUGHTS ON DRIVE HOME: I have Gisela's phone number. I wonder, if I called it, who would pick up the phone? Would it be Gisela? Would she tell me the weather in Germany? How do you say, in German, my levels are lower than they were before? Would I hear in the background the sounds of the beer from the taps being poured into steins when I called? Would I hear the German? The strong glottal stops harsh-sounding, or would those sounds just be the interfering signs of static common to an overseas connection?

WHAT THE WIFE ASKS ME AT HOME: Well, was Greg Springer your man?

WHAT I SAY: There is no way for me to know. How could I know a thing like that from kneeling next to him in some straw?

WHAT THE WIFE SAYS: Is it going to stop now? Every time you go on a call, you come back thinking you know the man who did it. I'm getting worried about you.

WHAT I DO FOR THE FLIES AT NIGHT: I turn the light off and open the window. I am sick of them buzzing by my head while I read the paper in bed. I am tired of them buzzing inside my lampshade making a tock-tock-tock sound as they slam into one side of the taut linen shade and then the next. There is a bright full moon out. Shoo, I say to the flies. Can't you see the bright moon? I say. I cup my hand and move it behind them, trying to direct them to the cool air outside.

WHAT THE WIFE SAYS: Can I read? Haven't we sat in the dark long enough? It's getting cold in here, she says. Shut the window. I close the window and turn the light back on, but the flies haven't vacated our home. In a second I can hear them buzzing inside the lamp again. The tock-tock-tock sounding louder than ever.

WHAT THE WIFE IS READING: A book about coma. There's a syndrome, she says, that occurs in children, who, after waking from it, display delayed recovery of consciousness. Apparently the psychological stresses of being in the hospital keep them sleeping, she says.

WHAT I SAY: That won't happen to Sam. When he wakes he will wake right away. He will want to know which sister played with his games. He will want to eat chocolate right away. He will want to know if it's still deer season.

WHAT THE WIFE SAYS: I can't remember, did his MRI show swelling? Midline shift? Mass lesions? I shake my head. She has asked me these questions before.

WHAT I SAY: Remember his Glasgow score. Remember how high it was?

WHAT THE WIFE SAYS: Look at that, ladybugs. I look to see where she's pointing. There are ladybugs crawling on the sills of all the windows surrounding our bed. At least they don't buzz, I tell her, but then I see how she sits up quickly and starts shaking out her hair. Bastard, she says, and with its small wings spread out a ladybug hops onto the blanket. And that is how our night is spent. One of us, every once in a while, waking up and shaking our head to get a fly or a ladybug out from crawling in our hair, then there is the sound of us wiping the sheet to knock the insect off and onto the floor, where no doubt we will step on it on our way to the bathroom.

WHAT SARAH SAYS IN THE MORNING: I bet you don't know what ambrosia is.

WHAT I SAY: It's a fruit salad mixed with whipped cream.

WHAT SARAH SAYS: No, it's whale vomit and it's used as a preservative to keep perfumes smelling good.

WHAT I SAY: You mean ambergris.

WHAT SARAH SAYS: Whatever.

WHAT MIA SAYS: Poppy, make ambrosia.

WHAT THE RADIO SAYS: Beep-di-dah-beep-di-dah-beep-beep-beep.

WHAT THE WIFE SAYS: STOP. I AM GETTING A TRANS-MISSION. IT IS IMPERATIVE THAT WE GET A HEAD POTTY CLEANER AS SOON AS POSSIBLE. OUR MIS-SION CANNOT CONTINUE WITHOUT THIS VITAL PO-SITION BEING FILLED.

WHAT THE CHILDREN SAY: Too bad about the mission. Guess you'll have to leave without us, Mom.

WHAT THE WIFE SAYS: Who will wash your dishes and cook your food and serve you and pour your milks and collect your dishes and wipe the countertops and do the laundry and do the food shopping and pick up your dirty socks and hang up your coats and take your wet towels off your beds and put away your toys and turn off the lights you left on in your rooms? Who will do all of this if I'm gone? the wife said. I'm going on the next flight, the wife says. The socks will be easier to pick up in space, I won't have to bend down and throw out my back. I'd like to see how wood burns in space, I wouldn't mind stacking wood in space, I could lift a whole cord in space.

NEWSPAPER ARTICLE I READ TO SAM WHILE I SIT BESIDE HIM EATING OATMEAL RAISIN COOKIES WHOSE CRUMBS FALL INTO HIS HAIR: The bats are sick. The bats are flying in daylight. The white fungus disease is evident on their mouths, as if they've been trying to eat snow. The paper says they've been roused from their winter sleep because they're weak and starving. They've been seen drinking water, and flying low over rivers and ponds where the ice has melted.

WHAT THE BATS SAY IN THE DAYTIME: I am sick, I am thirsty, I am hungry, I am dying.

WHAT THE DAY NURSE DOES: She comes in and flicks off the oatmeal cookie crumbs from Sam's head onto a paper napkin, then she takes out a small black comb from her pocket on her uniform and starts combing his hair, forming a part where he has never had a part, making him look like some kid I didn't know, making me think maybe this is not really my son who is here lifeless in a hospital bed but some other man's son, and I should go home now. I should drive up the driveway and find my son throwing snowballs wildly at his sisters from a snow fort he has built into the side of the hill. I should see his face red from the cold. I should see snow in his hair, and his eyes glistening and bright from his onslaught against his screaming sisters.

CALL: The hospital. Sam is sitting up. Sam is talking. Sam's foot is a live wire.

ACTION: Run to the car. Start driving off with wife, Sarah, and Mia barely having time to sit down in their seats, the car doors still open as I start to drive. Drive with wife incessantly asking if I want her to drive because she thinks I am driving too slowly. Don't expect a miracle, I tell her. Don't expect him to be completely re-covered, I say, driving past the Bunny Hutch preschool, watching other children swinging high into the sky while sitting in yellow and red plastic swings.

RESULT: Sam wants to know what the dis-dis-gusting thing was by his ear. He wants to know which one of his sis-sis-sisters thought he should be sleeping with a cooked chicken heart next to him all this time. He wants to know who has been made Head Potty Cleaner while he was gone because he wants to know if he is off the hook and doesn't have to take the j-j-job.

WHAT THE TESTS SAY: Sam's speech, although slurred, will slowly get better.

WHAT THE DOCTOR SAYS: Children recover much better from being in a coma than adults. By the way, the doctor says, did you ever find the hunter who did this? I tell him no, I never did, and that I didn't think I would ever find out, either. You'd be surprised. He might turn up at your door one day, the doctor says.

HOW WE CELEBRATE: The girls use scissors and cut out shapes in paper bags and then put candles in the bags and place them on the driveway in two lines, one on either side of the driveway. When I drive home with Sam our driveway looks like a runway instead and Sam says, "Either we're coming in for a landing or we're taking off."

WHAT WE EAT FOR DESSERT: Ice cream sundaes, the sprinkles hard and like sand between our teeth. The children are too excited from all the sugar to sleep at bedtime and so we play charades, propping Sam up in an easy chair and piling blankets around him and Nelly laying on the part of the blanket that trails on the floor. With her powerful large head at his feet she reminds us of a lioness content to have her pride back up to its original numbers. The girls act out snakes and elephants, and then move on to acting out teachers at school. After charades, I carry Sam up to bed. It's a full moon and the eerie white pours itself on his pillow, lighting it up, as if waiting for him to lay his head down right onto it.

CALL: The woman who works at the checkout wants to know if I've seen her horse.

WHAT I SAY: Your horse?

WHAT SHE SAYS: Yes, I put an ad in the paper to sell the horse and these people called and they said they'd come over to buy the horse. Well, I got back from doing errands to meet the people and the horse was gone. The horse has disappeared, and I thought maybe, if you were visiting other farms and you spotted my horse, you could tell me, because I could really use the money, she says, and then she sniffs and I wonder if it is because she is crying or because she has a cold.

WHAT I SAY: I haven't seen your horse. If I see it I'll call you. By the way, I say, how is the job at the market? Are you still learning unusual things about people from what they're buying?

WHAT SHE SAYS: I quit that stupid job. Bad people buy baby diapers and good people buy knives, you know. You can't learn anything about people from what they buy. I was all wrong about that, she says.

WHAT THE WIFE SAYS: That's strange, don't you think? A horse just disappearing into thin air?

WHAT I THINK: Not so strange, no stranger than a hunter shooting my son and never fessing up.

WHAT MIA SAYS: I think the spacecraft took the horse.

WHAT I THINK: Maybe the spacecraft took the hunter, too. Maybe all bad hunters are locked inside the spacecraft and made to float around for eternity, looking in the windows of homes at all the lives they destroyed.

WHAT WE WATCH ON VIDEO THAT WE BORROWED FROM THE LIBRARY, NOW THAT WE DON'T SPEND MONEY AT THE VIDEO STORE: A *Christmas Carol*.

WHAT I REALLY LIKE: How Marley, Ebenezer Scrooge's partner, moans horribly while holding his chains and presenting his ghost-like form to Ebenezer on Christmas Eve.

WHAT MY WIFE WANTS TO KNOW: Whatever happened to Ebenezer's wife, and did she die from some awful lung ailment from working so closely with those people in the poorhouse after he divorced her? And it wasn't really a happy ending at all, was it? my wife says, except for Ebenezer Scrooge being kind to Tiny Tim and his family, and giving them a huge turkey bigger than Tiny Tim himself, and Scrooge being reunited with his niece and nephew, and giving a coin to a beggar on the street. It's a terrible ending, because where is the wife? The one he hurt so much? my wife asks. And it's true, there's no more mention of the wife, the one he stopped loving in lieu of money, and it's a terrible ending. I agree and thank God, I think, it's not Christmas that we're watching this, because it would really put a damper on our holiday spirit.

WHAT THE WIFE COOKS FOR DINNER: Salmon baked with butter and paprika, and green beans cooked with chopped-up bits of bacon and couscous cooked with broth and bits of green olives stuffed with pimentos.

WHAT MY WIFE IS CRAZY ABOUT: Green olives. She puts them in bean burritos and she puts them in tuna fish salad and she puts them in ham and cheese sandwiches and she puts them in stir-fry. Sometimes I wonder if it isn't all the bits of green olives that first raised my levels.

WHAT SAM HAS STARTED READING OUT LOUD AFTER DINNER TO IMPROVE HIS SPEECH: *The Count of Monte Cristo.*

WHAT SARAH SAYS ABOUT DANGLARS: That man is pure mean, and I think how maybe the hunter who shot my son could be as mean as Danglars.

WHAT THE RABBIT DOES WHEN SAM READS: She goes into his lap and starts biting the pages.

WHAT THE WIFE SAYS SHE COOKED FOR DINNER: Flounder breaded in panko and fried.

WHAT I SAY: What's panko? Panko is bread crumbs, she says. Then why didn't you just say bread crumbs? I said. Because they are different bread crumbs, she said.

WHAT I THINK: What's happened to the world? How could a thing like bread crumbs go from being simple to complex?

CALL: I just wanted to know, a man says. I just wanted to hear your voice, he says, and then he hangs up.

CALL: A goat can't deliver her kid.

ACTION: I asked my wife to ask Mia and Sarah if they wanted to come with me on the call. Wouldn't they love to see a kid delivered? I said to Jen. Jen said the girls were tired and that they should stay home. All right, I said, and I drove to the farm alone. The farmhand was there, standing by the pregnant goat. His hands were bloody. I have tried, he said. I have been trying for hours, he said, but the baby does not want to come out. I put my hand inside the goat. The first thing I can feel is how the uterine lining is ripped. The farmhand had pulled too hard. He had been too rough.

RESULT: This baby is dead and the mother will die from the ruptured uterus, I said. The farmhand looked at me. Do me a favor, I said. Tell Marie, the owner, I have to put the goat down. Tell her I have to shoot it. The farmhand nodded, wiping his hands on his pants as he walked toward the house where I could see Marie standing in the doorway with the door open and with her oxygen attached to her nose, the clear tube trailing behind her, attached to her tank standing somewhere in one of her darkened rooms. She reminded me of an astronaut, the tubing keeping her from floating off while out on a space walk. I knew Marie would be okay with me shooting the goat instead of giving it an injection. Marie was poor, and she knew the bullet was free and the euthanasia solution cost money. Marie was always thankful when I saved her money. I reached into the goat again, wanting to be sure my diagnosis was right. I could feel the tear in the uterus easily, because it was so big. The goat screamed in pain. It sounded like a woman's voice. I took my hand out and I patted the goat's back. I told her the pain would be gone soon. When the farmhand returned he nodded his head. "I told her," he said. I looked at Marie in the doorway and she was also nodding her head, giving me the okay to put the goat down. I took the goat to the back of the barn, where no one driving by could see. I had my .38 and I put it on her forehead and then I pulled the trigger. The bullet must have entered her sinuses, because smoke from the gun blew out through her nostrils, swirling up toward the sky.

WHAT MARIE DID: She waved me into her house. It seemed like I was an astronaut, too, the way I floated across the ground to get to her doorway. I floated because shooting the goat and having the smoke blow out through her nostrils was surreal, and it all seemed like a dream. Marie had me come into her house and she closed the door behind me, letting the farmhand take the goat away in the cold. You want me to pay you in veal or mutton? she said. I could have my pick. The meat would be ready in a few weeks. I'll think on it, I told her. I was dizzy. I wanted to sit down, but I didn't. Marie hobbled over to the window and looked out at the farmhand carrying the goat in his arms. I don't like him, she said. Something inside her oxygen tank clicked, and I wondered why. Was that a signal it was running low? Then I looked and realized it was one of her black and white border collies' tails that was hitting against the tank; it was happy to see me, and had come into the room to meet me. He walked over to me and fit himself right up under my hand. I think I leaned on him a little. I was thankful to have him there, taking on a little bit of my weight, lightening my load.

WHAT I SAID: Why don't you like him, Marie?

WHAT MARIE SAID: Just a feeling I have. He didn't help with that kid. That mother would still be alive if he hadn't ripped her. I walked over to the window and watched the farmhand drop the goat onto the ground. He dropped it from a height higher than I would have dropped it, even though it probably didn't matter because it was dead. The goat slightly bounced after it was dropped so hard. Marie turned away. I guess I can't begrudge him too much. He bagged a buck this year and gave me all the meat.

WHAT I SAID: What's his name?

WHAT MARIE SAID: Jim Bushway. He's from up north. He doesn't have any friends here, I don't think. When he's not working for me, he's hunting, but he doesn't keep the meat. He'll shoot rock tiger and just leave 'em dead where he shot 'em.

WHAT I SAID: Rock tiger?

WHAT SHE SAID: You know, chipmunks. They always run across the rock walls here. He shoots 'em and leaves 'em there on the rock wall and says the coyotes will come get them. I know he's right, but still, she said.

THOUGHTS ON DRIVE HOME: It was a good thing I didn't take Mia and Sarah with me. I don't want the veal. I don't want to eat something killed before it has had a chance to mature. I will take the slaughtered sheep.

WHAT WE SEE IN THE SKY AS WE STAND OUTSIDE OUR HOUSE LOOKING AT STARS: The bright lights again, the object moving in the sky.

WHAT THE WIFE SAYS: Funny, I didn't get a transmission.

WHAT THE CHILDREN SAY: Come inside, quick. We're scared!

WHAT THE WIFE AND I DO: Watch the object moving low in the sky.

WHAT THE CHILDREN DO: Rap on the windows, and beckon us to come inside. I look at Jen and she looks at me. Is there a moment we think that if it landed we could go up inside it? Make our children come with us, guiding them on board, then take off into the night sky? We would look out small windows, try to see down below, the frosted land, the still north, the cloven tracks of deer dark like leaves that floated down side by side on the snowy land.

The bright lights sail away, and I hold out my hand for Jen to take. I call her name. She comes and we walk into the house, stepping on the wooden porch, opening the doors and going inside. But I don't stay inside with her. I go back out, telling Jen I will take the dogs for a walk. I run down to the field. Maybe the pilot can tell me what he saw the day my son was shot. Maybe there are pictures he takes, a camera made of indestructible metal soldered to the spacecraft's sleek underbelly. The spacecraft is low now, but not low enough for me to see a window, to see the face of the pilot. I flail my arms. Bruce and Nelly think this is a game. They jump on top of me. They try to catch my large gloved hands in their mouths. Get down! I say. I hear their nails ripping down the shell of my coat. Then I yell up to the spacecraft, "Tell me!" I say, but there is no possible way for the spacecraft to hear me, the dogs are barking loudly now. This is such a fun game. Their curved long-haired tails having brushed on the ground are frosted with snow now and sparkle the same way the stars up above are sparkling.

WHAT THE WIFE COOKED FOR DINNER: Gypsy soup.

WHAT MIA SAID: I do not like Gispy soup.

WHAT I TELL THE WIFE ABOUT: Jim Bushway, the rock tiger killer.

WHAT THE WIFE SAYS: Rock tiger?

WHAT I SAY: Maybe Jim Bushway is our man. Marie doesn't like him.

WHAT THE NIGHT SAID: You cannot even see out of your windows for all the fly shit that's stuck to the glass. How do you expect to tell if what you are seeing is really stars?

WHAT THE WIFE SAID: I can't stand these flies falling on my head at night and getting caught in my hair and buzzing all around. I will sleep with the mosquito netting over me, even though it is the middle of winter, so that the flies don't land on me. Jen let the netting settle over her and she was hazy behind it, reading a book.

WHAT THE KIDS SAID THE NEXT EVENING: Pop, where is my mouth guard? Sarah and Mia had a basketball game. We drove to the game taking the back roads that looked so different in the dark than in the daytime. The kids sat in the back and when they spoke to us it was hard to understand them, because they were wearing their mouth guards and chewing on them the whole way there.

WHAT STRUCK ME ABOUT THE BASKETBALL GAME: They played really good music at halftime. And who would have thought that in a small gym of a small school in a small town the music would be so good?

WHAT WE SAW WHEN WE DROVE HOME UP OUR DRIVEWAY: The spacecraft again.

WHAT THE WIFE SAID: Stop the car. She got out. She watched it for a while. Maybe it would tell her, I thought. Maybe a loud voice would cut through the night saying the hunter's name. Could it be Venus? Sarah asked. I shook my head. It was moving closer to us. Get back in the car, Mommy! Sarah yelled. It's just a spaceship, Mia said. It was a cold night. My wife dug her fists into her coat pockets, then she opened up the door and got back in for the rest of the drive down our driveway to the front of our house. The spacecraft was still flying in the sky.

WHAT SARAH ASKED: Who do we tell? Do we tell the police? My wife and I shook our heads. No, I said, remembering how helpful the police were in finding the hunter who shot Sam. It's probably just one of the drones the air force practices flying at night. Don't tell anyone, I said. I wanted the spacecraft for ourselves. I felt good about telling the kids that no one else needed to know about it. I also liked the idea of having our own spacecraft because it seemed like a rite of passage, a natural course of events for an adult—first you get married, then you have the house and then the kids and the dogs and the rabbit and now the spacecraft.

CALL: Arlo has a cow with diarrhea.

ACTION: Drove to Arlo's in the snow that was slippery. Stopped first to get the mail at the post office. A man came up to me. Is that your truck? he asked. I smiled, and told him it was. You could be arrested for that, he said. I was still smiling. I could not imagine what I could be arrested for. It's illegal to drive with snow on your roof. What if that snow blew back onto the windshield of another car? What if it slid off onto your windshield and you crashed into someone? the man said. The man was not smiling back when I smiled. I nodded. All right, I said. Are you high? the man said. High? I said. No, I'm not high, I said, still smiling because I did not want to have words with the man. I got back into my truck and drove off without removing the snow from the roof of my truck. When I turned into Arlo's driveway, I sped up and then stopped short, to see if the snow would come cascading down the roof and onto the windshield. The snow did not slide off. It stayed on the roof of my truck.

RESULT: At Arlo's I took a blood on the cow. What do you think it is? Arlo asked. I looked at the cow. Her heart rate was down. She had a slight fever. It may not be good, I said to Arlo. Arlo shook his head. You should have decked that guy who told you about the snow on your roof.

THOUGHTS ON DRIVE HOME: Will the snow fall off now? Will the snow fall off now? Will the snow fall off now?

WHAT I TOLD ARLO WHEN THE BLOOD RESULT CAME BACK POSITIVE: Arlo, you've got to put her down or else she'll give it to the rest of the herd. Arlo did not want to do it. He liked his Chianina cow. He toyed with the idea of keeping her separate from the herd, but it might be impossible to do. She might still infect the others and he could not afford that. As it was, he would not be able to slaughter her and sell the meat. The meat would be considered tainted and unfit for humans. He sent the white cow off to be slaughtered. Days later he got a call from a man who sells cows. Arlo, have I got a cow for you. It's the kind you like. It's a Chianina, the man said. Arlo made the man describe the cow and then he had the man read the number on the tag in the cow's ear. It was the same number as the number of the cow he had sent off to slaughter. A mistake had been made along the way. Instead of it being slaughtered, it was auctioned off. There would be the risk of it infecting other cows now, and the risk of it infecting humans if the humans ate the beef. I could punch you, Arlo said he said to the man who wanted to sell him back his own cow. The guy sounds like bad news, I said. He's a crook, Arlo said. Who knows what else he's done in his lifetime. I'll call the CDC for you. I'll report him, I told Arlo. You don't have to do that, Arlo said. That's not your job. You're not a cop, he said. No, please tell me his name, I said. Maybe I'm all wrong about this, Arlo said, maybe what he did is not so wrong. Come on, tell me his name, I said. Arlo looked at me, You're pretty itchy, Doc, to put a man behind bars.
WHAT I SAID: You're right. I am. I'm angry for you.
WHAT ARLO SAID: You're just angry, period.
WHAT I SAID: Sure I am.

WHAT ARLO SAID: I can't say I blame you. His name's Passen, and put him the hell behind bars.

WHAT I LEARN ABOUT PASSEN: He's been arrested before for the same thing. He hunts. He hunts grouse. I go with the CDC to his farm. We have a permit to search. There are stuffed grouse perched on his mantel. There are shotguns in a glass case and a drawer beneath the case with boxes of bird shot shells. There are freezer bags in the freezer in the barn labeled "grouse meat." I think this man could be the man who shot Sam. The CDC finds papers in Passen's house, papers he signed that show he knew that the cows he bought were diseased. The CDC can arrest him again.

WHAT THE WIFE SAYS: Thank God, now can you stop searching for this man? He'll be arrested. Your son's alive.

CALL: An owner says her horse is lame.

ACTION: Drove to farm with Sarah. The horse had a swelling on its hind ankle, and the swelling had begun to progress to the hock. I began massaging the tissues above the hock, slowly working my way down the swelling. I asked Sarah to hold the flashlight and shine it on the leg. She shone it on the wall, she shone it on the beagle who had trotted in after us, she shone it on the corner post where a spider had begun to spin its web. Hey Charlotte Web, I said, keep the torch on the horse.

RESULT: Worked the leg with my hands for forty-five minutes so that I moved some of the swelling down. Told the owner that if it wasn't better in a day or so, we'd come back with antibiotics.

WHAT I ASKED SARAH ON THE WAY HOME: What do you want to be when you grow up? You ought to start thinking about that now.

WHAT SARAH SAID: Are there any jobs for people who want to get paid for sleeping, because Sam could get that job.

WHAT THE WIFE SAID: There is always the Head Potty Cleaner job on the spaceship.

WHAT THE WIFE COOKED FOR DINNER: Steak sandwiches she said were really Martian gut sandwiches.

WHAT I AM ORDERING: Fifty dollars' worth of seeds. Among other things there will be fingerling potatoes growing in our garden this summer. I know what they will look like. They will look like fingers growing up from the ground, as if the dead were buried in our garden and they are trying to claw their way out.

CALL: No call. I drove to Arlo's farm. Arlo, I wanted to say, what about that spacecraft. You've seen it, haven't you? I wanted to tell Arlo that it knew who shot my son. That I had dreams of the military footage locked at a base somewhere, the picture of my son's attacker in the films. I wanted to tell him I was almost sure if those films were found, it would be Passen's face in them. I wanted to tell Arlo I had solved the mystery.

WHAT I ASKED ARLO INSTEAD: How are the Chianinas? How are my favorite cows?

WHAT ARLO SAID: I'd like to preg-check a cow.

WHAT I SAW DRIVING HOME AFTER PREG-CHECKING THE COW: A half-dozen does crossing the road. They ran, then stopped right in the middle of the road and I could have sworn they were all looking up, looking to where one night they had seen the spacecraft and looking to see if it would show up in the same part of the sky once again.

THINGS I HAVE SAID TO THE WIFE OVER THE YEARS: You're

mentally incompetent. Maybe you have a mitochondrial disease. You've got a slow learning curve. Your hands are as cold as death. The operative word is *Fuck off,* but you already know that I said that once.

THINGS SHE HAS SAID TO ME OVER THE YEARS: Fuck you, Fuck off, Go fuck yourself, You're a Nazi, You're a prick, You're a shit, Eat shit.

CALL: A voice on the phone that sounds like my own, only younger. Hello, is this the residence of Dr. David Appleton? the voice asks and I am elated. I have achieved space-time travel and here I am calling myself from the past. Are you the David Appleton who lived in Williamsburg, Ohio? Are you the David Appleton who went to _____ high school in '75? my young voice asked. I wondered where I was that I was calling myself from. Was I at my childhood home? Was I in the kitchen with my mother? Was the smell of her vegetable soup cooking on the stove? The smell of her peanut butter cookies baking in the oven? Was my brother beside me, punching my arm? My father in his La-Z-Boy chair smoking his pipe?

ACTION: I actually held the phone away from myself and looked at the mouthpiece thinking there would be some shred of me, some image of myself, coming out from the small holes in the plastic.

WHAT I WANTED TO SAY: Eureka! Yes, by God you have achieved space-time travel. You did it! I did it! I wanted to shout and I wondered when in the future I would actually be achieving this amazing feat of being able to travel through time, because as of yet, I hadn't a clue how to do it.

WHAT I SAID INSTEAD: Why yes, you've reached Dr. Appleton's residence.

WHAT THE VOICE SAID: Thank you. Thank you very much, and then the caller hung up the phone.

WHAT THE WIFE ASKED: Who was that?

WHAT I ANSWERED: I really don't know. Someone who wanted to know who I was, but they already knew who I was.

WHAT THE WIFE SAID: Did you tell them? Maybe you shouldn't have told them anything. You don't want everyone knowing who you are. Maybe it was that Passen, or one of his men, calling you from jail. Maybe he's out for revenge. I wish you hadn't called the CDC on him. I wish you had left well enough alone.

WHAT I SAID: Yes, maybe it was just Passen or one of his men.

WHAT WAS TALKED ABOUT AT TOWN MEETING DAY: The three streetlamps in town. Voters wanted to keep them on at night because they cut down on crime. Voters wanted to get rid of them because they cost the town money in electricity bills.

WHAT I WANTED TO KNOW: What was the lunch? What really is red flannel hash? Who sitting here has shot my son?

WHAT WAS DISCUSSED: Wattages and the cost of replacing standard bulbs with LEDs.

WHAT SOMEONE'S NAME WAS IN TOWN WHOM I DIDN'T KNOW BEFORE: Boogie, and I wonder, of course, if Boogie who lives on the next hill over from us knew who shot my son and also if she had seen the spacecraft. I thought how if the spacecraft returned it might show up at town meeting, floating above us, hovering still over the school where we have the meeting, coming in low every once in a while, peering through the gym windows, blinking its lights, giving its own ayes and nays to the passages of bills and amendments, and taking on, too, the smell of the red flannel hash cooking in the kitchen that we all seem to carry on our clothes and that hours after, we can still smell even when we are in our own homes.

CALL: A man and his wife have a borzoi who's sick. I told them I don't usually do small animals. Oh, no, they said. Jordan is quite tall. Please, would you come?

ACTION: I drove to their home. Jordan was happy to see me. Are you sure he's sick? I asked. The woman nodded her head. He wouldn't get up this morning. He lay at the foot of the bed. That's not like Jordan, she said. He seems all right now, I said. Jordan sniffed my pants, smelling the scent of my own dogs. I took his temperature. It was normal. I felt his abdomen. There was no unusual swelling. While I was there he walked over to his food bowl and ate what was put out for him in the morning.

RESULT: I told the couple that I thought he'd be all right. Whatever he had, it seems to have passed, I said. I talked to the couple for a while. The woman said she did not ever leave the house, she was too afraid. The husband wore clothes that looked like rags, but the couple was rich. I could tell by their beautiful home. The man showed me his bookcase. It was filled with rare books. He showed me his photographs. He had an original photograph of Custer on the wall in his hallway. The man knew many things. I asked him about building a chicken coop and he told me to use cedar, as it would repel water and be lightweight. He wrote down the name of the store to buy the materials at, but his wife did not want me to keep the paper. I'll write it for you, she said, and then she took the paper the husband had written on and stuffed it into the pocket of her cardigan.

THOUGHTS ON DRIVE HOME: What really became of the Zodiac

Killer? And what better place to move to except here, to a small town in the woods out here where no one might know who you are. Maybe you meet the girl of your dreams and you tell her who you are and she forgives you and she spends the rest of her life protecting you, because you are forgetful. You leave bits of your writing around without remembering that it's your handwriting that could condemn you, but your wife remembers.

WHAT YOU TELL YOUR WIFE WHEN YOU GET HOME: I have met the Zodiac Killer.

WHAT SHE SAYS: Eat some soup.

WHAT THE KIDS SAY: Who is the Zodiac Killer?

WHAT I SAY: I'm lucky to be here. What if they saw the look in my eye that meant I realized exactly who they were. I wouldn't be here, I said. They would have bludgeoned me to death.

WHAT THE WIFE SAYS: What was wrong with the dog? The dog, I say, was fine. But I tell her it reminds me of what I just learned. Guess, I said, what is the closest relative of the whale?

WHAT THE WIFE SAID: The dog? The horse? Humans?

WHAT I SAID: No, no, no. You would not believe it but it's true. Cows are the closest relative of whales. When I said it, it made sense. I could see cows floating peacefully in the ocean waves, their large eyes moving side to side, taking in their water world.

WHAT SAM SAYS: Poppy, do you know what a female bear is called? It's called a sh-sh-sh-she bear. Can you believe that?

WHAT THE WIFE SAID: Who left these dishes in the sink? Can't anyone wipe the stove top? What kind of husband are you? I bet the Zodiac Killer at least leaves his shoes outside the living room. I bet the Zodiac Killer empties the dishwasher. I bet the Zodiac Killer buys his wife a flower on Valentine's Day. Where's my flower? My card? My anything? the wife says.

WHAT I DO: I go upstairs. I think maybe Sam was shot by the Zodiac Killer. I think maybe, in a sick way, that's kind of cool. I mean if you're going to get shot, it might as well be the Zodiac Killer and not some slovenly hunter with bad aim and a high blood alcohol content.

WHAT MIA DOES: Gives her mother some chocolates from a heart-shaped box her mother left at the foot of her bed on Valentine's morning.

WHAT I SAY TO THE WIFE: See, there are your chocolates. We didn't need to spend money on more.

WHAT THE WIFE SAYS: I need a mammogram. I need a Pap smear. I need these things I haven't had in years. I'll go to the clinic with you the day of your appointment.

WHAT I DO: Work on a chicken coop with the kids. I have not bought the cedar the Zodiac Killer recommended I buy because the cedar was too expensive. I have bought pine, but I realize, as I'm trying to fit the boards together to see how the end product will look, that the pine is very heavy and I wanted this chicken coop to be the kind of chicken coop two people could pick up and carry to a new spot in the field every day so that the chicken poop wouldn't destroy the same section of grass every day, but darn if the Zodiac Killer wasn't right about the cedar. The pine weighs a ton.

WHAT GISELA WANTS TO KNOW: Is there anyone who will go to Tübingen with her? (Gisela is no longer after me about my levels.)

••••

CALL: The man who had a horse I had to put down and who speaks German has another horse that is a little lame. The man tells me that his uncle, who is not right and who lives in the apartment above their barn, has seen the spacecraft, too, and that he did not believe him. Now, he says, he has a new perspective on his uncle, and he doesn't want to have to think about it but maybe, just maybe, more of what he has said over the years is possibly true. The man still has three horses, and they stand in the field, their manes whipping in the wind, in a wind the man tells me is the fiercest in these parts and he swears there are no other fields, no other hillsides that could quite compare. Maybe it's true, I think, I am so cold up here. I zip my coat up as far as it can go, so that if I bend my head down, the zipper digs into my chin. "Furchtbare Kälte," I say to the man who speaks German. Ah, yes, very good. I understand you. You just said it's very cold out. Your German is coming along well, he said. You will know when you are really good at speaking a language when you start dreaming in the language. Have you dreamt in German? he asked. No, I answered.

RESULT: I X-rayed the foot. I could not see any damage, just a slight swelling. It could be the shoes, I said. The man who spoke German nodded. I will have the farrier come pull them, he said. What kinds of things? I asked the man who spoke German. What do you mean? he asked. What are the things that your uncle has said over the years that maybe you believe now? I asked. Oh, well, he believes there are people in the woods watching us. After the man who spoke German said it, I thought of the shape I saw form out of the leaves by the bonfire I built behind my house. The uncle was right, I thought. I wanted to meet him. You can't, he doesn't like people. He won't talk to anyone, except me and my wife and our children. He talks to the children quite often, more than he talks to us. He has pointed out the people in the woods to the children. They see them, too. But of course, I thought the children were just playing along with their uncle's game.

THOUGHTS ON DRIVE HOME: Maybe this uncle knows who shot my son, and now I think how it's two people who know the man. One is a spaceman, and the other is a man who only talks to children and won't talk to me.

WHAT I THINK I HAVE TO DO IN ORDER FOR THE SPACECRAFT TO COME BACK SO IT CAN TELL ME WHO SHOT MY SON BECAUSE THE LAST TIME IT HAD COME I HAD DONE THIS: Test my levels.

WHAT MY DOCTOR IS: So happy to see me when I get to his office, he gives me a handshake/hug and I'm pressed up against his breast cancer pin that digs into my own breast. Right, he says, he smiles so broadly. His favorite patient is back. Let's have a look at that prostate, shall we? He likes to talk about other things while he's palpating me. He likes to talk about sports and he is amazed I'm not well informed about scores and that I don't have television reception to watch sports. I don't know why, but I think about the zebra we have in our town when he's examining me. Yes, we really do have a zebra. It's someone's exotic pet they stable like a horse. The zebra has its own barn. The zebra has its own paddock. The zebra is alone on its hill, its black and white stripes not blending in at all with the tall-reaching pines on the fringe of the forest beside the rails of the paddock. Whenever we drive on the road by the barn with the zebra, my children open the windows and stick their heads out of the truck and yell "Free the zebra!!" because no one likes to see something that should be in Africa here instead.

I always laugh when my kids yell out when we drive by the zebra, and so I laugh while the doctor's palpating me. My laugh isn't loud, it's more of an exhalation of breath with a little of the sound of my voice trailing with it. The doctor asks, Does that hurt? and I can hear he's a little anxious when he asks, because he asks so quickly, and he bends his head close to mine, so that when I answer, he won't miss what I'm saying. No, not at all, I say.

At the end of the visit, the doctor scratches his head. I'm miffed, he says. I've found nothing unusual once again, but your levels, still considered high, are slightly lower. He looks sad, and I want to tell him something funny to cheer him up. I wonder if the zebra story would do it. Is the zebra story a rib-tickler to others? I wonder. I don't tell the doctor a story before I leave. Instead I tell the doctor how much I appreciate him taking the time to see me. I shake his hand, and he holds on to it for a while and I think he wants to take a look at my hand, too. Maybe he wants to palpate it as well. He wants to find a lump on me somewhere, on my palms, on the bit of skin between my thumb and forefinger that looks like a bat's wing. I promise him I'll come back in six months, for more tests and more exams. You never know, I say. My levels might mean something after all. He looks happier after I say it. Yes, I look forward to seeing you then, he says.

WHAT THE WIFE SAYS AFTER HER VISIT WITH HER DOCTOR THE SAME DAY: Hallelujah. There was nothing out of the ordinary about my exams, either. My breasts are perfect, but you already knew that, she says, laughing. We drive home on the winding road from the hospital back to our town. It is coming on maple syrup season. The days are warmer, but the nights still cold. On their land, most people have tapped the maples and the metal buckets that hang from taps hammered into the trunks look strange, as if the ceiling of the sky were leaking and the buckets were set out to collect the rainwater.

CALL: A one-and-a-half-year-old shire has a respiratory infection.

ACTION: I drive to the farm, taking my wife along with me while the kids are at school, and even Sam's back in classes. We drive on the dirt roads thinking how our dirt roads are prettier. Our dirt roads are more like lanes than roads, the narrowness of them making our roads seem quaint. We drive talking about our children. When we are alone we like to tell each other how wonderful our children are, but it is something we do not tell others. We tell each other with abandon, things we have lately seen in our children that prove how smart and wonderful and cute they are. We puff each other up with the glory of our children, we talk about how beautifully Sam is recovering, his speech not half as slurred, as if this were a sign of some sort of intelligence, but the minute we pull in to the farm, our conversation changes and we both know that it will be a while again before we are alone, without being interrupted, for a long period of time where we can brag so shamelessly to one another. It is a relief to do all the bragging, it's cathartic, as if we need every once in a while to do this bragging, or so that we remind each other of how right it was for us to have married each other.

When we get to the barn the shire is already standing there, with the crossties snapped to her halter. Shires are gentle, big, glossy, black-coated draft horses with massive hooves covered in white feathering. The owner isn't there, but the farmhand named Anna is. Anna is tall and blond and speaks quietly. She says she gave the shire a little bute, but not much. The shire's eyes look a little cloudy. I listen to the shire's lungs. They are clear, but she has a little temp.

RESULT: I give her gentamicin and penicillin and take some blood samples, just to see what virus she might really have. I have been to the barn before. I have treated other horses here. I ask Anna about the last horse I treated, and if she and the owner had decided to kill it because of its crippling hoof condition. Anna says, in her quiet voice, that she wishes I wouldn't put it that way, that I hadn't said "killed," because it was a big decision for her and the owner to have the horse finally put down, but in looking back, Anna says, it was the right thing to do. Anna says that everyone called the owner names for putting his own horse down. They called him a murderer, Anna says. But he's not. You can only let the animal go so far on a hoof like that. No extra time in the stall or soaking in Epsom salts or different shoes is going to change it. It all depends on how you look at it, and it's not until something like that happens that you realize how many people look at things differently than you do. It's as if they'll only be happy if the owner comes out and admits he did something horrible, and then in the meantime they shake their heads. They say what a shame. The poor horse, they say, but what about the poor owner? That's what I think Anna says, and then Anna leans over the shire and hugs the shire's neck and the ponytail of Anna's long summer blond hair lies flat against the black coat of the beautiful shire. Then Anna stands up straight. You shouldn't care who shot your son, she says, surprising me, I didn't know Anna knew. I can feel my wife getting angry beside me.

WHAT THE WIFE SAYS: Of course we should care.

WHAT ANNA DOES: She shakes her head. It's a waste of energy. Care about your son instead, she says.

THOUGHTS ON DRIVE HOME: Everything's melting now. Patches of grass can be seen among the snow and the patches look geographical, like the shapes of the continents played out on people's lawns.

WHAT THE WIFE SAYS WHILE WE'RE DRIVING: Do you think Anna knows who shot Sam? Do you think it was her boyfriend or something? Do you think she's trying to throw us off? Cover something up? What's her boyfriend's name, anyway? Does he hunt? Do you have that list still with the names of the hunters on it? she says. I bet he's on it, she says. Imagine telling us not to care, she says. Who is she? she says. Turn around, she says. I want to talk to that girl again. I want to ask her some questions. Goddammit, turn around, she says.

WHAT I DO: I keep driving home. I don't turn around. I drive home up our driveway, and Mia comes running out to greet us. She runs to her mother and Jen picks her up and buries her nose in her neck and breathes deeply, and I know she will stop wanting to know now the name of Anna's boyfriend. Mia has wiped the anger away so quickly it is amazing, and I take Mia from Jen, and I want to breathe Mia in, too.

WHAT THE WIFE COOKED FOR DINNER: Chicken burritos.

WHAT MIA SAID SHE WOULD EAT: A chicken burrito without the chicken.

WHAT SARAH NOTICES: That the burrito shells have shrunk in size, but we all agree it's a good thing since there was too much burrito shell to our burritos before anyway, so even though we know we're being cheated, we don't feel so bad.

WHAT THE NIGHT SAID: The streams are fuller now, the snow having melted. You will not be able to hear the owl hooting from the tree now, with the rushing sounds being so loud. You will not hear the occasional coyote yip. The snoring of Sam in the next room will blend in with the rushing sound. The snoring sound of your wife right next to you, though, can't be masked.

CALL: No call. I just drive to Dorothy's house. Dorothy is the woman with the sheep whose name is Alice. Alice is the sheep who follows Dorothy around like a dog. Alice is the sheep Dorothy took to church one day. I stop on the way to Dorothy's house. I need gas. With a fill-up I get a free peanut butter cup. Is this good or bad? There's been a scare. Peanut butter from a plant somewhere has been linked to illness in a handful of children. I eat the peanut butter cup, my fingers tasting a little of the gas from the nozzle I just used at the pump.

ACTION: I asked Dorothy if she had seen anything unusual. I asked Dorothy if she had seen the spacecraft in the sky. Dorothy called Alice over to her. Alice put her head in Dorothy's lap, in the hammock created by her floral cotton skirt and her knees. Yes, Dorothy said, Alice has seen the spacecraft, too, but I haven't, Dorothy said.

RESULT: I thanked Dorothy and I left.

THOUGHTS ON DRIVE HOME: I was still hungry. I wished I could fill up my gas again and partake in some more tainted peanut butter.

CALL: No call. I drove to the farm where the minis, Molly, Netty, Sunny, and Storm, lived. The owner was not home. I petted the minis. I asked them if they'd seen the spacecraft. The minis whinnied. I took that for a mini yes, a mini sharing of our common experience.

WHAT I PASS ON THE WAY HOME: The zebra. He is outside standing on the snow bathed in the yellow moonlight. I put the window down. Free the Zebra! I yell. I see the zebra turn and look at me. The brush at the bottom of his tail moves from side to side.

MORE THOUGHTS ON DRIVE HOME: Maybe rockets could be propelled by small, portable CERN accelerators, and man could travel from planet to planet without having to use fuel, relying on the power of magnets instead.

WHAT I DO ON THE WAY HOME: I stop off in front of the school. The sign is out by the road, the sign that has the letters that the bad kids can move around and make any words they want to and that they did once turn into COME TO THE FALL BOOB FEST. I sit looking at the letters that are there. VENISON DINNER TONIGHT, the sign says. I think what I can do and then I do it. I get out and change the letters around and then remove a few. I make the sign say, VEIN DINNER TONIGHT. Then I think how I wish I had some B's and O's because I'd really rather spell something with *boobs* instead.

WHAT I READ ON THE WAY HOME: The sign the local taxidermist leaves outside his house. SPECIAL: SKULL CLEANING HALF PRICE. I think how the sign is the same kind of sign that the school has, where I could change the letters around, but how could I come up with something better than SPECIAL: SKULL CLEANING HALF PRICE? And then I think how maybe one day a sign somewhere like that along the road will read LOW LEVELS GUARANTEED and I'll be sure to drop in.

WHAT I SAW WHEN I GOT HOME: The spacecraft again. Maybe my going back to the doctor worked. It was flying low over our house. I stopped and waved to it, and it seemed almost to wave back, I thought, because it seemed to flash back red and green lights, but then it zipped away. I went inside. I didn't care any longer if it could tell me the name of the man who shot Sam. I was just glad to see it back in the sky. Later, in bed, I looked for it again. I couldn't see it. It must be down in the town by now, floating over Phil's store, floating over the school, floating over the local taxidermist's house, the Zodiac Killer's house.

WHAT THE WIFE SHOWS ME WEEKS LATER: The brochure for the swimming team that the children have been on. Now there's a master's swim team for adults.

WHAT THE WIFE SAYS: The doctor says Sam needs the exercise. He should be on the team again, and your levels want you to join, too. I look at the brochure. I like how the sunlight comes in through the glass walls and lights up the pool water, making it look like water somewhere else, like water in Ecuador maybe, like water in Maui or Palau.

UPDATE OF THINGS MY WIFE THINKS MY LEVELS CAN DO SO FAR: Beg, talk, appreciate food, join a swim team.

WHAT I TELL MY WIFE: All right, I'll join if you'll join. I do anything now. I am so happy that the only thing I have to worry about now is my levels that it makes me appreciate having my levels. I am so happy to just look at Sam in our home again. I am happy to see him on the couch, his huge feet on the arm, dirtying the cloth. I am happy to hear him stomping upstairs across the floorboards and whipping towels at his sisters after he has showered. I am happy to hear him screaming for no reason, bounding down the stairs, reaching the bottom and wildly petting Nelly, shaking her head back and forth, and calling her a good girl. I think how it doesn't matter who shot my son. My son is back. If the hunter were to knock on my door now, I don't think I'd want to meet him. If the spacecraft were to suddenly blare out his name into the night sky, I wouldn't want to know what it was. I wouldn't want to be reminded of when Sam wasn't.

WHAT HAPPENS AFTER A FEW WEEKS: Most nights we crawl into bed, after having swum on our teams, smelling faintly of chlorine with a good kind of tiredness spreading out from our bones. I have tried to think like a dolphin. After all, this is what I have learned is the best thing to do in order to improve my fly. Think like a dolphin. These are happy, fast thoughts. These are undulations celebrating flight underwater. My wife and I have lain in bed in the dark before sleep talking in whispers about stroke and turn. Our arms, glowing silver in moonlight, have moved through the room, bent as we are on perfecting entry and recovery. We demonstrate for one another our aquatic techniques. Backstroking we remind ourselves to roll, keep our heads back and straight, our kick from the hip. Freestyling, our fingertips skate across the surface of the water right before we plunge them in for the pull. Breaststroking, we are moving our hands out in front of us, held in the shape of us at our prayers, our heels nearly touching our rears for the kick. Butterflying, we are trying to move like a dolphin, but it is difficult to do in bed, the weight of us heavy on the sheet coarse with grit the dog brought in on her feathering when she slept on our bed while we were out for the day.

And it is not just the night when we are in bed thinking about swimming, but it is at the breakfast table when we make Sarah or Mia or Sam (yes, Sam!) stand up from their French toast and we take them by their wrists and show them how in the recovery of the fly, their arms don't go straight back underwater, but out toward their sides, pushing away the water for maximum speed. We take their small thumbs, and we tell them to keep those thumbs down when entering the water. They don't listen. They grumble. They don't want to be corrected. They say they'll be late for school, and even your wife doesn't care if they'll be late for school, the whole family's standing now, arms straight up in the air, practicing the dolphin rhythm, pushing their hips in and then out, moving the smell of the sweet maple syrup through the air, over toward where the dogs are, making them bark, making them want what we have on our plates.

WHAT JANET EVANS SAYS: When doing the backstroke flip turn, flip over onto your belly and then take the allowed one hand stroke before flipping at the wall. It will help you flip faster and increase your speed.

WHAT MISTY HYMAN SAYS (THIS IS REALLY HER NAME, EVEN THOUGH IT SOUNDS LIKE A NAME YOU WOULD FIND AT THE BOOB FEST): Think like a dolphin.

NUMBER OF SIT-UPS JANET EVANS DID EVERY DAY WHILE IN TRAINING: 1,000. Core strength is everything in swimming the fly, the kick not so much from the hip but from the whole body. Your body is a whip.

WHAT THE CHILDREN SAY: Enough, enough, enough of swimming!

WHAT WE SAY: Never enough!

WHAT GISELA LIKES TO DO: Go swimming.

WHAT THE COACH IS: A Seventh-Day Adventist.

WHAT I HAVEN'T FIGURED OUT: What it means to be a Seventh-Day Adventist.

WHAT I HAVE FIGURED OUT: The coach is a really good coach. The children have their swim team practice with him first. Then the wife and the team and I have our practice.

WHO HOLDS MY PAGER WHILE I'M SWIMMING IN CASE THERE IS AN ANIMAL EMERGENCY: Mia, who keeps the pager clipped to the waist of her pants, but she is so small and thin, the pager weighs her pants down and she has to keep lifting them up. When there is an emergency and the pager beeps, she comes to the end of my lane and throws a kickboard on my head to get my attention.

WHAT I DO WHILE SAM IS SWIMMING: Just watch him sometimes, the water sliding off his smooth back, the catch of his stroke underwater, speeding him along, the breaths he takes from both sides, his body working beautifully.

WHAT I FEEL AFTER I'VE SWUM: That my levels are low. I will live.

WHAT THE WIFE SAYS: Victoria told me about the place in Costa Rica where they let you stay in cabins for free so long as you help with the turtles.

WHAT I SAY: What turtles? (Victoria is a woman at the pool who is always telling my wife things.)

WHAT SHE SAYS: The turtles that have come to the shore to lay their eggs in the sand. The eggs need moving before the tide comes and steals the eggs away. Let's go, Jen says. Let's stay in the cabins and stay up all night and help the eggs.

WHAT I SAY: That's a vacation?

WHAT THE WIFE SAYS: Victoria said you can freeze chicken eggs. I never knew this before. You can crack them into ice cube trays to store them in the freezer. People don't know these kinds of things, she said.

CALL: It's the voice of the man who calls and hangs up. This time I am ready. After he says hello, I start talking. I tell him the schools I went to. I tell him the places I've lived. I tell him the name of my first stuffed animal. Now tell me, I say, just who are you that you keep calling my house and why do you want to know so much about me? The voice lets out the breath again, the breath that sounds like a seashell, and then the caller hangs up.

WHAT THE WIFE SAYS: I think I'll work at the kids' school.

WHAT THE COP SAYS WHO TAKES HER FINGERPRINTS SO SHE CAN WORK AT THE SCHOOL: You have almost no swirls on the pads of your fingers. I once knew a potter with the same problem. Working with the clay at the wheel had worn her pattern away. Are you a potter? the cop asks Jen.

WHAT THE WIFE SAYS: Why, no. I type a lot, though, she said. I have maybe worn off the pads of my fingers with all of my stories.

WHAT I SAY: Sounds like you could commit a murder and get away with it.

WHAT THE WIFE SAYS: Who did you have in mind?

WHAT I SAY: Why that doctor, of course. The one who wears pins, the one more gung-ho about my levels than our parallel universe.

WHAT THE WIFE SAYS: Oh, I thought you'd say that hunter. Sam's hunter, she says.

WHAT I SAY: No, not him. I am done with him.

WHAT THE WIFE WONDERS: When you take your ice cube tray full of frozen eggs out of the freezer, do you have to defrost the eggs first before you cook them, or do you just throw them onto the pan and they skate around on the surface before the heat of the flame starts to melt them?

CALL: No call. The phone hasn't rung for two days. You see, I tell Jen. Nobody can afford to treat their animals anymore.

WHAT THE PHONE SAYS: Hah-hah-hah.

WHAT THE WIFE SAYS: Your fly looks so fast!

WHAT I AM TRYING TO DO: Lift my head up above the water only high enough to get a breath in that pocket of air. My chin is really still in the water.

WHAT I AM THINKING: I am a dolphin.

WHAT THE DOCTOR DOES: Calls my house and talks to Jen.

WHAT THE WIFE SAYS: It's been weeks, shouldn't you go back to the doctor?

WHAT I DO: Shrug.

WHAT THE WIFE SAYS: All they want to do is test your levels again.

WHAT I AM: A dolphin. My feet are my tail. My body is in the shape of a sine curve.

WHAT THE WIFE SAYS: Maybe your levels are lower. Don't you want to know that?

WHAT I WANT TO KNOW: How Misty Hyman keeps her head so low and her palms facing up to the sky in her recovery. I cannot keep my palms up to the sky for long because it hurts in the shoulders.

WHAT I SHOULD DO: Watch my Misty Hyman video over and over again.

WHAT VICTORIA SAYS: If your ring finger is longer than your forefinger, you're good at competitive sports.

WHAT MY RING FINGER IS: Slightly longer than my forefinger.

WHAT VICTORIA SAYS: People who are fat are inflamed all the time. The fat presses in on them, causing the inflammation. Their bodies react to this. Their bodies are always working hard to fight the inflammation. Their bodies always feel like they're sick.

WHAT MIA THINKS WOULD BE A GOOD NAME FOR THE MASTER'S SWIM TEAM: The Sea Slugs.

WHAT THE TEAM IS ALREADY NAMED: The Manta Rays. The logo on the swim caps, instead of looking like a manta ray, looks like a sperm traveling through its liquid medium.

WHAT THE COACH DOES: Takes care of a young man named Ted. Ted is in a wheelchair.

WHAT I DON'T KNOW: Why Ted is in a wheelchair. Ted is not right. It seems like whatever happened to him, happened long ago, before he was born, and just as his cells were beginning to divide.

WHAT TED SAYS TO ME: I do not know. I cannot understand Ted. While I am sitting in a chair on the pool deck watching the children swim, he sometimes holds a magazine or a catalog and he wheels his chair over to mine and points to the pictures and says something I do not understand. Sometimes the pictures are of cell phones or of cars. Maybe Ted is trying to tell me that he wants a cell phone, or that he wants a car.

WHAT TED DID ONE TIME: Fell into the pool in his wheelchair. He was removed quickly. Everyone jumped in to help him. He was smiling when we brought him up, and still holding onto his drenched catalog. Coach thinks that Ted may have released his brake on purpose. Ted likes the water. Ted likes to swim. Coach sometimes straps a flotation device to Ted's waist and Ted gets into the pool and moves his arms to move through the water. Ted is always smiling when he's swimming.

WHAT I THINK TED IS THINKING WHILE HE'S IN THE WATER: That he's a dolphin.

WHAT MY WIFE AND I SOMETIMES WATCH ON OUR TELEVISION WHILE WE'RE DOING SIT-UPS AND PUSH-UPS: Old episodes of *The Twilight Zone*. Oh, he was profound, Jen says, because after every episode Rod Serling will quote Shakespeare or some famous philosopher like Kahlil Gibran, who tells us what true love truly is. We watch the episodes on DVD because we don't have television reception and you can tell when there's a pause in the episode, that that is when a commercial was planned to air and Jen pretends it really is a commercial and she pretends we are our parents watching the show, and she says, Dahling, time for a cig and a martini. Because that's all our parents seemed to do when we were young, was smoke and drink, and they were not, as my wife and I are doing, huffing and puffing and strengthening our muscles so that they could have a stronger fly, a faster turn, lower levels.

WHAT COACH MAKES US DO: Swim underwater two lengths of the pool without taking a breath.

WHAT I CAN'T DO: Hold my breath for even one length. I am sorry. I just like to breathe, I tell coach.

WHAT I AM ASKED TO SUBSTITUTE-TEACH: Art. I don't know anything about art.

WHAT I TELL THE KIDS IN ART CLASS: I don't know what art is. I just know it when I see it.

WHAT I DO DURING ART: Sit at the teacher's desk and study German.

WHAT THE WIFE SAYS: Maybe your levels are telling you to take it easy. Maybe you shouldn't be cutting enough wood for the next ten years.

WHAT I SAY: What is your fascination with my levels? Do you miss Sam being in a coma? Do you miss constantly worrying about someone's health in the family? And besides, maybe my levels are saying, "Cut, cut, cut away!"

WHAT THE WIFE SAYS: That's not what your levels are saying. Your levels have more common sense than that.

WHAT IS SURPRISING: That according to Jen, not only can my levels beg, talk, appreciate food, join a swim team—they now have common sense.

WHAT THE CHILDREN SAY WHEN I GET HOME: Poppy, we are expecting ten inches of snow.

WHAT I SAY: Good, then when you stay home from school I can teach you math and German and violin and history. I can tell you about the Russian Revolution, about the czars killed in the basement and no one knew where their bodies were buried because they did not want some people to dig them up and put them in a tomb and worship their tomb and wish for the old regime to resurface. I can tell you about the Nazi war criminals, who when they were killed, were buried in unknown places for the same reason, so that no shrine would be created that worshipped the perpetrators of the Nazi killing machine. I can tell you about first position, and drawing your bow across your strings using your wrist and not sawing your elbow back and forth. I can tell you about angles, how in a parallelogram opposite angles are equal.

WHAT THE WIFE COOKS FOR DINNER: Mushroom barley soup.

WHAT THERE IS MORE OF IN THE SOUP THAN MUSHROOMS AND BARLEY: Carrots.

WHAT I SAY TO THE WIFE: My levels are saying where are the mushrooms?

WHAT THE WIFE SAYS: Tell your levels they can cook dinner next time.

WHAT THE HOUSE SAYS AT NIGHT: I'm closing you in, and buttoning you tight.

WHAT THE WIFE SAYS: What's that noise? Oh, it's the rabbit drinking her water, she says.

WHAT I, FOR A SECOND, THINK THE RABBIT CAN DO: Cure me. The all-seeing rabbit some kind of swami, some kind of medicine man. Is it the soft touch of her whiskers on my face when I'm lying on the carpet that can lower my levels?

WHAT SARAH SAYS WE SHOULD MAKE A MOVIE ABOUT: Rabbits running the country, and doing a good job of it, considering they are peaceful and vegetarian.

WHAT THE SNOW SAID: I will fall out to sea, steer clear of your green mountains, leave you still with your old snow, now yellow with piss from your dogs. You will have no snow day with your children, you will not teach them German, violin, and the demise of the czars. Sit alone in your house, listen to your Newfoundlands snoring loudly by the fire, wait for the phone to ring.

WHAT I THINK I COULD HAVE BEEN: A professional swimmer.

WHAT TED, AT THE POOL IN THE WHEELCHAIR, BROUGHT IN TO SHOW ME: A magazine with a picture of a man with a moose head mounted on his office wall, and then on the other side of the wall, reaching into another man's office, the moose's body was hanging in the air, above the man's desk. I had to laugh. Ted laughed, too. I don't know why I think it, but I do. I sometimes think that Ted could be Jesus Christ and I don't even believe in Jesus Christ, but maybe he is.

WHAT THE COACH TELLS US: That because so many people are losing their jobs, we may have to defend ourselves from people coming into our homes and taking what they want from us. We may have to have our guns ready, he says. We are sitting in a hot, crowded gymnasium at a technical school. We are waiting for our kids to compete in their swim heats. Coach is telling me this and above him hangs a basketball hoop that is missing its net. It looks like some kind of halo impossibly far from his head. Around us kids play video games, and read, and eat, and drink Gatorade, and run around playing tag, all waiting for their heats.

WHAT I THINK WE MUST BE: Crazy to spend an entire weekend waiting in the gym of a technical school, but I know years from now we will look back and say these were good times, maybe the best because we were with our children all the time. Sam is stronger every day. He's almost what he once was and nothing else matters. I look at my wife across the gym, leading Mia to the concession counter to buy a drink. I see my wife turn and look out across the sea of people and I wave to her and it is amazing that she can see me, but I know she does because she waves back.

WHAT THE WIFE COOKS FOR DINNER: Nothing. We are far from home, and go to an Italian restaurant where the waitress forgets to bring us bread.

WHAT THE HOTEL ROOM SAYS AT NIGHT: I have curtains and I can shut out the moon. I have windows you can't open, and I can shut out your air. I have a television and I can shut out your thoughts.

WHAT THE WIFE SAYS WHILE THE CHILDREN ARE SLEEPING, SOFTLY SNORING AROUND US: Did you make the appointment?

WHAT THE CHILDREN DO: Stop their snoring for a moment as if in their dreams they want to hear my answer.

WHAT I SAY: Yes, I made the appointment today. And I am telling the truth. I have made another appointment and I will have it soon. Sam is all right, and I will do things for myself now. I will take care of my levels. I think I can hear Jen nodding in approval, her head in the dark making a swishing sound on the stiff hotel room pillow.

WHAT THE WIFE SAYS THE SHOWER REMINDS HER OF: Guatemala. The pounding of the massage showerhead on her neck sounded like a turboprop plane and she remembered the last time she was on a turboprop plane and that was when she went to go see the ruins at Tikal. She remembers walking up the crumbling stone steps, but she says she doesn't remember much else.

WHAT EVERYONE DOES: Yells and cheers for their children in the race.

WHAT THE CHILDREN SAY THEY HEAR WHILE THEY ARE RACING: Nothing, just nothing.

WHAT THE CHILDREN SAY: The blocks at this pool are slippery. The water is cold.

WHAT MY SON ASKS ME ABOUT WHILE WE'RE DRIVING HOME: Turkey hunting.

WHAT THE WIFE SAYS TO THE SON: No, no more hunting for you.

WHAT I KNOW ABOUT TURKEY HUNTING: Nothing.

WHAT EVERYONE TELLS ME ABOUT TURKEY HUNTING: Turkeys are smart. They know when you are holding a gun. They will walk out in front of you on the road when you are not holding a gun, but the moment you have the gun, they will not appear. You can call them with a turkey call and sometimes that will work. Most turkey calls sound like fingernails running down a chalkboard.

WHAT TED DID AT THE POOL: Took a long flotation device, called a noodle, and floated in the shallow end, slapping it on top of the water. The sound was loud, and Ted liked it. He smiled broadly, showing his wide, white teeth. The sound drew attention to him, though, and the more he slapped the noodle on top of the water, the more people looked at him, and so he slapped the water even harder and faster. The lifeguard looked at Ted and took her hands and, palm down, lowered them a few times, letting Ted know he should calm down.

CALL: Coach has yellow Labradors that he breeds and the puppies need shots.

ACTION: Drove to coach's house. Noticed the long ramp leading to his front door. The ramp's wood was blond pine and reminded me of a newly built boardwalk. I pictured Ted wheeling himself up onto it, and the sound of the wheelchair's wheels making a rhythmic sound like breaking waves as they rolled across the boards and the spaces between them. In the air I thought I could smell the fish and salt smell of the ocean, and the smell of sun-warmed rocks exposed on the white dunes, but when I looked around me of course all there was to see was the mountains, dusted in white snow and the pine trees looking pointy and sharp. I saw the cute sand-colored puppies and I lifted them up and gave them their shots in their skin under the scruffs of their necks.

RESULT: Coach and I talked about the puppies. He would sell them all by the time they were nine weeks old. I looked at coach's house while we talked. Through an open window I could see Ted sitting inside in his wheelchair. He was looking out at what must have been the mountains, and he was smiling, sitting with his eyes closed and his head lifted, as if he were on the beach himself, taking in the warmth of the sun.

THOUGHTS ON DRIVE HOME: What the hell was that? Realized, quickly, that it was the snow finally sailing off the roof of my truck.

WHAT THE CHILDREN SAID WHEN I GOT HOME: Come on, Poppy. Let's go to the bank.

RESULT: I drove them, with their pickle jars filled with dollars and coins on their laps, to the bank so they could open their own savings accounts. The teller was patient. There were many pennies to put into piles and count. There were many dog hairs mixed in with the coins that had to be separated, everything smelled faintly of brine, the pickle jars not being washed out so well.

WHAT THE WIFE COOKED FOR DINNER: Gypsy soup she did not have all the ingredients for so she had to rename it Bedouin soup or Nomad soup, whatever the children preferred calling it.

WHAT THE WIFE SAID AT NIGHT IN BED: I can't move.

WHAT I SAID: Don't move. I'll do it all. And I did, taking care not to hurt her back she said she threw out bringing in logs for the woodstove in her office. I made love to her and every time I was just about to enter her, she scooted to the side, the time of the month being bad, or good, depending on how she said she looked at it, or how others looked at it. I was gentle with her, I was tender. I had, just days ago in a fight told her, "The operative word here is *Fuck off*," so I felt I owed her a little kindness.

WHAT COACH HAS US DO: Keep ourselves afloat by having our arms raised out of the water and just dolphin kicking. Keep ourselves afloat by just flutter kicking. Keep ourselves afloat with our hands clasped behind our backs and our legs crossed. The last one doesn't work and all around me in the pool I see people on the team start to sink down, the rubber of their caps disappearing under the water, I see Jen sinking too and then we all start to laugh and we are all choking and what in the world is coach trying to do to us and then I see him on deck raise his hands and laugh and say it was just an experiment he had in mind and I feel we have fallen for the oldest swim coach joke in the world and who knew there was one?

WHAT I SEE ON DECK: Ted sitting in his wheelchair and laughing at us too and clapping his hands together, only both the palms of his hands don't seem to touch when he claps, and mostly it's his fingers that meet together, and so his clapping doesn't make a sound.

Part Four

Spring

Spring

CALL: No call, just a voice I heard in the evening. I knew the voice. It was the one I had heard before on the phone. It was the voice like my own. The voice was calling my name. I had just come inside. I had just seen the spacecraft flying over our pond. I opened the door, and in the dying light I could see a young man walking up to our house. I didn't see his car. I wondered where he had come from. Was Sam's doctor right? Had the man who had shot my son decided to show up at my door after all? Had this man come from the spacecraft? Was he a spaceman? Was he the pilot? Had our radio beeped him in, had it divulged our location? I wanted to go back into the house, where the children were settling in for the night, brushing their teeth in the bathroom, pulling out footie pajamas from their drawers and arranging hordes of stuffed animals around their pillows on their beds.

WHAT I SAID TO THE SPACEMAN: Hello.

WHAT THE SPACEMAN SAID TO ME: I hope I'm not disturbing you.

WHAT I THOUGHT: We were doing nothing. The wife was starting the dishwasher. I could hear the detergent being squeezed from the bottle. Was the spaceman here to take me up in the spacecraft?

WHAT THE SPACEMAN SAID: My name is Mark Howell. Then the spaceman shook my hand. Even though it was cold outside, the spaceman's hand was warm. They must have good heating on that spacecraft, I thought to myself. May I come inside? the spaceman said.

WHAT BRUCE AND NELLY DID: Greeted the spaceman like he was one of us. They tried to jump on him. I had to pull them down. They wanted to lick the spaceman's face. The spaceman didn't mind Bruce and Nelly. He did not mind their smell or their size or their hair.

WHAT THE SPACEMAN SAID: Well, I made it all the way here. It took me a long time.

WHAT THE WIFE DID: She came to the door, wiping her hands on a dishrag. She looked at me. She looked at the spaceman. I introduced the wife to the spaceman. This is Mark Howell. He has come a long way, I said.

WHAT THE WIFE SAID: Oh, won't you come inside?

WHAT THE SPACEMAN DID: He stood in our kitchen. He looked around the house. He looked at me. This is it, I thought. This is when the abduction starts. I could hear the children screaming at each other upstairs. They were not going to go to bed quietly. They would be part of the abduction. The spaceman had already heard them. He pointed at the ceiling. Kids? How many? he asked. Three, Jen said. Can I offer you some water or juice?

WHAT THE SPACEMAN SAID: I'm beginning to think that maybe I shouldn't have come. But the spaceman sat down right after he said that. He sat down in one of our kitchen chairs with a cushion on it. The cushion was not the cleanest thing. The children often dropped their food, and crumbs of it collected in the dimples where the buttons on the cushions were sewn. Jen looked at me, I looked at Jen. We sat down at the table with the spaceman. He ran his palm over the wooden tabletop. It was a table my father had made. The wood was maple. The knots in the wood drove my mother crazy when her eyes started to fail her. She had tried many times with a sponge to rub them out, thinking they were stains from certain foods. The spaceman said he had come from Philadelphia. He had driven straight through without stopping. He had known my name and my address for a while now and it was just recently he decided to come.

WHAT I THOUGHT: The spaceman and his kind have been looking for me for a long time. They have observed me from up above. They have traveled with me to farms. They have watched me treat horses and goats and llamas and cows and lambs from the sky. Now they need me on their planet. There is some kind of animal they have that is dying, that is going extinct, like our bats. Maybe there is a man on earth who can help them. I am their man.

WHAT THE SPACEMAN SAID: You are my biological father.

WHAT I THOUGHT: Or the spaceman and his kind need help with gravity, and they think I'm their man. Their planet is losing their field, and they think I can help them restore it.

WHAT THE WIFE SAID: How can that be?

WHAT THE SPACEMAN SAID: He was a donor, a long time ago. Twenty-seven years ago, to be precise. My mother wanted a medical student. She had seen his picture. He was handsome. He had scored well on tests. She decided on him.

WHAT THE WIFE SAID: Why?

WHAT THE SPACEMAN SAID: Money. One hundred dollars for a sperm donation was the going rate. I think we look alike, don't you think? the spaceman said to Jen. Jen looked at the spaceman, then she looked at me. Yes, a little, she said. Excuse me, she said. I have to check on the children. And it was a good thing she went. Sarah was screeching. It seemed that Sam had stolen her tooth that she had left in an envelope for the tooth fairy and Sarah was chasing him with a broom, ready to smash the handle on top of his head. Alarm! Alarm! Sam was screaming in a German accent, and running through the upstairs of the house.

WHAT THE SPACEMAN SAID TO ME: I'm sorry to tell you this way. While driving up here I imagined a million ways I could do it. There didn't seem to be a good way. I guess I could have written you a letter. But what if you didn't answer? I tried calling a few times. I asked who you were, but then I hung up. I'm sorry. I know it must be a shock. But I want to tell you how happy I am to finally meet you. The spaceman smiled. His teeth looked very straight.

WHAT I SAID: Your teeth are so straight.

WHAT THE SPACEMAN SAID: Yes, I had braces as a child.

WHAT I SAID: You've got a cleft in your chin.

WHAT THE SPACEMAN SAID: Yes, I can see I inherited that from you.

WHAT I SAID: How did you get here?

WHAT THE SPACEMAN SAID: I drove. My car's out there. The spaceman pointed out the window, into the darkness. You may not have heard it, the engine's electric, the spaceman said.

CALL: A horse that needs stitches above its eye. It was the same horse that I thought for a second I had put a stomach tube down its lungs instead of its stomach.

ACTION: Asked the spaceman if he wanted to go with me to sew up the horse. Spaceman answered yes. Stood at the bottom of the stairs and yelled up to Jen that we were going out now to treat a horse. Jen yelled back, All right. But maybe she had yelled all right to Sarah, telling her it was all right now, and not to screech any longer, Sam would give her back her tooth for the tooth fairy.

WHAT I NOTICED WHILE WALKING TO MY TRUCK: The spaceman is the same height that I am.

WHAT THE SPACEMAN SAID: See, there is my electric car. And he pointed to a dark shape in the driveway.

We drove talking about his life. He had loving parents and a blue heeler. I wanted to hear all about the blue heeler, as I have always been fond of the breed but worried they would be too protective of their owners and would have a tendency to bite children. He said his blue heeler had indeed bitten a girl on her head, and years later, he found out the girl had fallen off her bike and so X-rays were taken and the doctors believed that she had a tumor and it wasn't until they operated that they found out that it was old scar tissue from the bite on the girl's head from his blue heeler. The spaceman said he knew it didn't make sense, him coming from a loving family, why he'd still want to meet me after all these years, but he did. There were some things that happened in life that he would never have the answers for, he said. And when he said it I wondered if he wasn't really Jesus Christ, too, and maybe Ted from the pool wasn't Jesus Christ at all, but this spaceman was because he talked so plainly and clearly. And what did that make me, being the biological father of Jesus Christ the spaceman?

WHAT I COULD NOT SEE IN THE DARK WHEN WE DROVE UP TO THE OWNER'S HOUSE: I could not make out, in the darkness, the hill the woman had once pointed to that her husband and son had climbed to hunt deer. I could not make out the front lawn, either, where the woman had said she had watched the buck while her husband and son were up in the woods with their rifles at the ready.

I introduced the spaceman to the owner. I told her, This is . . . , but she interrupted. Oh, your son, the owner said. Pleased to meet you. You look just like your father, the owner said and the owner shook the spaceman's hand. The owner said the horse was banged up pretty good. The owner assumed it was the mud he had slipped in. We were slipping in it, too. We slipped in it on our way to the barn, only the spaceman didn't slip as much because the owner showed him a board she had put down over the mud, so he could walk on it without slipping. He did not have the proper shoes. He wore deck shoes, the kind with the leather uppers and the useless bit of short leather lace that was threaded through the four eyelets, the kind that had the flat, treadless sole that was white or light colored, reminiscent of marshmallow. Do you sail? I asked the spaceman as he walked across the plank, and I walked beside him, my boots sturdy in the mud.

WHAT THE SPACEMAN SAID: I don't sail. I've been sailing, but other people sailed the boat. I'm afraid I don't know the first thing about it. I traveled the waters of Turkey in a schooner. Turkey is a beautiful country, he said.

WHAT THE HORSE WAS LISTENING TO IN THE BARN: Classical music on the radio. It was Dvořák, the spaceman said.

RESULT: I had to shave the hair around the horse's cut, so at first I gave the horse some tranq. Then I brought out my shears, but there wasn't anywhere to plug them in. I thought I could unplug the horse's radio, but the owner said not the music. Dvořák was one of his favorites. Sometimes I think the music calms the horse

down, the owner said. The spaceman and the owner searched for
another outlet. The owner found one behind some blankets that
were hanging up. The music still played while the shears buzzed
around the horse's cut. I could feel the spaceman watching me
as I worked. I sewed up as much of the cut as I could, but the
horse had lost a chunk of flesh, so there was a bit that I couldn't
sew, due to the lack of skin. I'm leaving this part open, I told the
owner. I think it will heal all right. It won't leave too big a scar.
The owner nodded. She said she expected it wouldn't. Then the
spaceman nodded, too, as if it were also his horse and he was
understanding what I was telling him. I wanted to ask the owner
if her husband and her son had any luck the rest of the season, if
they had bagged a deer, if they had ever bagged the big, beautiful buck she had seen by herself sitting in her house and looking
out her picture window. But I didn't ask. The spaceman was busy
talking to the owner about barrel racing. I hadn't known she was
a barrel racer. I had only pictured her in her free time sitting in
her chair, looking out her picture window at the deer. She started
talking loudly and quickly about barrel racing. She had learned
to ride as a girl. She never had lessons, she just sat on horses and
taught herself. She loved being at a complete stop one moment,
and then the next moment being at a full gallop and making the
tight turns around the barrels. There was a chest in the barn and
she pulled blue ribbons out of it that smelled of mildew. The
spaceman held the ribbons up to the light. The light was near
the radio, and it seemed as if Dvořák's music made the tails of
the blue ribbons flutter slightly. The spaceman said the woman
should hang her ribbons up where people could see them. He
fastened a ribbon to the barn wall by sliding part of the ribbon

into the space between two wooden boards. You wouldn't think the ribbon would stay up like that, with so little holding it, but it did stay up.

THOUGHTS ON DRIVE HOME: No thoughts. I spoke aloud. I spoke without thinking. Want to see the pool where we swim? I said to the spaceman. Sure, the spaceman said. The pool was closed, but you could still see in. The walls of the pool were glass. We leaned against the cool glass. Light from a streetlamp lit the place up. I told the spaceman how solar panels helped heat the water. I told the spaceman how the pool had very little chlorine and that ultraviolet rays were used to kill the bacteria. The spaceman said he swam on his high school team. The spaceman said that whenever he smells chlorine it reminds him of that time in high school. That's the time, he said, that he first decided he would someday meet his real father. The father he had who was married to his mother was not a good swimmer. When they went to a pool or the beach, the father would swim sidestroke, and even then, the spaceman said, his father would swallow the water and choke and sputter and cough and his mother would worry about him and his mother would send her son into the water, to make sure his father, his not-real father, was all right and would not drown.

WHAT THE WIFE TOLD THE SPACEMAN WHEN WE GOT HOME: Don't be silly, there's no need to stay in a motel. It's late. Spend the night here, she said.

WHAT THE WIFE TOLD ME IN BED IN A WHISPER SO THE SPACEMAN WOULD NOT HEAR: What does he want?

WHAT I SAID: Nothing. You know, just to see who I am. Just to know.

WHAT THE WIFE SAID: When is he leaving?

WHAT I SAID: In the morning, I'm sure. What does it matter? He seems nice. Did you know he used to swim?

WHAT THE WIFE SAID: What do we tell the children when they meet him?

WHAT I SAID: If they ask, I'll tell them the truth. The spaceman will have his curiosity fulfilled. He'll see I'm just an ordinary man and then he'll go home and appreciate his father whom his mother is married to. This will blow over, I said.

WHAT THE WIFE SAID: You call him the spaceman?

WHAT SARAH SAID AT BREAKFAST: You two look alike. You both have that thingy, that hole in your chins. Are you an uncle or a cousin?

WHAT THE SPACEMAN SAID: I'm your half brother.

WHAT SARAH SAID: One whole brother is bad enough.

WHAT SAM SAID WHEN HE CAME DOWN TO BREAKFAST: Cool, I always wanted a brother. I'm sick of my sisters. Are you going to live with us?

WHAT THE SPACEMAN SAID: No, I have an apartment in Philadelphia.

WHAT SAM SAID: You might like it here. We get lots of s-s-snow and the sledding is good. Mom's an okay cook, that is if you like green olives.

WHAT SARAH SAID: Sam was in a coma and now he talks funny. Sam, say Sally sells seashells by the seashore.

WHAT SAM SAID: Bugger off, Sarah.

WHAT THE SPACEMAN SAID: A coma?

WHAT SARAH SAID: Yes, he was shot and fell out of the tree stand.

WHAT MIA SAYS: They thought he was a bird. Show him your scars, Sam.

WHAT SAM SAID: Bugger off, Mia. See how annoying my sisters are?

WHAT THE SPACEMAN SAID: That's terrible. Who did it?

WHAT SARAH SAID: Someone in town, but we're not sure.

CALL: One of Arlo's Chianina cows with porcupine quills stuck in its muzzle.

ACTION: Spaceman and I set off in my truck to the farm. Spaceman wanted to know about my son. Is it true, he said, you don't know who shot your son? I shook my head. In this little town, you don't know? I shook my head again. I can't be sure. It might have been a guy named Passen, but he's in jail for something else now. I'll never know for sure. It could have been anyone. He put your son in a coma for weeks? the spaceman asked. Yes, I said. I didn't want to shake my head again. I was looking past the field where I had seen a coyote trotting across before, and I wanted to see if he might be trotting this way again. The spaceman whistled. I thought at first it was going to be a tune, but it was not. It was a whistle of surprise. A whistle of incredulity. Oh my God, he said. You and your wife must have been sick with worry. When he said it I remembered how Jen would sit up in bed at night, not reading, just staring at the windows that were dotted with cluster fly shit. It's not too late, the spaceman said. You can still try to find out who it was. No, I said. I said it quickly and loudly. The spaceman shook his head. He looked out the window. I felt bad for saying no the way I had said it. We drove on the road where the taxidermist had his sign that said SKULL CLEANING HALF PRICE. I pointed it out to the spaceman. I laughed. Can you believe that sign? I said. The spaceman nodded his head. I can believe it, he said. If you're not sure who it was, if it was Passen or not, then why are you still making these vet calls, and you're not out knocking on everyone's door trying to find out exactly who did that to your son? What are the police doing? he said.

There was no evidence. There were no telltale footprints in the woods that anyone could find. There was no car parked by the side of the road, no tire tread marks that could be traced. No way to trace the gunshot. The police did what they could do, I said. The spaceman worked his jaw. He shook his head. He exhaled loudly.

When we drove up the road to Arlo's, we could see his white Chianina cattle standing on the hillside in the early mist. They're beautiful. They look like ghosts, the spaceman said, while shaking his head and smiling. I introduced the spaceman as Mark Howell to Arlo. Arlo showed us the cow. She had about seventeen quills stuck in her nose. I tranqued the cow. While I pulled out the quills Arlo held the cow and murmured to her, telling her to be still and calm. The cow was so tall that Arlo just had to turn his head to talk into the blackness of her white ear. He did not have to bend down to her. I told Arlo that the spaceman was from Philadelphia. Arlo said he had never been to Philadelphia. He said he had never been away from here because he liked the trees here and the trees were enough for him here. He did not need to leave his state and see other trees. He did not need to travel to see mountain ridges with tree lines that were not his. Arlo laughed at himself. You'd think I was goofy about trees, he said. The cow shook her head. The tranq was wearing off. I gave her a little more. I gave the spaceman the quills as I pulled them out. The spaceman lined them up on his palms, the tapered ends all facing the same way. Arlo wanted to know if the spaceman

was a doctor, too. Oh, no, I teach, the spaceman said. The spaceman taught Spanish in a public school. The spaceman said he had
learned it in Spain, and so there was a time when he got back from
Spain that not even the Puerto Rican postman understood what he
was saying because when speaking Spanish you sound out the Z's
like they were *Th*'s and the way the Puerto Rican postman looked
at the spaceman when he spoke Spanish with his lisp you'd think
he did not speak Spanish at all. You'd think, and yes here the spaceman said it, You'd think I was from another planet. Then the spaceman said, What about the doctor's son, Arlo? Do you know anything
about who shot his son, almost killed him, and then put him into a
coma for weeks? Arlo shook his head. He patted the hind end of his
cow with a hand that was deeply lined, and the veins popping out
on the backs of his hands looked as large as earthworms as he patted
the cow. I think you do know, said the spaceman. This is too small
a town not to know.

I laughed. I had to say something funny soon or else I knew
Arlo might want to turn and punch the spaceman in the jaw. But
what was there funny to say. Was it funny to talk about the zebra?
The other day, I said, my wife called Sarah a wench because she
was being mean to Mia. Well, Sam had never heard the word
wench. He said sarcastically, "Hah, that's really funny, Mom, calling Sarah a wrench. What are you going to call me when I'm
mean to Mia, a screwdriver?" Arlo looked at the spaceman, then
he looked at me. That is funny, Doc. Do you think this cow will
be all right now? Do I need to Betadine her nose or anything? I
think she'll be fine, I said.

THOUGHTS ON DRIVE HOME: No drive home. No thoughts. We drove
to the pool. Let's get in a swim, I told the spaceman, even though I

did not sound right to myself saying "get in a swim" because I had never said it that way before and I had always ever said to the wife or the children, Come on, let's go swimming. The spaceman wore the extra swimsuit I carried with me and he borrowed the extra goggles I carried with me and they fit him well. While we changed I asked him how his students behaved. Did they talk to each other while he taught? Did they have their headphones in and listen to music or talk on their phones while he taught? You see, I told him, the children I teach have done these things. The children I teach, some are horrible, I said. The spaceman laughed. Yes, he said, I have had the same kinds of children. But there are just some children whom you will not be able to teach. You will not reach them, he said, but you must always try. The same with your son. You must try to find out who shot him. I'll help you, he said. I already looked, I said. I knocked on doors. I asked questions. It could have been that guy Passen, and he's in jail now, so it's over. Don't you fucking think I tried? I said. I banged my locker shut. It made a very loud noise. The spaceman opened up the locker, then shut it again quietly while he talked, as if to teach me how lockers should be shut. You were alone then. You had seen your son shot and then in a coma. You couldn't possibly have done a good job looking. But I can help you. Together we can find out who did it. Maybe it was Passen, maybe it wasn't. But we can find out. How many people in this town? Six hundred? Six hundred is not so many. Someone knows something and they are not telling. They are protecting someone. It is heinous what the man did. It is heinous that the man probably knows you in a town this small. What's the old saying, Don't shit where you eat, or should I say, Don't shoot where you eat. I thought you were a teacher. Now you're a detective? I said. The spaceman put his hand on my shoulder. His hand was as large as mine, maybe larger. The weight of his hand on my shoulder felt good and strong. I would have liked some of his strength. Was some kind of alien transfer going to take place from him to me, I wondered. We'll find the man together, he said, and when he said it I became excited. Maybe he was right that I hadn't done a good job looking. I had gone knocking on doors asking if owners had seen the spacecraft, when maybe I should have been asking more about the hunter who shot my son. Maybe the man could be found after all.

WHAT HIS BUTTERFLY WAS: Really good. When he came up for a breath, he moved his head to the side, and I thought how Misty Hyman wouldn't have done it that way. Misty Hyman would have gotten her breath from directly in front of her. But the spaceman's way seemed to me like an efficient way to breathe. He did not always have to be searching for that hidden pocket of air. The way he lifted his head from side to side, the air for him was easy to find. The air was all his.

WHO WE SAW AT THE POOL GETTING IN A SWIM: Coach. He brought Ted and Ted sat in the wheelchair waiting for coach to get in his swim. The spaceman got out of the pool before I did. I could see him talking to Ted in the wheelchair on the deck of the pool. The spaceman knelt down in front of Ted and Ted put his hand on the spaceman's shoulder. What were they talking about? Were they trading religious insight? Was the spaceman being ordained? Later, in the locker room, I told the spaceman I could never understand Ted, and so I didn't try to talk to Ted too much. The spaceman said he could understand Ted. He once worked with others like Ted and had learned to understand their speech. He said that all Ted was telling him was that his foot hurt, and that his sneaker

was on too tight, and so the spaceman had reached down and loos-
ened Ted's laces for him. The spaceman handed me back my bath-
ing suit that he had borrowed, and when I took it he covered my
hand with his own. I wondered if this was how the boys, the bad
boys, the gang boys, shook hands at the school he worked in. We're
going to find the fucker who did that to your son, the spaceman
said, and when he said it I could feel my heart race. It almost hurt.
I remembered the alpaca who had died from the sound of the clap
of thunder. It was like fear, him saying it. Yes, I thought, maybe
this spaceman is right. Maybe this spaceman with the beautiful
fly is someone I've been waiting for all along. Someone who can
help me. Let's find him, I said, and for a moment I let myself feel
the anger all over again that I felt right after my son had been shot.
WHAT WE SAW ON THE WAY HOME: The children's school. I pointed
it out to him. I showed him the apple tree where in the fall, during
recess, the children's teacher would let one child climb into the
tree and let the child shake all the apples to the ground, then the
teacher would let all the other children run under the tree and collect the apples. The children would put the apples on the ends of
long sticks and then throw the apples off the ends of the sticks, far
out into the field toward the base of the mountain, just for fun. Oh,
in Philadelphia, the spaceman said, there would be lawyers around
to stop that kind of play. But then again, in Philadelphia we don't
have people shooting each other out of trees.
CALL: Dorothy says her sheep Alice has a bad leg.
RESULT: Spaceman and I drove to Dorothy's, past a field where forsythia bushes grew, their buds about to bloom. I told the spaceman
that when I was little I thought forsythia was really "forcynthia"
and that it was named after a woman, the kind one would want to

give flowers to. Outside Dorothy's, the spaceman wanted to know where the barn was. No barn, I said. The sheep lives inside the house. Inside the house, Alice walked up to the spaceman and sniffed his knee, then she walked under the kitchen table and peered out at us from under the tabletop with her wide, kind eyes. Dorothy shook her head. It's something with her leg, Doc, she said. I looked at Dorothy. She looked more tired than the last time I had seen her. I noticed the hem of her dress had come undone in places, and the cloth that had been turned under for years was much more colorful than the rest of the cloth on the dress. Come over here, Dorothy said to Alice, and she said it as if she were talking to another person and so the spaceman thought she was saying it to him because he went forward a step. But Dorothy was looking at Alice when she said it and Alice came out from under the tabletop and put her head in Dorothy's lap. Dorothy rubbed Alice's neck. This sheep has gone to church and met the local pastor, I said to the spaceman. The spaceman nodded. She's a pretty sheep, he said. Both Dorothy and I nodded because Alice really was a pretty sheep and Dorothy kept good care of her and kept her wool clean. I knelt down and palpated the leg that Dorothy said hurt Alice, but I could find neither heat nor swelling. I did notice, however, that Dorothy seemed to be shifting her weight often while she sat in the chair with Alice's head in her lap. How about you, Dorothy? How is your leg? I asked. Dorothy shook her head. Well, it so happens, I've been having trouble with my leg, too. It hurts me all day and it hurts me all night. I guess, and now Dorothy laughed, I guess that means it hurts me all the time, she said. Dorothy, I said, it sounds like you should make the appointment to see the doctor. Have you got the doctor's telephone number? the spaceman asked, stepping closer to Dorothy now. Dorothy shrugged, I suppose it's on the fridge, but if I go to the doctor for my leg, he will probably find something wrong with my arm. Maybe not, maybe he will just fix the problem with your leg, the spaceman said. You think so? Dorothy said and Dorothy looked up at me and the way she looked up at me she looked just like Alice when Alice looked up at me from underneath the tabletop.

RESULT: I was getting ready to leave, but the spaceman wanted to stay and help Dorothy find her doctor's telephone number on her refrigerator. There were a lot of cards on her refrigerator door hanging there by the use of magnets and we looked through all of them. There were magnets so old they were cracked in half and some of the magnets had words on them advertising stores that had once been in the area, but had long since gone out of business. When we found the right card, the spaceman called the doctor for Dorothy and made the appointment. You'd think that Dorothy would be able to go to a doctor's appointment any day, but the only day she wanted to go to the appointment was on a Thursday, so the appointment was made for a Thursday weeks from then. Before we left, Dorothy asked if I wouldn't mind driving her to the appointment because her leg hurt her and she didn't think she could push down on the gas pedal. Oh, and, Alice, too, she's coming with me to the appointment in the back of the truck, Dorothy said. Okay, both you and Alice to the doctor's, I said, and then the spaceman made sure that I wrote it down in my book.

One last thing, the spaceman said to Dorothy. Did you know about the doctor's son? No, don't answer that. Of course you knew. This is a small town, everyone knew. Dorothy lowered her eyes to her linoleum floor. Yes, the poor boy, Dorothy said. Isn't that right, Alice, she said and she reached out for Alice so she could rub Alice's head. Well, said the spaceman, the police have said they're getting closer to finding out who that man was. They're very close. He doesn't stand a chance now. No one can help him now. It's almost water under the bridge, the spaceman said. Dorothy kept rubbing Alice's head. Who was that man anyway? He couldn't have been a churchgoer like you. You probably never saw the likes of him across the pew, did you? the spaceman said. Dorothy looked at me. There were tears in her eyes. Your son's all right now, isn't he? Tell us he's all right? Dorothy said, and I knew that when she said "us," she meant Alice and herself. I nodded my head. My son is fine. He's perfectly fine now, I said. It's time for us to go, I said to the spaceman, all of my excitement about finding the hunter who had shot my son gone now.

WHAT THE SPACEMAN SAID WHEN WE WERE BACK IN THE CAR: I think she knew. Everyone in this town knows, your Arlo with the ghost cows knows, this Dorothy knows. Hell, the sheep probably knows. It's pretty sickening, what they're doing to you, he said. You may not be from here originally, but still, you should be treated fairly. You live here and work here. You're nice to these people. You're probably not even going to charge her for that call, are you?

WHAT I SAID: She is so poor. I wanted to open her refrigerator to make sure she had food in there.

WHAT THE SPACEMAN SAID: You're not good for your own business, are you?

WHAT WE LISTENED TO ON THE WAY HOME: The bit on the CD about Gisela talking about how she did not want to go play chess or table tennis or go to the movies or go lift weights or go in-line skating or go on a hike. What is the matter with Gisela? the spaceman said after I translated for him. Why doesn't she want to go out? I don't know, I answered the spaceman. I guess that's strange, I said, but I think I knew why she didn't want to go out. I didn't want to go out, either. I didn't want to visit any more farms. I was very tired. I thought it would be nice to go home and sit by the fire and have my children read aloud to me. Sarah was now reading *A Separate Peace*, and I wanted to hear the description of the stately old school, and how even a thing like the hard stone steps could change and become worn from all the students over the years that had walked on them.

WHAT THE WIFE WAS COOKING FOR DINNER: A rib roast with baked potatoes and a salad.

WHAT THE SPACEMAN DID: Went up to Sam's room and played his race car set with him.

WHAT I COULD HEAR: The high-pitched insect sound of the race cars going around the track, and the spaceman and Sam laughing and yelling every time the race cars crashed and flew up into the air when vying for the single track around the turn.

WHAT THE SPACEMAN SAID TO SAM: That's the fun of this game, isn't it? The race cars crashing?

WHAT SAM SAID: Oh, yes. That's the best part.

WHAT I COULD ALSO HEAR: How both their laughter and their yells sounded almost the same. The spaceman sounding as young as Sam.

WHAT THE SPACEMAN AND I DID NOT EAT: A rib roast with baked potatoes and a salad. We had a call instead. We would grab food on the road, I told Jen. She nodded while slicing carrots on a bias while we walked out the door, leaving the roast on the table with the aroma and steam floating above it toward the rafters.

CALL: An owner, one I've seen before, thinks her horse has choke. It's the family that is so poor, the one where the boy sat on the tractor that looked like it had been driven up through the ground, the one where the mother sat in her car seat to talk to me, because there was nothing else to sit on outside, no lawn chairs or even rock walls.

ACTION: Drove to farm with the spaceman beside me. I asked him how he found me. Finding out who you were and where you lived was not so hard. There are places now that keep your information on file if you'd ever donated a sample of your DNA, the space-man said, and a relative of yours had done that, and it was through him I found you. It was a process of elimination, the spaceman said. I drove with the spaceman saying how he was glad, after all, that he had discovered who I was. In fact, you're more than what I had hoped for in a real father, he said. It's funny, but I wanted to meet you so I could see what I myself could become. You're like a benchmark for me, and I'm happy to see you're someone I can really admire, he said. We passed the fields at night where a coyote trotted by a tree line. I slowed the truck so we could see his yellow eyes in the headlights.

The boy was there and so was the mother. There was no barn, there was no electricity. The mother held up a kerosene lantern. The smell of the kerosene was strong. Maybe it had a leak, or maybe when the kerosene had been poured into the base, it dripped. I have a flashlight, I said. It might make it brighter. I was glad when the mother blew out the kerosene lantern and left it on the porch of the house, far away from where I could smell the kerosene. The boy held the horse while I took out my stomach tube. After I easily passed a stomach tube through him, I realized the horse did not have choke. If it had choke, I wouldn't have been able to pass the stomach tube through him. But it was too late. The spaceman had already touched the nose of the horse because it was a good-looking horse, with a blaze in the shape of a moon. Stand back, I told the spaceman calmly. This horse might have rabies. The horse was salivating. The horse was tilting his head back and to the side, the moon blaze looking like the moon being jerked by a string in the sky. The horse was not eating. He had gone over to his feed, but he had just lifted the hay in his mouth, and was not chewing it and was not swallowing it down.

RESULT: I asked the mother questions. I asked if she knew if the horse had recently been bitten by an animal, but the mother did not know. Has he been bit? she asked her son, who was still holding the horse. Her son shrugged his shoulders. There were marks on the horse. They could have been scratches from bushes or the fence. They could have been marks left from an animal's teeth days ago. I told the owner we just wait a few days and if the horse dies, then we have the horse tested. Do not get near the horse for the next five days, I told the owner. Sometimes these animals, in the furious stage of rabies, will come after you. The mother shrugged. She looked like her son when she shrugged and I thought how they were two of those people who looked alike not because they share the same facial features, but because they have the same mannerisms. The mother said she had a .38 in the house and she would just shoot the horse if it came to that. I wished she hadn't said that, because after she did, I knew that the spaceman would remember he was on a mission to find out who had shot my son. I spoke fast. I would not let the spaceman interrupt and ask her about the shooting of my son. Whatever you do, I told the mother, don't shoot the horse in the head, because it's the brain that's sent off to the lab in order to determine if it's been infected with rabies. If it is, then we know to treat everyone who came into contact with it with a series of rabies shots. Then it happened. He sidled up to the son. I could not hear what he said, because at the same time the mother was asking how much she owed me. She was holding bills that smelled like kerosene. The spaceman was whispering, and then I saw him pull out his wallet and show the son some bills. I almost ran to pull the spaceman away, but the son leaned over and whispered back into the spaceman's ear. What was he telling the spaceman? The spaceman must have seen me watching. He turned his back to me so I could not see the son at all.

WHAT I SAID TO THE SPACEMAN WHILE DRIVING HOME: I'm sorry I brought you here. I should have had you wait in the truck before I saw the horse. I've been vaccinated for rabies. I don't think I'm at risk. I'm not even sure the horse has rabies, though. It could be other things. It could be moldy hay—they may not have the money to feed it good hay—it could be botulism. Let's cross our fingers that it's not rabies, I said, and then I wondered when the spaceman would tell me what the son had whispered in his ear. Did the son say the name of the man who shot Sam? Would I now finally know?

WHAT THE SPACEMAN SAID: I'll be going home tomorrow. I have to get back to Philadelphia. Rabies is the least of my problems. I have something to confess, the spaceman said. I had two reasons for coming here. One you already know, because I wanted to meet you. The other is because . . . and I don't know how to say this, the spaceman said. The spaceman put his head in his hands.

WHAT I THOUGHT: Oh, don't put your head in your hands now, because look, there on the side of the road are two deer and they are looking at us, and see how beautiful they are, I wanted to tell the spaceman, but I could not interrupt his moment where he had his face in his hands. The deer ran off, leaping up the hillside into the darkness.

WHAT THE SPACEMAN SAID: There's a cop behind us.

WHAT I DID: I looked in the rearview and saw the flashing lights. I pulled over. The town cop rolled down his window alongside me. Hello, Ed, I said. How's your night going?

WHAT ED SAID: Fine, Doc. And how are you? Ever get that inspection?

WHAT I SAID: No, Ed. But I've been meaning to do it. I thought maybe I'd even go tomorrow.

WHAT ED SAID: Well, don't worry about it. Get it done anytime.

WHAT I SAID: Hey, did you see those two deer back there? Looked like a doe and her fawn to me, I said.

WHAT ED SAID: Oh, yes. I did see them. It might have been her fawn at that, but he was big. He might turn out to be a buck.

WHAT I SAID: What were all the fires about last week? Was it just people starting rubbish fires?

WHAT ED SAID: Yes, that was it. It's too dry now to start a fire, but people are fooled. They think because in places there is still snow on the ground and mud on the roads that it's wet enough. But it's not. The dead grass on the fields is like tinder, and the leaves from last fall on the ground are like paper. They go up like that, Ed said, while snapping his fingers in the space above his blinking radio in the patrol car.

WHAT I SAID: Well, let's hope the fires are over.

WHAT ED SAID: Yes, let's hope so. Well, I'll be seeing you then. Take care. And then Ed drove off ahead of me.

WHAT THE SPACEMAN SAID: What did that cop stop you for? Were you speeding? Was your taillight out? The town cop stopped you for nothing, but meanwhile he sits in his car and lets the man who shot your son freely wander the town? What kind of town is this? said the spaceman.

WHAT I SAID: Oh, no. That was just Ed, I said. Ed likes to chat sometimes. What is it you were saying before Ed stopped us? The spaceman leaned his head back on the headrest of the seat. He looked up at the ceiling of my truck.

WHAT THE SPACEMAN SAID: I've got kidney disease.

WHAT I THOUGHT: Was there someone he could see on the ceiling of my truck that he was talking to? Maybe I had left the shade to the sunroof of my truck slid open and he was talking to someone through it. Was his spacecraft up there floating above us, flashing its lights, talking back to the spaceman? Was he telling the space-craft that he had kidney disease?

WHAT I SAID: I didn't know that. I'm sorry to hear that.

WHAT I WANTED TO SCREAM: Alarm! Alarm! in a German accent, and I wanted to lower my truck to the safety of the depths of the sea.

WHAT THE SPACEMAN SAID: I've been on the donors' list too long. My father, the other one, he offered to donate one of his, but we're not a match. I could have told them that at the hospital before all the tests, that we were not a match. It was something I knew from a long time ago. Maybe something I figured out while watching him swim, the way he swam only sidestroke that we were not a match, but he insisted on trying. He is that kind of father. Then the spaceman looked at me. I knew he was looking at me because we were going past the third streetlamp in our town and the streetlamp was on. It hadn't been turned off to save the town money yet. The spaceman said, while he was looking at me, that he bet that he and I were a match. I bet we are a good match, he said, and then he put his face in his hands again. We now had turned up a road that eventually would take us home. It was one of the reasons I came to see you, to ask you, he said into his hands. The road we were on was dirt, and in the headlights I could see how the mud had turned the road into a washboard of ruts. The truck bounced over the ruts and I could see how the spaceman's hands were moving up and down his face from the bouncy ride and then the spaceman took his hands off his face and set one on the armrest and one on the console between us. I noticed after I drove over a very deep rut that the CHECK ENGINE light in the truck went off, and I thought, finally, something's been fixed, and I wondered if I were on some kind of streak and maybe my levels would be the next thing to be magically repaired. I started driving up our driveway, but I didn't drive all the way up. I didn't want the spaceman to have to get out of the truck and be close to the house, where the children might come running out to see us. One of them, probably Sarah, would see his face and ask right away why he had been crying. I stayed parked at the start of our driveway with the engine off.

WHAT I TOLD THE SPACEMAN: I think you're very brave to come here and ask me this and I will think about it. Right now, though,

we had better drive up to the house and we better see what there
is to eat because I've forgotten that we didn't eat. I forgot that we
had said we would get something to eat on the road. Are you ready
to drive up to the house? I said to the spaceman. He nodded and
wiped his eyes and then said *mierda*, Spanish for *shit*, because he
had lost a contact lens while wiping his eyes and I had to turn the
truck light on above our heads so we could find it. It was on his
knee the whole time; I saw it winking there like a splash of water. I
told him I didn't know he wore contacts and that I wore them too
and that without them I was blind. He said he was also blind without his. I then told him how I could see perfectly without them.
I just had to hold whatever I was looking at very close to my eyes.
I told him that sometimes my wife made fun of me while I was
reading without my contacts and she would push the magazine or
whatever I was reading even closer up to my face so that it knocked
into my nose. But it was just as easy to make fun of her, I said,
because she now needed glasses to read. When she wasn't wearing
them she held the book or whatever she was reading very far away
from her. She would stretch her arms out as far away as they could
go and sometimes when she leaned over my shoulder to read the
same article I was reading, I would hold the article close to my
nose and she would try to push it far away and we would fight that
way for a while, just trying to read the print.

WHAT WE ATE FOR DINNER: The cold roast.

WHAT SARAH ASKED THE SPACEMAN: Why are your eyes so red?
Were you crying? Would you like to hold our rabbit? She can make
you feel better.

WHAT I SAID: Sarah, isn't it your bedtime?

WHAT SARAH SAID: Oh, Dad, Lyle says he knows a boy who eats bugs.

WHEN THE SPACEMAN LEFT: Sometime in the middle of the night. I didn't hear his car, but I did hear what I thought was the top of the rabbit's cage being opened. Maybe the spaceman had taken Sarah's advice after all and was petting the rabbit.

WHAT THE WIFE SAID SHE HEARD: Something whirring outside in the dark, and she thought it might be the spacecraft. I figured it was his electric car.

WHAT I THOUGHT: I would not find out the name of the man who shot my son now. The spaceman is too upset. The spaceman should be upset. I should not bother knowing the name of the man who shot my son when the spaceman is this upset. I don't really even want to know who shot my son. I am okay not knowing. I can keep going on calls if I do not know. It is a good trade to make. I can keep admiring Dorothy's sheep and Arlo's ghost cows if I do not know. I can visit the calm Belgian whose throat I incised so that he could breathe from the plastic handle of a milk jug for the rest of his life. I could visit the woman with the hair so long it always became stuck in the buckles of her horse's bridle. I could still visit the Zodiac Killer. He is full of advice. I'd like to know what design for a barn he'd suggest. I could still go to Phil's. I could walk down his well-worn aisles where the floorboards creak and heave and I could stand in front of his glass meat case and I could order sausage he had made himself and bacon he had cured on his own. I could visit Arthur still and listen to the horse's talk through him and watch the geese land on his pond, their feet out in a pose to brake, their wings not beating, coming down on water flat as glass on a windless day. I could still visit the Mammoth Mules and I could still see the minis, Molly, Netty, Sunny, and Storm. What a good life I have not knowing the name of the man who shot my son.

WHAT THE WIFE SAID WHEN I TOLD HER THE SPACEMAN NEEDED MY KIDNEY: No.

WHAT THE DOCTOR SAID WHEN I CALLED HIM ON THE PHONE: I'm so glad you decided to call. I told him I wanted to schedule a time to talk.

WHAT THE DOCTOR SAID: That's a wise thing to do.

WHAT I SAID: No, not for me, I mean not for my levels, for my kidney. I'd like a discussion, I said. Is it possible to talk over the phone?

CALL: Jen screaming, telling me there's a bat in the sink drain. She went into the bathroom to wash her face, and there in the sink was a small bat, nose crammed into the space between the drain and the metal stopper.

ACTION: Called the children to the scene of the emergency. The bat is obviously sick, I said to the children. I sent Sam off to find a plastic container. Tore off a piece of cardboard from a Tampax box and scooped the bat up into a plastic container that Sam brought that once held fancy greens. Told Sarah to fold up toilet paper to put inside the plastic container to keep the bat warm. Sent Sam and Mia off to catch flies in our house. The bat needs food, I said. Sam and Mia were more than happy to go up to the window glass where the cluster flies were clinging and pinch the wings of the flies and put them inside the plastic container. We gave the bat water, but he was too weak to drink.

WHAT THE WIFE SAID: Rabies!

WHAT I SAID: Not everything has rabies. It might be white fungus.

WHAT THE DOCTOR HAD SAID OVER THE PHONE THAT I RE-PLAYED IN MY HEAD AS I LOOKED AT THE BAT THROUGH THE CLEAR PLASTIC CONTAINER, BREATHING EVER SO SLIGHTLY, HIS HEART IN HIS CHEST MOVING NO MORE NOTICEABLY THAN A VEIN IN A WRIST: You can live just as well with one kidney.

WHERE WE KEPT THE BAT FOR THE NIGHT: In the pantry, on a shelf with a jar of green olives, next to a pipe the hot water ran through and where it was cozy and warm.

WHAT I THOUGHT THE BAT WAS THE SIZE OF: One of my kidneys.

CALL: The children are all calling for me. Jen is sitting on the toilet with the lid down. She is crying. The children have all come running to me to tell me they have found their mother this way.

ACTION: I walk upstairs. I see her sitting on the toilet.

WHAT I SAY: You may want to lift the lid before you pee.

WHAT THE WIFE DOES: She looks up at me. I see the tears streaming down her face, mixing with her hair. Very funny, she says. I put my hand up on the top of the glass shower door to rest it there and look down at her. What's the matter? I say, feeling how what I'm leaning on is slippery, probably because up high on top of the glass shower door is where I keep my bar of soap so that it doesn't wash away and disappear while the shower is running.

WHAT THE WIFE SAYS: I don't think I can do it again. I can't have someone else in this family in the hospital again. You can't give your kidney away. You will not give it away. Your children need a healthy father. Your levels might skyrocket after losing a kidney. This kid, this spaceman, you didn't raise him. You didn't even know he existed a week ago. This is not about you! she says.

UPDATED LIST OF THINGS MY LEVELS CAN DO: Beg, talk, appreciate food, join a swim team, have common sense, skyrocket.

WHAT I THINK: I wish she were just screaming about the house being dirty, about the dishes in the sink and the clothes on the floor. Then I could just run outside. The kids could join me. We could run to the back field and check on the small trout as small as their hands in the stream. We could check on the brush piles we created last year and look into the dark of them to see if there are any beady pairs of black eyes staring back at us, it being a happy home to some furry creatures.

WHAT THE WIFE SAYS VERY QUIETLY: Please.

WHAT I THINK: That what I'm seeing is already in the past, she has already cried, and maybe the crying is over. Maybe now she has stood and wiped her nose and brushed her hair on the way out of the bathroom. She has made herself presentable. She has pulled down her sweater so that it lies smoothly over her pants. She has checked herself in the mirror. She has checked her eyeliner and with her fingertip she has smeared away any blurring black smudges. She has smiled into the mirror and has checked for telltale signs of food between her teeth.

WHAT THE WIFE IS STILL DOING: Sitting on the toilet with the lid down. She has not risen, she has not arranged herself. The tears still fall. Things that I'm seeing may be in the past, but the past just happened so quickly, it wasn't long ago at all. Is there a way to make the past longer, or the present further away? I take my hand off the top of the shower wall. Sure enough, there is mucky green deodorant soap on my polar fleece cuff now. I try not to look at it for too long. If I do she will know I am not paying enough attention to her. She will think I am not taking her seriously. I cannot reach for a washcloth and wet it and try to wash the mucky green deodorant soap away now. At best, the only thing I can do is hold my arm out a little to the side, so as not to get the rest of me covered in the mess.

WHAT I SAY: It's not the same. It won't be the same as it was with Sam. I'm not going into a coma. Jen interrupts me. Why? Why? Why? She yells and so of course I think for a minute that she wants to know why it won't be the same, and why I won't be going into a coma, but I know better. I know she wants to know why I feel I have to do this for some kid who showed up at our door a week ago. I shrug my shoulders. I do this by first bringing my arms in close to myself. Now the mucky green soap is definitely smeared on my side. I shrug again and again. It doesn't matter now, I have turned into the mucky green soap monster. When I go back down and see my children they will want to know what it is. Is it horse mucus? Is it cow cud? Is it alpaca spit? they will ask. I think I will tell them it is rearranged electrons from space-time travel, and maybe that is what it really is anyway because all of a sudden Jen is standing. She is saying, "Fine, they are your kidneys, do what you want with them," and she is lifting the lid of the toilet and throwing wadded-up tissues she used to blow her nose into the water in the bowl.

WHAT I SAY: It's the right thing to do. What that hunter did to Sam, that was the wrong thing to do.

WHAT THE WIFE SAYS: You don't owe this kid anything. You didn't shoot him.

WHAT I SAY: I gave him life.

WHAT THE WIFE SAYS: Oh, Jesus fucking Christ, you're not fucking Jesus, you know.

WHAT I SAY: Okay, it sounded like too much, but I am part of the reason why he's alive now.

WHAT THE WIFE SAYS: I married an egomaniac.

WHAT I SAY: I'm not. Then Jen says, Oh, sure, and she takes a washcloth and wets it and starts wiping off the mess of the green deodorant soap that is on my sleeve and on my side. She uses such strong strokes to brush the soap off that my body turns to the side with her every downward stroke. When she's done she wads up the washcloth and throws it down onto the basin of the sink and says, Dinner is ready.

WHAT DINNER IS: Great. It's breaded pork chops cooked to tenderness in broth and sweet potatoes mashed with butter and cream and maple syrup and green beans sautéed with oil and garlic. I want to tell her how good it is, but I can't. She will think I am just trying to smooth the waters between us. So at first I am thankful for when Sam starts to say, Mom, this is delish-delish-delish, but I wish he didn't have signs of slurring when he's trying to say it because while he's trying to spit it out the wife looks at me as if to say, And this proves my point, here is an example of how precarious life is, it has left us with our son who still slightly slurs and if you give this space kid a kidney, the aftereffects may be worse. So I say, Delicious, ending Sam's sentence for him and noticing that the green beans may not be that good after all and they might be somewhat burned and a little bitter tasting.

WHAT VIDEO WE RENTED FROM THE LIBRARY: How we love the library and leave it with armloads of books and movies, even if the service at the library is slow, and the librarian who has been there for years always looks at the scanner gun for a few moments first before he uses it on our books' labels as if he's never seen the scanner gun before. And I know this librarian and he is also on the master's swim team and I have seen him in his swim trunks, and there is a huge scar on his belly that even pulling the waistband of his trunks way up past his navel does not hide and I wondered what part of him was surgically removed or rearranged. He is a very slow swimmer, and it seems as if he goes backward instead of forward in the water, or that he goes nowhere at all. It was the librarian who recommended the video to Mia. The video was about mammals and Mia had watched it first and then wanted me to watch it with her. The cheetah, I learned, will let one of her offspring share her kill with her even years later, even when the offspring is an adult she will remember it, but she will never let any other adult share with her. Isn't that amazing? Mia said.

WHAT I SAID: Yes, it really is amazing, and I hugged Mia on my lap while I said it and I smelled her hair that smelled faintly like our house when we walk into it after we've been away for a few days. It smells good, like wood smoke and meringues made with cocoa, and it smells earthy, too, maybe of the small pine needles the dogs trail in with them on their fur after hiking with us in our woods.

WHAT SAM WANTS TO KNOW: What the wife and I were fighting about.

WHAT I SAID: Fighting?

WHAT HE SAID: Yes, you know, her crying on the toilet with the lid down, the way she always does when she's upset with you.

WHAT I TOLD HIM: Everything. How the spaceman wanted my kidney. How the spaceman knew the name of the man who shot him by accident. How I had seen the spaceman bribe my client's son, and the son had whispered the name of the man in the space-man's ear. Sam looked outside when I talked. Was he looking at our pond, noticing the snow beginning to melt on the surface? When I was finished talking, he nodded his head. What if it were me, he said? Would you have given me your kidney? Of course, I said. Then you should give him yours. What happened to you while you were in a coma? I wanted to ask him. Had a part of him changed? Had he been visited by a higher being? This wasn't the boy who called his sisters jerkface and cheesebutt. He sounded older. He cleared his throat. He's your son, too, he said. It doesn't matter that you didn't raise him here with us. You can help him, that's all that matters, he said. Besides, it's cool. How many kids have dads that saved a man's life?

WHAT I SAID: What about your mother?

WHAT HE SAID: She should learn how to cry sitting on the toilet seat without the lid down. At least that way she could pee and cry at the same time and be more efficient.

WHAT I SAID: What about the name of the man who shot you. Do we want to know that?

WHAT SAM SAID: I don't want to know. I don't care. You make mistakes while hunting. It happens all the time. Did you know there was a kid who shot an old man sitting on a tractor because he thought he was a deer? What are you going to do anyway, shoot the guy? I'd rather say my dad saved a life than took one away.

WHAT I WANTED TO DO: I wanted to take Sam everywhere with me, I wanted to put my hand on him the way Arthur put his hand on the horses and had them talk through him. I wanted everything I said to be what Sam said because he said it so well, no matter his speech was slightly slurred.

WHAT SAM SAID WHEN I HUGGED HIM: I bet now is a good time to ask for the new computer I want.

WHAT THE HOUSE SAID AT NIGHT: Give the spaceman a kidney.

WHAT SARAH SAID IN THE MIDDLE OF THE NIGHT: Poppy! Poppy! Did you hear that?

I thought that she too had heard the house telling me to give the spaceman a kidney. Hear what? I said. The house, it's falling apart again, she said.

WHAT I SAID: No, it's not. This house will never fall apart. Go back to sleep now. In the morning you can come with me to see the lambs.

RESULT: The bat was dead in the morning.

WHAT SAM SAID AS HE LOOKED AT THE FLATTENED BAT IN THE PLASTIC CONTAINER THAT ONCE HELD FANCY GREENS: He looks like a wilted lettuce leaf.

WHAT I SAID: Really, I thought he looked like a kidney, curled the way he was.

WHAT THE RABBIT SAID WHILE I LAY ON THE FLOOR AND SHE WAS SNIFFING MY HAIR, SNIFFING MY EARS: Give the spaceman your kidney.

CALL: Yes, there were sheep I had to go see. Their lambs were there, too. Over sixty of them hopping in the fenced-in pasture. Sarah and Mia walked into the field with them and ran with them, sending them this way and that way like a school of fish, only there was no body of water, just the new grass on the ground, a strange bright green that would not last. It was only this unusual color now from the snow it had been buried under for so long and that had suddenly been exposed to warmer currents, the displaced air from flapping tips of newly arrived robins' wings. The next week it would be a greener green, already older and closer to the dull, tough grass blade summer green it would soon become. The girls' rubber boots looked so big on them, gaping around their thin legs as they ran with the flock that moved like a school.

ACTION: The sheep's mothers needed shots and I looked into their eyes and told them hush, to keep their bleating down, while I injected them.

RESULT: Mia and Sarah came out of the pasture with the lambs following behind them, asking me if we could take one home. Just one. How about the littlest one, Mia said, and pointed to what was surely the littlest one, who was so little even the short new blades of grass reached high above his dainty hooves.

THOUGHTS ON DRIVE HOME: With the melting of the snow appeared beer cans that had been tossed onto the side of the road during winter and now protruded from roadside mud. If deposits for cans were raised to twenty-five cents, the problem might disappear. Who would throw away twenty-five cents so easily? And if they did, there would be more people out looking to collect the cans and make money.

CALL: The spaceman saying on the phone how he hadn't much time now. He had wanted to come back and visit me again, but there were problems with the battery of his electric car, so he had let weeks pass, and now, he said, he was flat on his back in the hospital with the doctors and nurses hovering. I pictured his spacecraft parked in a space at the indoor garage of the hospital, its lights not blinking and not moving at all. I could hear, in the background, the sound of ambulances and fire trucks. I could hear the wheeling of a cart and the closing of a door. I thought he might also remember to tell me the name of the man who shot my son, but he never did. Of course he's not going to tell me now, he's worried about his own health, I told myself, and so I told him, Here's the good news—that horse never had rabies, it was just moldy hay, I said. Oh, yes, I remember that horse now, the one with the moon on his head. That is good news, the spaceman said. The spaceman coughed. It did not sound like a cough from a respiratory infection. It sounded dry and I thought of fallen leaves when I heard him cough and I thought of Ed, the town cop, and how he said the fallen leaves were as flammable as paper and I pictured the spaceman, my son, up in flames on his hospital bed, the pillows puffy behind him, the white bedsheets taut around the mattress burning, leaving shattered-looking holes from the scorch. I'll give you my kidney, I thought. I can live with just one.

ACTION: I wrote the wife a note. I told her where I was going, just to visit my son. I got in my truck and drove and I took it as a good sign that throughout the whole way, my CHECK ENGINE light never came on. When I got to the hospital, I saw that he looked like he had lost weight. The cleft in his chin I thought looked shallower somehow, as if once it could fit a whole green pea but now could only fit the half of one, a split one. There were many forms to fill out. I filled them out in the waiting room, using a magazine for support. The front of the magazine had a picture of a covered bridge that was not far from my home, that was not far, in fact, from the imprisoned zebra.

RESULT: It was no use, leaving my wife a note like that. She was onto me fast. I had her speak to the doctor I was assigned. I had him reassure her I would be all right. My wife, while crying, wanted to know about the calls, how she should handle them. I told her over the phone that there was not much to do, considering the small number of calls I had been having, but that there was one thing

I'd like her to do and that would be to drive Dorothy and Alice to the doctor's on Thursday. Who are Dorothy and Alice? my wife asked, and why do I have to drive them to the doctor's? Just as a favor, I said. You'll like them, they're both very nice old ladies, I said. There were antigen tests and the spaceman was right. He and I were a perfect match. It didn't seem to matter about my levels being high if I donated a kidney. They weren't a concern to my doctor in this hospital. He pooh-poohed my levels. He shrugged. He said tests like that these days for levels caused the patient more worry than did the patient good. I liked this doctor. He wore a white lab coat, but he did not wear the breast cancer pins. He also wore a fishing cap, with a feathery fishing fly attached to it, but the metal hook had been removed. He wanted to know what I caught up where I lived. Was it brookies? Was it bass? I liked this doctor because he let me know he knew about other things than being a doctor. He knew about fish, about walleye. His answers were made from a broad spectrum of information he had gleaned from doing so many different things and having so many different interests over the years. I asked him if he'd recently read what I had read, that maybe the dinosaurs never disappeared, but they're still here. They're just chickens and other birds now. They've just evolved. The doctor thought that sounded reasonable to him. He considered the wrinkled wattle on the turkey. He considered the scaly appearance of chicken feet. I wished he were my doctor at home. I looked out the hospital window at the people walking in the streets and realized that looking out the window I saw more people in one minute than I would see in an entire day at home.

WHAT THE FATHER WHO WAS MARRIED TO HIS MOTHER SAID WHEN HE SAW ME: Thank you. His eyes were filled with tears

even before he reached my bedside. He grabbed my hand, he was
so thankful I was going to give his son a kidney. I could tell by
his handshake that he was not a good match for my son. His was
not a strong hand that could stay cupped, pushing water aside in
order to swim fast. There was no close blood match or antigen
match here.

WHAT THE MOTHER SAID WHEN SHE SAW ME: I told Mark years
ago not to contact you. I told him that we should protect your pri-
vacy, but now I'm glad he didn't listen. Is that what you're like, too,
do you not listen to what your mother or your wife tells you to do?
That's not something you wrote down on your application when I
considered you for your DNA, she said with a smile. I also smiled,
thinking how she was right. I don't listen. I didn't listen to the wife
when she told me not to come here, told me not to give up one of
my organs.

WHAT THE HOSPITAL COOKED FOR DINNER: Meat loaf with tan-
colored gravy.

WHAT THE SPACEMAN COULDN'T EAT: The meat loaf or the tan-
colored gravy. He had to eat a low-sodium, low-protein diet before
the surgery.

WHAT MIA SAID TO ME ON THE PHONE WHEN I CALLED HOME:
Poppy, I have lost another tooth and now there is an *L* in my mouth,
see, she said. But I could not see, I could imagine her tilting her
head sideways, while still holding the phone, to show me how the
spaces in her mouth formed the *L.*

WHAT THE SURGERY WAS: A laparoscopic nephrectomy.

WHAT I DIDN'T WANT TO THINK OF WHEN I WAS GOING UNDER:
If I would ever come up.

WHAT I THOUGHT OF WHEN I WAS GOING UNDER: The yellow

junko I had seen in my birch tree in the front yard before I drove down to the hospital. Spring is almost here, I thought. I thought if the ground was still frozen and what the temperature of the soil was, as I wanted to get my seeds in early, my fingerlings started, our growing season is so short. I wondered if I could use my rectal thermometer that I used on my horses to insert into the soil to take the temperature. I figured I could.

WHAT I WAS SURPRISED TO SEE WHEN I WOKE UP: That the spaceman wasn't next to me in the room. Wasn't my side just split open and didn't I just give him a part of me, and shouldn't we be close to one another, wouldn't that make the acceptance of my kidney into his body that much easier? Weren't we like Siamese twins now, and separation would be traumatic? Maybe my body needed to be close to my kidney, and close to the new body it now lived in. Then I realized it was just the spaceman I wanted to be close to. I wanted to know if my son was all right.

WHERE THE SPACEMAN WAS: Down the hall. They wanted us walking up and about as soon as possible. They figured we would be more likely to do so if we had to walk a ways to visit each other.

WHAT I SWEAR BY: Morphine.

WHAT THE SPACEMAN SAID HE SWORE BY WHEN I TRUNDLED DOWN THE HALL WITH A WALKER TO VISIT HIM: Morphine.

WHAT THE SPACEMAN WAS HOLDING UP: A bag of urine my new kidney in his body had produced. He was very happy, as he had not produced his own urine for a while now. Through his bag of yellow urine I could see out the hospital window. I could see trees in a small park and the trees looked anemic and looked as though the branches could barely carry the weight of the fat squirrels who were fed peanuts by the lonely old men on park benches and did not look like our svelte squirrels who had to gather their food. I thought of Arlo, who said he never left his home because he didn't want to see other places' trees, and now I knew what he meant and I longed for my own trees, and the view of the trees I had on the hillside beyond the pond.

HOW MANY DAYS I WAS IN THE HOSPITAL BEFORE MY WIFE TOOK THE TRAIN DOWN TO DRIVE ME HOME: Four.

WHAT I SAID TO THE SPACEMAN BEFORE I LEFT: Good luck, take good care of my kidney. I will, said the spaceman. Come visit us if you can, if we are still living where we are living and haven't moved off the grid to a small house in the thick of the woods to avoid paying high taxes, I said.

Don't move, he said. I like your house.

You don't really have to visit if you don't want to, I said, and I meant it. I didn't want him to have to think that he should have to visit me. I did tell him though that turkey season was coming on and that we didn't have a blind, just camo clothing he could borrow and a shotgun that was once my father's that we could wrap in camo masking tape. I said, Come visit in the fall, not in the spring. I'm not keen to hunt in spring turkey season as I believe the turkeys don't taste good then, after a long winter with little to feed on. Come visit in the fall, when the turkeys would have had time to fatten up, I said.

You're not really much of a hunter, are you? You're always concerned about the animals, he said. Yes, I said. I wouldn't feel right about shooting a dinosaur anyway, not when we thought they'd all gone extinct for so long. Listen, I said, don't bother visiting. Just send me postcards from exotic places, from the tops of the tallest mountains, from the pyramids and glaciers. I want to know my kidney is going places. Write to me you are in the finest health, I said.

WHAT THE SPACEMAN SAID: I'm sorry we never found out the name of the man who shot your son. We can still do that, you know, when I'm out of here. I can still help you, he said. It's the least I can do.

WHAT I SAID: I thought you already know. I thought that boy . . . . I thought you paid him, I said.

WHAT THE SPACEMAN SAID: Yes. I did give him money. I don't know what for. For the windows, for the horse that was so skinny. Don't you think that if I had known the name of the man I would have told you?

WHAT I SAID: It doesn't matter. I've already given that man a name. I call him Danglars. I don't ever want to learn his real name.

WHAT THE SPACEMAN SAID: Are you sure? The man should pay for his crime, he said, looking again at his bag of yellow urine hanging on its hook.

WHAT I SAID: I'm sure.

WHAT THE SPACEMAN SAID: Maybe there's hope for us yet, I mean humans. Maybe if the dinosaurs didn't go extinct, then we won't. We'll just evolve, the spaceman said.

WHAT THE WIFE SAID WHEN SHE SAW MY SCAR: So the spaceman really did abduct you. And then my Jen punched my shoulder and said, That was for making me drive a sheep to the doctor's.

WHAT I SAID TO THE WIFE: Tell me, do I look like our librarian now? The one with the scar? The one who swims in the pool but never looks like he goes anywhere?

WHAT THE WIFE SAID: No, you look good. The scar is small.

WHAT I NOTICED ON THE TREES AS WE DROVE CLOSER TO

HOME: Buds on the tips of branches looking like the flames of torches that, instead of burning with flame, glowed with the pale warmth of new green.

WHAT I DID: Opened the window wide to smell the melting snow and the roadside's fresh mud which was veined with narrow streams whose water was from the melting snow of nearby hilltops and mountain peaks.

WHAT SARAH SAID WHEN I GOT HOME: Where were you?

WHAT MIA SAID: Mommy got a transmission to give the spaceman a kidney and Poppy gave him one so the spaceman wouldn't die.

WHAT SARAH SAID: Good, then the spaceman will live.

WHAT SAM SAID: Maybe we shouldn't turn on the radio anymore.

WHAT BRUCE SAID WHEN I GOT HOME: He kept barking at me, maybe he was trying to tell me all the things that had gone on while I was away. I sat down on the hearth and let him stand in my lap and I hugged him and told him he was a good old dog, the best.

WHAT THE WIFE COOKED FOR DINNER: Chicken quarters on the grill.

WHAT THE CHILDREN SAID WAS FOR DINNER: Barbecued dinosaur, aka "Dino on the barbie." The day was unusually warm, even though we still had patches of dirty snow on the property. I sat by the pond wearing shorts and I wore a straw hat my wife said made me look like a Floridian. I saw how my white legs looked like death. I rested and watched the children paddle around in inner tubes on the pond and try to push each other out. The water was still as cold as snow, but the sun burnt their arms and gave them red cheeks.

CALL: Another goat in labor can't deliver.

ACTION: Drove to farm on a windless, sunny day. The owner walked me through the barn. Along the way we passed long rows of tables and on the tables were hamsters and rabbits and rats in cages. The owner said they raised them for sale. The primary customers of course being pet shops. I stopped to look at a rat and the owner told me how affectionate rats were and how they would never bite you unless they had a litter of rats and they were trying to protect their young. You can understand that, can't you? the owner said and I said that I could. When I saw the goat I was disappointed. I was hoping she'd be big and helping deliver her baby wouldn't be too difficult. I was hoping this delivery wouldn't turn out like the last one, but the goat was very small. The owner said, I hadn't planned on breeding her, because she was so small, but one day the farmhand let the male goat out with the nannies by mistake. I put my hand inside the goat. I could feel how the legs were presented first. I pushed one leg back to turn the goat around, headfirst. I explained to the owner while I was doing it how my children wanted a pet rat, but that my wife was against it. Jen thought that rats smelled. It was not so easy. There was not much room inside the goat. At one point I felt something hard, and realized I was feeling the baby goat's teeth and then I was able to pull the baby goat's head down, where it ought to be. This delivery would not be like the last one. The mother goat was able to push on her own now. I would not need my .38 today.

RESULT: The baby goat was born and the afterbirth delivered and I washed my hands with cold water from a hose while the mother goat licked her baby. The owner, on the way out as we walked through the barn, tried to give me a rat as payment. She picked up a cage and tried to make my hand hold the metal handle on the top of the cage. Oh no, I said. My wife would kill me.

THOUGHTS ON DRIVE HOME: They shouldn't have lowered the gasoline prices. They should have kept them the way they were, and all the extra money could have been put toward a slush fund for the development of alternative energy sources.

WHAT THE CHILDREN SAID WHEN I GOT HOME: Poppy's home! They ran to me. Sarah jumped on my back. Sam gave me a hug. Mia grabbed on to my leg.

WHAT I SAID TO THE CHILDREN: I almost got you a pet rat, but I knew your mother wouldn't have liked it.

WHAT THE WIFE SAID: Rats stink.

WHAT THE CHILDREN SAID: A pet rat! We want a pet rat! Can we have a pet rat please?

WHAT I SAID: If you keep a rat's cage clean, then it won't stink.

WHAT THE WIFE SAID: Yeah, well, we have a rabbit and nobody's cleaned the cage in days, and the rabbit cage stinks, so why do you think these kids are going to remember to clean a rat's cage? No, I would end up having to clean the rat's cage, Jen said. Maybe going to space would not be such a bad idea after all, she said. There I would not have to clean the rat's cage. I would not have to carry wood. I would not have to cook the meals, pick up the dirty socks, the wet towels . . .

WHAT WE DID: We attacked the wife. We all ran up to her and hugged her. I kissed her where I could, she was shaking her head so much, not wanting to be kissed. I felt generous. I wanted to give her whatever I could, the way I gave my kidney away. I felt I had evolved, and up to the task of unquestionably helping fellow mankind. A lung. Could I give her a lung? Could she breathe deeply then, relax, love being touched? Sarah tickled her sides. Mia kissed her on the belly. The wife began to laugh. Leave me alone, Jen yelled, laughing. Oh, going off to space without us, we said. No way, we said. We're going, too. We half picked her up and half pushed her out the door. We stood in bright sunshine right outside the door, slipping on the melting ice dirty and matted with New-foundland hair from where the dogs sometimes sat and kept watch, looking down our driveway and out over our field to the pond. We managed to get Jen over to the field beneath the apple tree, where there was still a patch of snow. We threw her onto it. We landed on her. The dogs joined in, barking and grabbing at our sleeves with their tails wagging, wondering if they should stop what was hap-pening or let it continue because it was fun. The snow wasn't so soft, but more like gritty crystals that stayed in Jen's hair as she lay, still laughing, on the snow. Sunlight came through the branches of the apple tree and the children, breathless, lay back on the snow beside Jen and let the sun hit their faces. I lay back too and we all closed our eyes. What I heard was the sound of Bruce and Nelly panting as they lay next to us, and farther away I heard the sound of a car driving on the slick muddied road, its tires sending up the top layer of brown water and making a splashing sound.

We were quiet for the longest time. Even though the windows were closed I could hear the cluster flies in the house buzzing in the corners of the window frames. They were active and happy with all the solar heat circulating in our rooms that faced south. I let my thoughts wander. I thought about gravity again—how it wasn't really a force and how its effect was caused by the curvature of space—objects inside of space spun in the same way a marble would spin inside the curved sides of a bowl, always going down. I thought about Einstein, how only twelve people were left alive who understood his theory of relativity, and I thought how I would devote the rest of my life to understanding it, just so there would be thirteen. I felt grandiose. It would be my debt to society to understand it fully. Jen and the children might someday come to understand why I would do it. Why I would give up on the calls, why I would give up on the substitute teaching, why I . . . and then Bruce licked my face. It was horrible. His breath stank. His tongue was huge and slobbering. He then moved to my ears, using his front teeth very gently to nibble and clean out whatever wax embedded in my conch-like swirling cartilage he could find. Besides being horrible, it tickled. I laughed then, too. I could not help myself. I tried to push Bruce away, but the more I did, the more he pressed his 150 pounds into me, intent on my ear. When I caught my breath, I said, Damn you Bruce, get away!

WHAT DRIVES UP THE DRIVEWAY WHEN I AM AT HOME ALONE WITH SAM: A loud pickup truck.

WHAT COMES OUT OF THE TRUCK: A man.

WHAT I SHOULD DO: Go outside and greet the man, but I already know what the man wants. I already know who the man is the way his eyes are cast down, the way his wife remains in the truck, staring straight ahead. I already know who he is by the way he knocks quietly on the glass of our front door. This is the man who shot my son.

WHAT I DO: I open the door and the man tells me who he is. I am Jason Lane. This is my wife, Carol, in the truck, he says, and he motions toward his truck. I know who she is. I have seen her before in the post office. She has retrieved her mail from a box that is right next to mine. We are postbox neighbors.

Jason Lane has a mustache whose top hairs are lighter than the rest, probably bleached by the sun. He is a man who has spent most of his days outdoors. Jason Lane shakes his head. Even in coming here it's like I'm doing it for myself, doing it because I can't stand the guilt, he says. He smells like chain saw oil. I haven't hunted since then, he says. I won't hunt again. It's not enough for you, is it? It would not be enough for me if I were the father of your boy.

WHAT I THINK IS FUNNY: That for so long I wanted an apology from this man and now I don't want to hear him say anything more. His wife in the car, Carol, looks out over where our garden grows in warmer weather. Jason Lane nods his head. It sure would not be enough, he says, and then he says, Call the police now. His eyes are bloodshot and blue, the kind of blue that either goes right through you or the kind you think they are so clear blue there is nothing behind them, no intelligence in the man. Or I'll call them, or she will, he says, nodding his head toward his wife. So where is the phone? he says and he makes his way past me into the house. Bruce and Nelly are on him in a second, wagging their tails, getting in his way, slobbering on his coat front because to them everyone who walks through our door is a friend. Then Sam comes downstairs. Sam is tall for his age and is strong from all the swimming he has been doing. His shoulders are wide, and he does not look like he has spent time in a hospital bed cocooned in a pale blue blanket with legs that were once as skinny as arms.

This is Jason Lane. This is the man who shot you, I say to Sam. Sam holds out his hand. I'm Sam, pleased to meet you, he says, and I know how Sam has a strong handshake, I have felt him practicing it on me before and I have felt the bones in my hand grinding against one another when he does it.

Jason Lane shakes his head. This is all wrong. This isn't the way I planned. If you'd just give me the phone, I could get this over with the way it should be gotten over with. I could turn myself in, he says.

How did it happen? Sam says, excited by a hunting story. Did you hear the grouse first, did you lead your gun just by hearing where it was he flew up from and then there I was sitting in my camo in the tree stand?

Yes, that's how it was. I lead the grouse right after I hear them, they are so loud when they beat their wings. I've been hunting all my life. I know just the right amount of distance to aim in front of them, he says.

Then Carol, his wife, is at the door. I open it for her but she does not look at me. She looks at her husband. Did you do it? she says to him.

Yes, he's made the call, I say to her. Go on home now, I say to Jason Lane.

Go on back to the car, he says to his wife and she leaves.

Jason Lane turns to me. There is more he wants to say to me, but I don't want to hear it. The day is warming up outside. Sam and I could take the dogs through the fields, we could breathe in the smell of last summer's grass melting beneath the snow, warming up in the sunshine, and we could breathe in the smell of a milder wind blowing through the needles of the pines.

Go home with your wife, I say to him, and then he leaves and the smell of the chain saw oil is gone, too. I am glad to be free of the smell. It was the smell of a machine and there is nothing mechanical taking place. What is taking place is as layered as something in nature. I won't ever be able to figure it out. It is the pond surface rippling, the meandering grooves of bark on a tree, the tall grass and milkweed leaning over in a strong wind looking like the form of a man lying down in it, only there is no man.

Summer

Summer

CALL: My wife, in summer. I can hear her voice. She is calling us into the house while the kids and I are by the stream. Sam, in his shorts, stands in the shallow water trying to catch trout in his hands, and laughing because he can't, because Bruce and Nelly have bounded into the water with him, muddying the water, scaring the trout away, making them dart up under the shadows of the shore. Sarah is low on the bank, peering into the dark places between piles of brush, calling to foxes or voles, any creatures she hopes live inside. Mia rides on my shoulders as we head back to the house and my big hands fit all the way around her thin sun-warmed ankles. "Watch your head," I say to Mia as we enter the house and Nelly and Bruce, wet from the stream, push their way past us, to be first through the door. Jen serves us casserole made with zucchini fresh from the garden and while we eat I look out at all of them, happy to see their faces, the steam rising off their plates making me want to wave it away, making me want to always be able to see them as clearly as I can.